Zenith Rising

by Michael Goodell

PublishAmerica
Baltimore

ISBN: 1-60703-732-7
PUBLISHED BY PUBLISHAMERICA, LLLP
www.publishamerica.com
Baltimore

Printed in the United States of America

To Mary, who never stopped believing, even when I did.

Chapter One

Always, always this big pregame feel. Me and the boys, headin' onto the field, and this time we gonna win. We gonna kick some ass big time.

Zenith Police Sergeant Dunnington Jefferson gazed back at the pair of flak-jacketed troopers in the back seat. White eyes shining in black faces, black as the night. Blacker than the soul of Kong. Demetrius "Kong" King, boss dog of the Wrecking Crew. Well tonight you ass is mine. No more messin' up my kids with your crack cocaine.

The rain-slicked road reflected in the headlights as the car moved silently through the darkened streets. Jefferson glanced at Peters. "Fuckin' rain."

"Rain's stopped," Peters replied. "It's all peaceful like now."

Jefferson glanced back. "How 'bout the others?"

"On our tail."

"No mistakes tonight. Everything goes right and we put that mutherfucker away for a long, long time."

"Got the warrant?" Peters asked again.

Jefferson grunted. "Warrant, visual ID on Kong, wiretap says he's there right now. Can't nothin' go wrong now."

The other three murmured their agreement, and Jefferson knew the eight men in the trailing cars were doing the same. Last minute safety drill. Check your kevlar, everything snug. One more time with the game plan. We gonna kick off then we gonna run right over them. He hefted his shotgun again. Checked the safety. Off. Two minutes to show time. He squirmed on his seat.

"Take it easy, Sarge," Dalrymple grunted from the back seat.

Jefferson faced him. "You know how long I been waiting for this guy? How many times I been so goddam close? No way can I take it easy. Not 'til it's over. Not 'til we get into the end zone."

Then it was time. Peters pulled up at the head of the block, and Jefferson got out to direct traffic. He sent Baker's crew down the alley, and motioned Reynolds around the block, come in at the other end. Sixty seconds now. Then Reynolds pulled in, flashed his lights once. "Now," Jefferson whispered over the radio, and both cars surged ahead, converging on 633 Brookstone, a red brick, two-story house with a sagging wooden porch and solid steel front door. Jefferson was going in the side door, and Peters and Dalrymple were coming in with him. The others were gonna sit tight. Blast the shit out of the house if they had to, otherwise wait for his word.

Both cars slithered to a halt at the foot of the driveway, and all eight doors burst open. As Jefferson ran around the front of the car he heard the unmistakable, gut-wrenching rattle of an automatic rifle. It came from the alley, where Baker was supposed to be. "Shit," he cried. Jerking his head at the noise, his foot slipped on the slushy drive and he went down. His elbow jarred on the pavement and a shotgun roared. Both barrels connected, the shells ripping into the back of Peters' head. He never knew what hit him.

Suddenly everyone was shooting in the dark. The front porch light went on and the door swung open. Jefferson, still down, watching hell break loose, rolled at the burst of light, pulled his revolver free, and let loose three shots at the body flying through the door. Then he screamed. Screamed and pounded his head on the pavement. Screamed and cursed God and Kong and every fuckup on his team. Screamed and stared in horror at the body of the three-year-old girl.

The shooting stopped. The wails began, and sirens began to ululate through the darkness. The little girl's mother flew out of the house, shrieking "My baby, my baby!" She fell upon Jefferson, beating him with her fists, scratching at his eyes until Dalrymple pulled her off. Jefferson just sat there.

Reynolds took over, sending two men in to secure the house, one to call for an ambulance, and two to check on Baker and his crew in the alley. He stood over Jefferson. "The fuck happened Dunn? You killed a fuckin' kid." He shook his head and walked away.

* * *

Zenith Police Chief Ernest P. Slaughter slammed down the phone and hurled an ashtray against the wall. Once upon a time he had welcomed crises. There'd been nobody better in a fight. Nobody got on top of things faster, and rode them as hard. But once upon a time he hadn't been pushing sixty-two. Once upon a time his job had been easy, at least a hell of a lot easier than it was now. Once upon a time he'd been in law enforcement. Now all he was doing was damage control. Chief Slaughter was tired. So goddam tired. By all rights he should be sleeping off another round of golf in his condo down in Florida. Instead he was going to be babysitting the media until noon.

He put in calls to Peter Jensen and Avery Douglas, and tried again to brew a decent cup of coffee. Angie performed miracles with the ancient machine, but he couldn't see ruining her sleep just to avoid having to drink tepid dishwater. While he waited for the latest caffeinated travesty, he reviewed the report on his desk. Another abortive raid. Three more officers dead. That made fourteen already this year, and it was still March. He grimaced and stared out the window, where dawn had begun to paint the sky.

He shook his head. He wouldn't let the sunrise fool him. On the way downtown the radio had warned that another storm was on its way. This was the snowiest, coldest and longest winter in Zenith's history, and there was no end in sight. Cold as it was, however, the streets of Zenith kept getting hotter. The Wrecking Crew had spent the winter wiping out the competition and nothing the police did seemed to slow them down.

When the machine grumbled its readiness the Chief sampled his handiwork. Another failure, only this time it was hot, bitter mud which greeted his jaded palate. Oh well, at least it would keep him awake. He ran his hands through his wiry gray hair and maneuvered his bulk around the desk.

He picked up the report again, as if this time an answer might appear. But no, just the same hard, cold, brutal facts. Someone had tipped him off. No way Kong could've figured it out. Somebody tipped him off and there were five dead. Three of his boys, some piece of shit crackhead, and that little girl. He shook his head. That fucking Jefferson. Slapping the file on his desk he swore again and tried to figure it out.

Somebody leaked and the leak had to have come from inside. How many knew? He shook his head. Counting the men on the raid, no more than fifteen. He could exclude himself. He knew he hadn't done it. So who? Jensen? Douglas? No, it had to be one of the twelve. Actually, take away the three dead and you were down to nine. He was willing to bet the traitor made it through. Traitors always did, the bastards.

"I should've been there," thought the Chief, against all reason. He had no place in the field anymore. He was out of shape and out of training. He would have been a liability, a hazard to his and everybody else's health. "Maybe I would've got killed," he mused bitterly. That would have gotten him out of this morning's press conference. It was going to be a bitch. The public wanted something done about the mayhem in the streets. He didn't blame them. Hell, they were his streets, too. He just didn't think putting his head on a platter would accomplish anything.

Slaughter knew the only reason he still had his job was a lifelong friendship with Mayor Jeremiah Brown. He also knew the uproar over this latest fiasco might prove too much even for an alliance cemented on the front lines of the Civil Rights movement. Jeremy might be his closest friend, but he was above all a shrewd political animal. He wouldn't hesitate to jettison an old comrade to keep his own career afloat, and Slaughter wouldn't expect him to.

"Have to save my own ass," he decided, and settled back to wait for Douglas and Jensen to arrive. The heads of Internal Affairs and Media Relations ought to be able to come up with something between them. He was especially interested in Douglas' input. They'd sift through the nine live bodies and find one to throw to the wolves. And they'd find him before 11:00 a.m. He needed a break. He needed something big, something to show that the Police Department was on top of this one, something to keep them from eating him alive.

Chapter Two

The remnants of yesterday's storm loomed black and brittle above the dawn-scuffed Zenith sky. The day, resigned to duty, inched slowly forward. Lightening in the east, pushed by the sun, night surrendered its hold on the sky. Low clouds caught the yellow light and scudded beneath the slate. Gradually brightening, they rose to rose, then pink, then brilliant red. Finding a gap in the overcast, they lingered against the glowing blue, celebrating, in spite of themselves, the return of the sun.

On the ground, darkness ebbed more slowly. In Wellington Lakes, men and women stirred, dragged from slumber by relentless alarms, by radios shattering the peace with manic laughter from "The Morning Crew," or the reedy voice of Steve Inskeep on NPR. It was time to start anew, to roust the kids and cook them breakfast, to remind their husbands that they needed to pick up Jake for his ortho appointment at 4:00, or that they wouldn't be home until late because of the Regional Sales meeting; they reminded their wives that Caitlyn needed to shop for a Prom Dress after school, or that they were supposed to meet with their attorney over lunch to set up a trust fund for Meghan.

Others woke up alone, forcing bloodshot eyes open against the grinding headache courtesy of those three Armagnacs in the bar with Kerry Pullman and Ron Philbert after another Country Club dinner. Or they were roused by the grateful ministrations of the latest divorcee whom they'd retrieved from the Wellington Grill. Or they awoke petulantly, suddenly aware that it was only dawn and they didn't need to be up before 11:00, only it was 11:00 in Paris, where they'd been until yesterday. Or they woke up alive and ready for action, clapping a beefy paw on the hip of their petite wife, who rolled away from them, and parried their clumsy groping without ever quite gaining consciousness, until the lumbering beast gave up and clumped to the bathroom, wondering which courtroom adversary was going to pay today because his bitch of a wife was colder than the remnants of the snow pack outside.

In the city, some women greeted the sun at their doorsteps as they headed out to catch the first of three daily buses which took them to their jobs cleaning the mansions in Wellington Lakes. Others moved quietly to the kitchen to make sandwiches for their children's lunches, slicing the baloney in strips so they could stretch three slices into seven sandwiches, reminded in doing so of Jesus turning five loaves and seven fishes into food for hundreds, and how comforting was Brother Rollins' homily on that very subject at Sunday evening service last night, and how disturbing to see her older boys turning away from the church. Others merely rolled over and went back to sleep. Let the kids fend for themselves today. I'm jus' too tired—again.

Some men caught the sunrise glow through the high, rectangular windows of the tool and die shop where their shift would end in another hour. Others, stumbling home from a night on the streets, in darkened houses, a flash of a knife or the barrel of a gun lingering a moment on the edge of their consciousness, searching for a conscience, until the memory was shrouded, then smothered, in the smoke from the pipe.

Others, rising in their highrise by the river, gazed over the troubled city beneath their feet, resigned to the fact that they hadn't died before they woke, confident there was no Lord their soul to take.

As the sun rose, the Ontanagon River flowed sluggishly southward, chunks of ice bobbing on the brown water, slowly melting on their journey to the sea. The sun rose, and the sky responded in a palette of color unseen by those still asleep, and even by most of those slowly wakening. Another day had dawned, a day like no other; a day like all those that had gone before in the dying city. A day that, before it ended, would wreak subtle changes in the mass of individuals who scratched out an existence, or who glided blithely along; who would grow older, grow richer or poorer, would gain wisdom or more likely not. For some it was a day pregnant with potential; a sale, a deal, a job or promotion waited to be closed, or sealed, or seized, or lost.

For some the day would be their first, born into wealth or poverty, or into the vast chasm of ordinariness which lay between, into a home filled with love, or despair, or indifference. For others the day would be their last, their final breath passing dry, withered lips from a body punctured with needles and trussed up with catheters and feeding tubes and electrodes, from a body criss-crossed with scars; a body which had been sliced and diced by teams of surgeons whose Hippocratic oath had mutated into a sadistic creed, who kept bodies alive long after the souls of their inhabitants had departed; their death a welcome denouement presided over by a jaded nurse or a loving spouse, or a mourning son only just arrived from the coast, eyes brimming with the tears of regret for all the things he'd meant to say but couldn't find the time or courage, and all the things he had foolishly said and now could never take back.

For others life would end suddenly, a chance glance, an ill-timed word tossed off at the bar triggering rage in a stranger passing through, or glancing down at the ashtray to crush out the butt, he runs a red light and plows into a gasoline truck. The explosion breaks windows three blocks away, and leads the nightly news, even taking priority over the three dead Zenith cops, because somebody videotaping his daughter's first steps just happened to catch it in the background.

* * *

Narrows Burton watched through the dirty windows of the terminal as dawn streaked the sky with salmon and peach. The gray between the clouds softened to blue. Dingy strays of leftover snow scarred the tarmac fringe and clotted the base of the terminal. He tapped Marissa's shoulder and nodded at the sky. She glanced up.

"Nice," she dismissed it. "What's with this line?"

"You've got plenty of time."

"I don't want to miss my flight. I've got a one o'clock meeting." She glared at a balding Pakistani when his bag bumped her shin. "I hate goddam lines," she muttered.

"It's always like this," Narrows conceded.

"Why don't you do something? Why don't you get a real airport?" She pushed a burst of air through pursed lips. "Jesus." Her petulance was a relief. It made it easier to say good-bye.

"We had some fun, didn't we?"

She turned to him, her face softening briefly at his tone. Dark eyes, heavy lids, brown hair severely cropped around her skull. Her lips parted when she smiled, white teeth. The tip of her tongue darted out to her lower lip. Then she shrugged.

"I've never brought anyone home before."

"Should I feel honored?"

"Feel anything you like—it's a start."

She spun away from him. "Look, why don't you put your damn bag in front of you like everybody else?"

The man turned and smiled apologetically. "So sorry." He bowed his head. In front of him were two other bags. "Too much suitcase," he offered.

Groaning, Marissa turned away.

"I'll be in San Francisco again this August." Don't be needy, Narrows chided himself.

"Yeah? That's nice," Marissa conceded, striding forward a step-and-a-half as another traveler moved to the counter. "I'll be there, too. At least I will be if this line starts moving. Otherwise I'll miss my flight which means I'll miss my meeting, which means I'll get my ass fired and I'll have to move back home to Modesto—" She broke off, nostrils flaring at the sound of his laughter.

"What's so goddamned funny?"

"Nothing," Narrows insisted, getting himself back under control. "It's just—you spin this whole tragic tale out of a slowly moving line."

"Well, it will be tragic if I don't make—"

"There's plenty of time."

"Not if we don't get moving."

"Look, there's only twelve of us in line."

"And there's only two goddam agents."

"And we've got an hour-and-a-half." He slipped his arm around her shoulders, as if to comfort her, or restrain her as one might a five-year-old.

"What if it takes ten minutes per customer?" she demanded. "Then I miss my flight."

"It won't take ten minutes. It won't even take five."

"Five minutes?" She let a little panic creep into her voice. "Five minutes times six is half-an-hour. And then what? I still have to get to the gate from this, this—" She studied the gray concrete walls of the ticketing hall, making no attempt to conceal her disdain. "This Quonset hut," she decided. "God knows how long that'll take."

"They're aluminum."

"What?"

"Or corrugated steel."

"What are?"

"Quonset huts."

"So?" She whirled to face him, kicking over the suitcase in front of her. Narrows studied her face, searching for but failing to find the slightest hint that she was putting him on. "Who cares what Quonset huts are made of?"

Narrows stepped forward to help the Pakistani right his unwieldy bag. "You called this a Quonset hut. I was merely pointing out—"

"I wasn't trying to describe it—"

"You got the shape right, though," he conceded, gazing at the barrel-vaulted ceiling.

A grudging smile glimmered on Marissa's lips. He decided to press the advantage. "Besides, what's the worst that could happen if you do miss your flight?"

"You mean beyond having to spend more time in this pit?"

He frowned. "Look, I'm just trying to cheer you up."

"Well, don't."

"You got it, babe," he decided. "No more cheering up. But why rip Zenith? I mean, granted, it's no San Francisco, but it does have its qualities."

"Besides you?" she asked, laying her hand on his cheek. Her fingertips lingered, so tender, so dramatically different from her spite, and then trailed slowly across his skin to his lips. This was why he'd invited her back, he reminded himself. Amazing how easy it was to forget it, even over the short course of a long weekend.

"Besides me?" he repeated, before pushing his tongue against her middle finger.

"Yes, besides you." She concluded the interlude with a light slap on his cheek. "You're a dear, Burt. You're clever, you're smart. You know your way around a winelist, and a bed."

He grinned, and slipped his arm around her shoulders again. "It's easy with a good guide."

She eased away. "Why waste your life, Burt?"

"What?"

"Why live in this hell hole of a city?"

"It's not that bad—"

Marissa tucked a wayward strand of hair behind her ear, glanced at her watch again, and sighed. "When I first got here I thought you'd lied to me."

"Lied to—"

She touched his cheek again, but this time there was no tenderness. "Just listen. When we made plans for me to visit, you told me how great Zenith is. And I was looking forward to see this midwestern jewel. So what do I find when I get here? A black pit of a hell hole surrounded by a couple of lakes and some pretty houses." She raised her hands, palms up. "Big deal."

"So what are you saying, you had a lousy time?"

"You just don't get it, do you Burt?" Her eyes narrowed as she tried to work it out. "We had some fun, sure, but I can't help thinking, you know, one weekend, Burt. One weekend and I've pretty much done Zenith."

"That's harsh."

"It's true."

"What about the Art Museum—you couldn't imagine going back there? You're done with that?"

"The Art Museum!" She burst out laughing. The little man in front of them turned, a smile on his face, thinking he might share in the levity. Marrissa's mirth cut short as she glared at him. "Do you mind?"

He shrugged and faced forward again, shuffling his bags ahead another three feet. Narrows counted the remaining flyers, wondering if he would make it to the end.

"So the ZIA didn't do it for you," he concluded.

"Burt, if that's the best you can do—"

"I thought you liked art."

She laughed again. "I do like art, Burt. I like sushi, too, but I wouldn't want to make a steady diet of it."

"You act like that's all there is to do in Zenith."

"It's not?" She nudged her bag forward. "You mean we could have wasted Saturday afternoon doing something else?"

"Look, Marissa." Narrows' voice turned cold as he fought the urge to scream at her. "I took you there because, yes, it's one of Zenith's great treasures. It's a hell of a museum, world class. I thought you'd like it. Hell, I love going. There's always something new, some gem, some delicacy you can climb inside." Like I thought you were, he didn't say, some little piece of perfection I could get lost in for a very long time.

She stared blankly, taken aback by his intensity.

"After all," he reminded her. "We met in an art museum."

"That was work, stupid." She fumbled in her leather purse-cum-attache for her ticket as they neared the front of the line. "I was there for business, the Commercial Real Estate Conference, remember?"

"I remember you giving me a tour of the Japanese wing. I remember the Graphic Arts show and the Jackson Pollock retrospective."

"And business? You remember that?"

"Of course I do. I pitched Oak Grove, got some interest. I just didn't—"

She smiled condescendingly. "Oh, right, your—what is it? Your environmentally correct subdivision?"

"It's more than a subdivision, Marissa. It's a town, a whole community, built to scale, with the aesthetics, the parks, those things that make a community, built in from the start, not slapped on like an afterthought."

She gave his cheek a tender, valedictory pat. "I love your passion, Burt. It's a pity to waste it, and your talent, in this pig sty."

He took her hand in his, removing it from his face. "It's not a pig sty. Zenith was a great city, and it will be again."

She smiled skeptically. "And you're going to rebuild it?"

"Damn right I am. Right after Oak Grove."

Marissa sighed. "At first I thought you'd lied to me about Zenith, just to get me here, like one of those Arab guys who marries an American woman and then takes her back to Algeria to be his slave. I wondered what else you lied to me about. Now I'm thinking maybe you weren't lying to me. Maybe you're lying to yourself."

"Maybe I was…" Narrows' voice trailed off. There was no need to continue. He nodded at the waiting ticket agent. "You're up," he said, then turned and walked away.

* * *

The paperwork, debriefing and cleanup kept Sergeant Dunnington Jefferson at the station until four a.m. After that was the trip to the hospital which duty prescribed, the torture of trying to encourage Baker's wife and Riley's girlfriend while they waited for their men to come out of surgery, and trying like hell to avoid the eyes of Sondra Peters. "I killed him," Jefferson kept saying to himself. "I killed him. The hell with that little girl, I killed Sondra's husband." His best friend. Oh, the hours at the bowling alley, fishing in the Ontanagon River, hunting up north. The nights at the bar, unwinding after another tough day of eating shit. "And now I can't even look at her."

He was on administrative leave, he knew that. Cap said he didn't know what was going to happen, but Jefferson knew. Administrative leave, that was S.O.P. in cases like this. And those fucks from Internal Affairs'll be all over me like stink on shit, ripping my life apart.

Jefferson stuck it out as long as he could, which was about two hours, and then he headed straight home. At least that was the plan, though he made a little detour to the Walloon Saloon, where he had the breakfast special, a shot and a beer, to try and kill the pain. And then he went home to his darkened house. Delia was a sound sleeper, he thought while filling a tumbler with Jack Daniels, but even if she weren't there was no way she'd be getting up. "Not for me," he muttered, tossing off half the drink in a single gulp. "Not for this fuckup." Things hadn't been good between him and Delia for a long time. Not since Dee started kindergarten, and that was—he finished the drink and poured another one—was it eight years? Yeah, eight years, 'cause tomorrow Dee was having her thirteenth birthday. Tomorrow, hell, it was already tomorrow, he thought, glimpsing the brightening sky through the kitchen window.

He couldn't help it, he thought about that other little girl. She was never going to have a thirteenth birthday party. Because of him. And because of her, he wasn't going to have a pension. No twenty and out for him. He could kiss that old dream good bye. The one about retiring to his fishing cottage up on Green Lake, just him and Delia and sunrise on the water. He finished the second drink and loaded number three. It didn't matter. That dream had died years ago, along with his marriage. Spending their twilight years together, just the two of them? There had to be worse forms of hell than that. He just couldn't think of any at the moment.

* * *

The walnut doors creaked shut and the elevator began its groaning 12-story descent. The lobby, in a display of outdated decorum, concealed its ornate decor behind a shroud of neglect. The plaster cornices begrimed by a decade of smoke and dirt, the crystal chandelier modestly sheathed in dust, the once young doorman now shoe-horned into his threadbare uniform, all greeted Seneca Doane III as he exited the car.

"Mornin' Mr. Doane," Wilson said, tipping his cap in a genuine show of respect. "Gonna gettem today?"

Doane nodded brusquely. He didn't bother trying to conceal his mood. It was one of the perks of celebrity. The doorman labored under no illusion regarding his right to civility from this giant of jurisprudence, this lion of justice, who reached deep into the pockets of rich, greedy corporations and distributed wealth to Wilson's unfortunate brothers and sisters. Some days Mr. Doane took the time to speak to him, to look him in the eyes, to make him feel more like a man than a piece of furniture. Most of the time, however, he was like he was this morning, already miles away, working out the game plan for another million dollar payout.

Wilson held the door open for the great Mr. Doane. "Your car's waiting," he said, pocketing the $5 tip.

If celebrity had its perks, it also exacted a price. While some might regard having a car and driver at his beck and call the apogee of significance, for Doane it was one more freedom bartered for fame. For every Wilson who viewed him as a hero, there were several who thought him despicable, and with each successive victory, they were more likely to come after him, with a gun, a knife, or a jacked up 4x4 Ford pickup.

It happened two years ago. Some yahoo from Merryvale, getting tanked after his shift at the Herringbone Truck plant, read about Doane's verdict against the Winston Brewing Company in "The Zenith News." He decided to exact some vengeance of his own, and drove to the attorney's office in downtown Zenith. It was just dumb luck that Doane was pulling out of the lot as the cretin approached. With his shock of bright red hair and his lunar landscape of a face, Doane was nothing if not recognizable. Making the connection through a haze of Winston Lager, Bo Jacobs floored it, slamming into the left rear door of the Mercedes. Doane could credit his survival to three factors: one, Bo's aim was atrocious; two, the 500 series was built like a tank; and three, Bo hadn't thought to put on his seat belt.

That was the last time Seneca Doane III drove his own car. That was also the first time he thought about retirement. It wasn't that he was intimidated, just that it wasn't fun anymore. It was nothing more than a game, a game for fools and losers, and he couldn't escape the nagging suspicion that he was the biggest loser of the lot.

Except maybe for Bo's surviving kin and heirs, who approached the attorney a week after the funeral to inquire about the chances of winning a settlement from Ford. "Well, what about the windshield company?" they asked when Doane finally stopped laughing. "Bo got cut up pretty good," which set him off again. Even now, climbing into the back seat of the limo, the memory brought a smile.

* * *

Harry Bachman woke with the rising sun as he always did. He eased himself out of the bed, careful not to wake Mya. She'd come in late last night from a poetry reading at the Zoo, and he figured she deserved to sleep in. Unfortunately, Mya being Mya, she'd let her clothes lay where they fell last night in her haste to get beneath the sheets her lover had been warming for her the previous two hours. Harry got his feet entangled in her jeans, and went down with a muffled curse.

The bedside light clicked on. "What was that?" Mya wondered drowsily.

"Nothing," Harry said. "I just tripped over—my feet, I guess." She laughed in that husky voice of hers. "What time is it?"

"Just past six."

"Oh, babe, come back to bed." Mya stretched luxuriously beneath the sheets.

"Can't, Button," he replied, shirking pleasure for duty. "Got that GA breakfast." Button was so far from describing Mya that it had been inevitable that it, or something similar would become Harry's nickname for her. It amused them both to think of how the recidivist feminist-cum-lesbian crowd to whom her poetry most appealed would react if they learned his pet name for her. It was horrifying enough, Harry speculated, that she was married to a man.

"Oh, is my big strong man off to save the world this morning?"

"Just a little piece of it this morning," Harry said. "I'll save the rest after lunch." He paused at the bathroom door, savoring her chuckle. "How was the Zoo?"

"Ah, wonderful," she sighed. "I had them eating out of my hand—everyone, even the grunge crowd who thought there was going to be a band."

"That's great, Mya."

"Dana was there," she announced.

"Dana your editor or Dana your old roommate?"

"Both," she said brightly. "But I meant Dana my editor. She liked my latest batch of poems and says it should be enough for a second book."

When Harry returned to the bed to give her a congratulatory hug, Mya wrapped her legs around him. "Maybe you should let the world save itself today," she whispered, snaking her hand down between his legs.

Harry extricated himself reluctantly. "You make it hard, Button," he said, kissing her forehead. "But Dave and Chelsea have worked so hard to set this up."

"I don't deserve you," she said with a mock pout.

"You got that exactly the wrong way around," Harry said as he padded to the bathroom. "Grasslands Alliance would never have gotten off the ground without your support."

Mya snorted. "You owe a lot more to old man Herringbone than you do to me."

Stopping in the doorway, Harry conceded the point. "Yeah, still hard to believe he funded the Industrial Ecology course."

"I wonder if he even knows what it is?"

Harry shrugged. "Hard to say. He's a funny old guy."

"A funny rich old guy, you mean." Mya stood up and stretched beside the bed. "Is he going to be at the breakfast?"

"Why? Do you want to come?"

"Come see my sugar daddy, you mean?"

Harry laughed. "The way you had him wrapped around your finger—"

She pulled her nightgown over her head, revealing her trim, athletic body. She shook her long, brown hair, and approached him. "You really think that's why he gave that grant to the university? Because of me?" She moved into his arms.

"Sure," he said, nuzzling her hair. "You explained it so well. The need to rethink consumer-based capitalism, the funding restrictions at Zenith University, the medicare cutbacks at the Medical Center, the need for research dollars. How could he not finance the Herringbone Transportation Safety Research Lab?"

"So I'm not just a pretty face?" Mya smiled up at him impishly.

"No, you're a pretty body, too." Harry bent to kiss her but she spun away from him. Pulling back the shower curtain, she said, "I know a way to save time."

* * *

When they reached the War Memorial, Seneca Doane told his driver he'd walk from there.

"You sure, sir?" he asked solicitously. "Want me to follow?"

Doane waved his hand. "Forget it, Jake. There's nobody around. Go get some breakfast." It was such a joke having a bodyguard, and a pretty sad joke at that. "Swing back by around noon, take me to the ZAC."

With that Doane left the car and scuffed through the accumulated slush that passed for an early-spring Zenith sidewalk. The giggling weather girl on the radio had said to enjoy the morning while you could. There was more snow coming. Hard to believe it, though, he thought, gazing at the brilliant colors only now starting to fade from the scattered clouds. It looked like a beautiful day.

He circled the War Memorial, admiring as always the heroic Midwestern bluster of the limestone sculptures. Commemorating the pride of Zenith, raw youth who had perished in the Civil War, in the Spanish-American War and in World War I, it didn't mourn their passing so much as it celebrated the city's productive power. Not just a world leader in automobiles and locomotives, in glassware and steel, it seemed to boast, Zenith also produces the bravest, strongest and most heroic soldiers around. Certainly the statues represented the high water mark of the male physique. These weren't boys, these were Gods. And now they are God's, Doane thought as he turned north to head for the office.

Though his thoughts remained focused on heroic gestures, they weren't the gestures of the honored dead, but the kind to cap his career. Something else on the radio this morning, about the shootout at the drug house. Three dead cops and a three-year-old girl. It held promise, he thought. It could be the basis of his final lawsuit. The notoriety would be on a national scale. And then he would walk away. Shake the dust of this pathetic city from his shoes and retire to a Tuscan villa. You wanted to go out on top. You didn't want to stay too long at the table.

How apt, he thought, to think these thoughts while walking past the plywood-covered windows of the Parisienne. Until recently, and for fifty years before, the Parisienne had been Zenith's premier restaurant. A seat at one of the four principal tables in the front room next to the bar had symbolized, more than money or power, true status.

Some people had devoted their lives to studying the arcane criteria Robert Rollins, Jr., the Parisienne's famed maitre d', utilized to determine upon whom to bestow the ultimate honor. Many sought patterns in the character of those who passed his muster. Others believed clues lay in the person of Rollins himself. Everyone greeted him with warm deference, hoping for a kind word or sign of recognition. While there were only a few whom he called by name, to these his familiarity was almost as great an honor as a seat at one of the coveted tables.

Though seemingly arbitrary, the sole characteristic of his judgement, all agreed, was its unerring accuracy. Harry Winston, of the Winston Brewing Company, merited a seat, as did Wilton Thurston, CEO of Zenith Steel. Old Man Herringbone had made the cut, but Ken Jr. never did. Not, that is, until he took his daughter Cindy to the Parisienne on her sixteenth birthday. On that night Rollins ushered them straightaway to Table #2. He even called him Ken. Thinking he had finally arrived, Ken returned the following night only to shrivel beneath Rollins' cool formality as he directed him into the back room. Cindy, on the other hand, returned again and again to reclaim what was rightly hers. Ken returned too, though never on the same night as his daughter, to take his place within the second echelon.

That was the power the Parisienne had in those days. No matter how frequent or painful the rebuffs, they always came back. Always, because you never knew when your luck might change. One day you were simply part of the crowd, the next you were a peer of Derrick Philbert, Marcia Perryman, Justin Meade, or Fred Thompson, of Thompson Properties. Or Narrows "Burt" Burton, Fred's rising protege, though there were many who said he was only there because of Cindy Herringbone.

They said some people marry money, but Burt had married a seat at Table #2. Whether or not they were right about Burt's status was never determined because by the time he and Cindy split up, Rollins had long since departed.

At the height of the Parisienne's glory, and Rollins' power, there were, on rare occasions, nights when none of those deemed worthy of prominent seating would attend. On those nights Rollins, in his wisdom, seated no one at the front four tables. People were kept waiting at the bar for a table in the back, casting wistful glances at the empty chairs. But it was better that way, they all agreed. It would cheapen the tables' status to confer them on the unworthy. If just anyone could sit there, they reasoned, then where was the prestige when their turn finally arrived?

As time went by the nights on which the front tables remained empty became more frequent. The writing was on the walls and Rollins had always been a good reader. When the position of Chief Steward at the Zenith Athletic Club opened up, he decided it was a good time for a career change.

Surprisingly, business was never better for the Parisienne than it was in the first few months after Rollins left. Suddenly anyone willing or able to slip a hundred dollars to Ariel Khartourian, Rollins' replacement, was deemed worthy of priority seating. Zenithites flocked to the restaurant to enjoy for just one night the magic, the prestige of being seated in the sanctum sanctorum of the Parisienne. They continued to come until they realized that the food wasn't really all that good, the waitstaff was actually quite rude, the whole place was starting to look shabby, and the truly elite didn't come there anymore.

So began the rapid decline of the Parisienne, a decline which mirrored that of Zenith as a whole. Still, each day when Seneca Doane passed the padlocked door on the way to his office, he mourned the Parisienne's demise. Not that he had ever enjoyed pride of place. Not him, not Seneca Doane. It didn't matter that he had real power, the kind that made the men and women at the front tables grow silent and glance away as he was led past them into the nether reaches which the regulars nicknamed Siberia. It didn't matter that he earned more each year than those old-money trust fund babies could imagine. Seneca Doane didn't count because of how he earned that money, and wielded that power. Still, it hadn't prevented him from patronizing the place.

In fact, his ostracism was the single most attractive thing about the Parisienne. It was the reason Doane chose to celebrate his ever increasing verdicts there. Nothing gave him as much pleasure as winning a

$2,000,000 product liability settlement from Zenith Steel and then flaunting it within spitting distance of Wilton Thurston himself.

The Parisienne wasn't the only plywood Doane passed on the way to his office. Although he only had three blocks to travel from the War Memorial, there were a total of eight shuttered shops and restaurants lining the narrow street, and three of the four high-rise office buildings stood empty. Reaching the door to the Alhambra Tower, a twenty story brick and stone structure featuring a Moorish entry lined with ornate tile mosaics, Doane paused to watch the handful of huddled forms who picked their way down the sidewalk. He gazed at the peeling paint on the once brightly painted murals lining the street, and laughed as he always did at the sight.

The murals represented one of Mayor Brown's greatest fiascos, an apt evocation of the man's ineptitude. In preparation for what should have been his greatest coup, landing the Kiwanis convention, one of the largest, and last, conventions ever to grace the city with its presence, Mayor Brown decided something needed to be done to dress up or conceal the preponderance of empty shops and broken windows blighting the city center. First he ordered city workers to cover the windows with plywood. Then he bought hundreds of gallons of paint and charged the city's high school students with the mission of transforming downtown Zenith into a living gallery. "Make a new start—With art!" was the slogan activating the most misguided use of students since the Cultural Revolution.

Doane never did figure out what it was that Mayor Brown had expected, pastoral scenes of grazing sheep or reproductions of Old Masters, but giant depictions of Malcolm X, Patrice Lumumba and Fidel Castro, along with their more sensational sayings, certainly weren't likely to appeal to the esthetic sense of twenty thousand white insurance brokers and car dealers from small town America.

Brown's decision to paint over the most offensive murals in the week preceding the convention was buffeted by cries of censorship, and ran aground when Jesse Jackson himself arrived to lead a mass demonstration against institutionalized racism. "Give us art, not apartheid," came the cry. It being too late to cancel, the Kiwanians came and cowered in hotel rooms scattered throughout Greater Zenith, venturing out only in the fleet of buses hired to shuttle them directly to and from the convention center.

The only good to come out of it, from Doane's point of view, was the $200,000 he managed to win from the city for the family of a student who broke his neck falling off a ladder while putting the finishing touches on Malcolm X's eyebrows.

Seneca Doane walked through the door of the Alhambra Tower, removed his hat and overcoat, and crossed the lobby to the elevators. He whistled as he walked and gave an overly loud greeting to Justin, the security guard dozing behind the desk. He had the feeling this was going to be a good day, a very good day.

Chapter Three

They called Sergeant Dunnington Jefferson in at ten that morning. Delia had to shake him awake. It took some doing. When he finally opened his eyes she said tonelessly, "They want you downtown."

"Wha-whassat?" he mumbled, blinking in the piercing glare of the forty watt bulb out in the hallway.

"Downtown," she spat. "They want you downtown."

"How come?" he wondered, trying to shake off his stupor.

"How the hell should I know?" Delia hissed. "Maybe you left a wake up call."

"What's that s'posed to mean?"

"It's your day off, Dunnington. It's Dee's birthday. You remember Dee, don't you? She's your daughter, your youngest daughter."

Jefferson sighed. He'd promised to be there for Dee's party. He'd promised, but this bitch was making it easy to break it. He got up slowly and began collecting the bits and pieces of clothing he'd scattered earlier while searching for the bed. "I gotta go. S'probly about last night."

"Go ahead and go then." Delia picked up a shoe and pitched it at him. "Go ahead, you bastard. It's the force you're married to, not me."

"Delia, please. Not now," Dunnington pleaded, mustering as much dignity as any hungover, middle-aged man ducking flying footwear could hope to. "Not now. Three of my boys were killed last night."

"It's a damn shame you weren't," she replied, and there was nothing in her face or voice to make him think she didn't mean it.

Dunnington limped out the front door, swore at the steadily falling snow, and slithered down the soggy, whitening streets to headquarters.

* * *

Narrows Burton slumped forward on a bench, his elbows resting on his weary, aching knees. He gasped for breath. Sweat beaded on his face. It gathered at the tip of his nose and dripped onto the floor between his red, swollen feet. He watched the drops darken the faded green carpet. He rocked back and forth, waiting for the pain to subside, waiting for the energy to finish taking off his clothes. He sighed. He leaned back against the damp, beige wall and shivered. He ran his hands through his bristling black hair and told himself it wasn't worth it.

"Still there, Burt? You're going to miss lunch." Denny Redmond toweled himself in the doorway leading from the showers. He stood in a way Narrows never could. Proud, uncowed by his nakedness, his lean body glistened with health. He didn't need to shed any weight. He didn't smoke, and if he drank as much as he pleased, he did so with few ill effects. What galled Narrows most was that at thirty-eight, Denny was three years his senior.

"You moved well today," Denny said in gracious tribute to the vanquished. "It always surprises me the balls you reach."

Narrows managed to laugh. "And you're always waiting on the 'T' for my return."

"That's the object of the game, buddy." Denny strolled across the locker room to the mirror, trailing the towel across his back to catch the last flecks of moisture. He whirled and launched the balled-up cloth into the towel bin twenty feet away. In a dozen years of weekly squash matches, Narrows had never seen him miss that shot.

Narrows shrugged, stood, peeled off his shorts and jock, and walked gingerly toward the stalls. Each step sent waves of pain through his swollen feet. His ankles were sore from frequent starts and stops in pursuit of Denny's irretrievable shots. Narrows had long since abandoned hopes of beating his friend. No matter how hard he tried, Denny dispatched him effortlessly. He continued to make the effort because the ordeal gave him the resolve to get into shape. If that resolve lasted only until his first post-game Heineken, at least he had made the effort.

As if to bolster Narrows' dwindling discipline, Denny greeted his return from the shower by asking him about his diet.

Narrows shrugged. "I like living too much." His eight foot underhand toss was off the mark again, and the towel landed on the shelf next to the bin. A flicker of a smile crossed Denny's face as he searched the mirror for some hint of imperfection. He was dressed in a tailored wool suit, dark gray with faint maroon windowpaning. His white shirt was crisply starched, and his navy blue and maroon silk tie was firmly knotted beneath the button-down collar. He brushed his thick blond hair straight back, then blew it dry, shaping it with skillful fingers until every strand was in place.

He paused at the door as Narrows shrugged into his slightly rumpled suit. "You know, it'd only take about twenty pounds," he offered, genuine concern overriding his usual reticence on personal matters.

Narrows groaned. "I know, Denny. I tell myself that all the time. Jesus, what's twenty pounds? A couple months at the most?"

"No. It's more than that, and less, too. You don't have to starve yourself, just make a few simple changes in your diet. Cut out bread and butter with dinner, give up salt, have water instead of beer with lunch. That's really all it takes."

"A few simple changes," cried Narrows. "You call giving up my midday beer a simple change?"

"You shouldn't laugh, Burt. This is serious. In just a few years you might..." Denny let the words hang. Having to pay attention to one's heart was maybe the final loss of innocence, the last threshold on the headlong flight from youth.

Narrows stared at the friend who had virtually adopted him upon his arrival in Zenith, fresh out of Kansas State University. The Zenith Steel Corporation had offered him a position in marketing. Having no reason to go back home to Pennsylvania, Narrows had accepted. When his father died, Narrows had sought a good investment counselor to handle his share of the estate. A colleague had recommended Denny, who turned out to be a sympathetic spirit. Over lunch they discovered a mutual interest in squash. Denny had sponsored him at the club, introduced him to his circle of friends and helped him make a series of shrewd investments. When Zenith Steel folded, Denny had pulled a few strings and landed Narrows in the commercial real estate department at Thompson Properties. Denny had even introduced Narrows to his future wife, but on the whole he'd been very helpful.

Now Narrows looked at the man who had been more like a father than an older brother to him, and he envied his youth.

* * *

The Men's Grill at the Zenith Athletic Club hadn't changed in the fifty years since Karl Bildenhurst underwrote its complete renovation. The second-generation German immigrant had grown rich during World War II. A contract to provide steel to Zenith's Herringbone Tank Works had transformed his Zenith Foundry into the Zenith Steel Corporation, the largest steel mill in the state.

Under Bildenhurst's guidance, the old, dark paneling was pulled down and the bleak, brooding oil paintings discarded (several had been salvaged by the Zenith Institute of Art to form the backbone of the now highly regarded 19th Century English Portrait Gallery). The stolid mahogany tables and chairs were dumped on antique dealers, who added a 1000 percent markup and moved the entire stock within a month. The threadbare oriental carpets met a similar fate. In their place Bildenhurst had installed low slung blonde wood chairs and tables of the latest design. The carpeting was made of the most modern synthetic fibers. The birch paneling was bright and lively. A series of brilliantly colored abstract paintings had completed the room's transformation into the most modern Men's Grill of any urban club in the nation.

When the renovations were finally completed, the members had all agreed that the new Men's Grill certainly gave the place a lot of pep, and proceeded to abandon it in favor of the dark, comfortable Old World ambience of the Great Hall.

Though longing to rectify their collective disgrace, the ZAC Board of

Directors had been reluctant to offend their benefactor. However, when Old Man Bildenhurst finally kicked off in 1972, they decided to restore the room to its original condition. It had taken ten years to raise the money, but before the architect could finish drawing the plans, the club succumbed to political pressure from the Zenith City Council, and a series of high profile demonstrations by feminist groups against its sexist policies. Funds earmarked for Men's Grill restoration had been applied instead to the construction of "separate but equal" women's athletic facilities.

Nevertheless, as the ZAC's sole remaining bastion of male exclusivity, the Men's Grill had enjoyed a renaissance. Its proximity to the men's locker room had given it added prominence due to an influx of athletic members following the demise of the Union Club. It grew so popular that it became necessary to appoint a full time steward. The call went out, and Robert Rollins Jr. answered it.

He occupied his post alongside the Men's Grill bar, wearing an inscrutable smile and supervising the trio of waiters and pair of cooks who constituted his crew. Small and lean, he wore his wiry hair short, and his crisp white jacket with pride. He greeted his guests with a polite restraint which, though dramatically different than the quiet arrogance with which he had reigned at the Parisienne, was highly appropriate for the Men's Grill.

Rollins nodded at Narrows as he came out of the locker room. He wore a gray herringbone tweed jacket over a pair of gray woolen slacks. His white shirt, though clean, wasn't likely to be mistaken for one of Denny's emblems of crisp efficiency. His red tie was knotted loosely, the top button open on his shirt. His face was still flushed and he felt the sweat beading on his forehead again.

His face was round, with a tendency towards jowls which age would accentuate. His skin was pale except after exercising. He tended to burn and so avoided the sun as much as possible, a habit which now put him in the unaccustomed company of the health-conscious. His mouth was unremarkable in repose, but broadened into a splendid grin and an easy laugh which transformed his entire face. His dark eyes widened and actually seemed to sparkle when he was amused. It made him great fun to be with, and a popular drinking companion.

On the other hand, when he was unhappy his eyes were penetrating, and even hostile. Casual acquaintances knew to avoid him when they saw him glower, and even good friends shied away when he reached for the scotch.

Narrows moved slowly through the dining room, nodding at various colleagues and stopping here and there to do a little unavoidable business with developers and investors. He paused to search for Denny in the congested room. Usually the luncheon crowd began tapering off at the end of March when most members' fancy turned to thoughts of golf, sailing, or a few weeks in their cottages up north. By June, Narrows and Denny often had the place to themselves. This year, however, everyone's habits were held hostage to the weather. It was hard to think about spring, let alone summer, when snow still lay on the ground.

After surveying the room a third time, Narrows spotted Denny at a table along the west wall near the end of the bar. He waved and angled to the right, choosing the most direct route, though it would take him past the Round Table, where Seneca Doane was holding court.

The Round Table was the largest table in the Men's Grill. Once a massive slab of highly polished oak, it had been the exclusive domain of the ZAC's wits and raconteurs. Unabashedly modeled on that more famous literary conclave, the Round Table had enjoyed a twenty-five year reign in the spotlight of Zenith's cultural and social elite. In fact, one of the table's founders, Dr, Harold Dunfees, had actually been invited to lunch at the Algonquin. A professor of English Literature at Zenith University, Dr. Dunfees had delighted in gracing the assemblage with the much-embellished witticisms of his friends, "Dot" Parker, "Al" Woolcott and "Bobby" Benchley. The Round Table's glory days ended about the time old man Bildenhurst replaced it with the formica-topped abortion which still sat in mockery of the twelve-foot-high leaded-glass bay windows.

Seneca Doane's presence at the Round Table was for Narrows an apt representation of the decline of civilization. The table remained the favored Men's Grill setting, but its humor was now given over to scatological puns and vicious swipes at Blacks and Jews, and its occupants were usually personal injury attorneys and smarmy manufacturer's reps.

And bloated real estate lawyers, Narrows remembered too late, as Rob Patterson loomed before him. He let the giant crush his hand.

"Still trying to play with the big boys, eh?" Patterson substituted scorn for his envy of anyone still capable of athletic competition. A former defensive end for the Zenith Barons, his four-year All Pro career had been cut short when he blew out his knee. Though a half-dozen specialists predicted that he'd never walk again, a year of painful physical therapy proved them wrong. Patterson regained the use of both legs. He finished college, and went on to law school. Now a respected attorney, he remained in Narrows' eyes an unrepentant jock who had never grown up and never stopped growing.

Neither his celebrity as a local sports hero made good, nor his notoriety as a condemnations specialist who had singlehandedly scuttled a series of major Zenith redevelopment ventures, could ease the pain of exile from the gridiron. The knowledge that city planners wouldn't consider the most insignificant tool and die plant expansion without consulting him first paled before the gnawing certainty that he would never again blindside a quarterback at full speed.

Patterson had plenty of money, a beautiful wife, and an eight-bedroom French Renaissance mansion on six acres in Wellington Lakes. Yet he remained bitter and self-destructive. He poured all his athletic aggressiveness into eating himself into an early grave. It was sadly ironic that, after successfully defying his doctor's prediction that he would never walk again, Patterson now defied his warnings that his knee couldn't continue to support his increasing bulk. Though already forced to rely on a cane, he continued to shovel enormous amounts of food into his gaping mouth.

His peers tolerated him only because of his power to destroy. His decision to take a case was based not on its merits, but on how much damage he could do to the other side: the City of Zenith, a corporation seeking a new headquarters, or a developer planning a subdivision. Because of the opponents he chose, the public saw him as a populist hero, taking the side of the defenseless homeowner, representing environmental groups, and standing up for the small businessman; he was loved and admired by all except those who knew him.

Narrows let Patterson crush his hand, breathe foully into his face and mock his athletic pretensions, because the attorney held the key to the most important deal of Narrows' life.

"How was the special today?" he asked, gazing longingly at Patterson's empty plate.

He belched in reply and said, "I was on the phone with Ted Jr. this morning."

Narrows winced. Patterson's gloating announcement was more painful than his handshake. "I'm not sure this is the right place to discuss—"

"It sure the hell is." Patterson's voice shattered the subdued civility which most guests brought to Men's Grill luncheons. "That's precisely the reason we come to this rathole. So we can take care of business without having to share it with the ladies." He grinned. "At least, that's what the bitches say."

Narrows shrugged. There was no point in arguing. Patterson's misogyny was well-established. "Why don't I call you this afternoon and you can tell me what Ted had to say."

Laughter rumbled up from deep within Patterson's belly. It was a rich, resonant sound which, if you didn't know the man, might lead you to think him congenial. "I don't anticipate returning to the office this afternoon." He gestured at the table behind him. "These gentlemen are going to try to get me drunk." His amusement was justified because his enormous bulk allowed him the luxury, or tragedy, of consuming prodigious amounts of alcohol without the slightest effect.

Inwardly seething at this man who would so blithely squelch a deal representing three years of intensive effort, Narrows suggested, "Then maybe I should call Ted myself."

Patterson moved closer, dwarfing him. "I wouldn't do that," he said mildly, the softness of his tone actually heightening the ferocity of his threat. He was equally capable of physical, financial or legal harm, and played upon his intimidating physical presence to keep his adversary off balance.

For once the strategy failed. Not because Narrows possessed extraordinary courage or superior legal knowledge, simply because he no longer cared. He had almost clinched the deal a year ago, then the old man died. Ted Jr. had been most reasonable at first. Then Patterson got involved. Now it was going on six months of humiliating and costly delays. His investors were getting impatient. They didn't like to see their money tied up in a wrangle showing no signs of being resolved. It was time to put an end to it.

"I've been talking to the Department of Natural Resources," he announced casually.

Patterson took a half-step backwards and gave an unconvincing laugh. "You wouldn't dare."

Narrows smiled at the weak rejoinder, and pressed his advantage. "They think the grasslands might have environmental significance." As he stepped around the big man, he added, "It's time to cut my losses."

"Why, you little shit."

"Give me a call." With that Narrows made his way over to his table. "Sorry, Denny."

He looked up from his feast of tuna salad, cottage cheese and fresh vegetables. "Rollins is holding the last special for you."

As usual on Wednesday afternoon, Narrows struggled against his conscience. Having just gone through hell, he faced this first hurdle on the road back to fitness. Every Wednesday, hedonism outflanked reason and undid whatever benefit he had gained from his ordeal. Today, after confronting Patterson's 350 pounds of self-indulgence, Narrows' gluttony faltered. He succumbed to dietary restraint. "I'll just have what you're eating," he decided. Denny pantomimed applause.

After Narrows' diet plate arrived, Denny said, "You ought to pick on someone your own size. I thought Patterson was going to have a stroke."

"We should be so lucky."

"You should be so lucky," corrected Denny. "Rob's one of my biggest clients."

"You're worse than a whore, you're a shameless whore."

Ignoring the barb, Denny continued. "So what was it all about—Oak Grove?" He frowned at Narrows' confirmation. "Scoring points off him won't help, Burt. You've got to wrap this up."

Narrows washed down a mouthful of cottage cheese with a gulp of water. "How can you stand this stuff? It's utterly tasteless."

"You get used to it," Denny replied absently. Then he added, "I'm getting worried, Burt. You're out a hundred grand already."

Narrows pushed his plate aside. "You agreed it was a good idea, Den." He shrugged. "I hate him."

"What are you going to do?

"What am I going to do? If you're so tight with the bastard, why don't you do something?"

Denny laughed. "No way, buddy. I'm strictly neutral on this one. Patterson's worth fifty grand a year in fees and commissions."

"A shameless whore," Narrows repeated. He gave another shrug. "If it's not wrapped up by next Friday, I'll cut and run."

* * *

Later that afternoon, Patterson and Doane found themselves sitting alone at the Round Table. The others had all returned reluctantly to their offices after a two hour lunch. Doane made an attempt to leave, too, but was waylaid by the big man's hand on his arm.

"Stick around, Counselor. We need to talk."

"Somebody you need me to sue?" Doane wondered. "Have a slip and fall? I noticed you're using a cane these days."

Patterson's face clouded over, and for a moment Doane thought he might have gone too far. But then the big man laughed. "Naw, nothing like that. How 'bout a game of chess?"

Both attorneys appreciated the challenges inherent in the game. It kept them sharp. Doane felt its benefits in the courtroom, Patterson in the maneuvering outside the chambers where he did his best work.

They moved to the game room, Patterson first ordering Rollins not to forget about them. Patterson picked white, and they began to play. "Still using the Sicilian I see."

"I'll keep using it 'til you figure it out."

"Is that so?" Patterson slid his king's bishop diagonally forward, and said with a chuckle, "And when was the last time you beat me?"

Doane laughed. "You're just lucky, that's all."

"We make our own luck."

"You mean like that stupid cop last night?"

"Wasn't that something?" Patterson shook his head. "You know, this city truly is a shithole." When his companion frowned he said, "You disagree, or are you confused by my rook?"

"Hell, Rob, I'm not blind. It's just, you know what Zenith used to be. What it was. I just can't help but think—"

"That's progress, anyway." The big man roared at his own joke. "But enough of that. Figured out who you're gonna sue?"

"What makes you think I'm going to sue?"

Patterson laughed again. "Why, Red Man, isn't that what you do? Somebody dies. Somebody gets sued. You make a lot of money."

Doane let out a sigh. "Sometimes, I gotta tell you, it gets old, being that guy. But you're right. I'm sniffing around." He chuckled, sadly. "I made contact with the grieving mother."

Patterson whistled softly. "Morning after. I'm impressed."

"She's a piece of work, let me tell you. And that guy, Kong. He's scary. I mean major league scary. That guy's got a screw loose."

"You met with Kong? Red Man, you're going big time for sure."

"Well, I didn't try to meet with Kong. I didn't plan to meet with Kong. What I heard, he's laying low, maybe took off for Columbus." Doane shuddered. "So I had Phil Chandler, my investigator, find out where she's staying, and he sends me over to some house just off Perryman. Not too bad a neighborhood, yet. She's sitting on this couch, sobbing out her eyes. My guy's there. He introduces me and she jumps up and starts screaming about how that fucking cop killed her baby. Then Kong strolls into the room—that's what he did, he strolled. Comes up to me, says 'What you want?' So I give him my card. Tell him a terrible thing happened, and I want to see justice done." Doane paused to diffidently nudge his knight forward. Patterson snorted, ran his queen across the board and announced, "Check."

Doane studied the board for a minute, then he said, "Kong went ballistic. He shoved me—shoved me, back against the wall. He got in my face and started ranting about "Don't need no white lawyer. Don't need no lawyer at all. Keisha be fine. She don't want that baby no how." Doane shook his head. "So I got out of there. You know what I think? I think that cop was right. I think she threw the baby out the door."

"So who else you looking at?"

Doane stared at his friend. "Did you listen? Did you even hear one word of what I said?"

"So, let me get this straight. You got a conscience now, is that it? You're going to go around and start judging people?" He shook his head. "Red Man, you surprise me."

Doane finally resigned the game. "You know, Rob. Sometimes I surprise myself. You know what I felt when I left that house? I felt dirty. I felt like I was somehow involved in their sick game. Let me tell you, it's not a good feeling."

* * *

By the time Chief Slaughter announced Police Sergeant Dunnington Jefferson's suspension without pay pending an investigation into last night's slaughter, the chief suspect in this case of "bribery and the betrayal of his fellow officers" was already throwing down shots of Jack Daniels at The Walloon Saloon, just around the corner from his youngest daughter's thirteenth birthday party. The storm became a blizzard, and he got stranded and drunk. He was still there when the five o'clock news came on. He peered through the gathering mists to see himself made infamous. There was his face, back when he used to smile, on TV screens all over Zenith. And there was his tearful wife telling a reporter, "It wouldn't surprise me one bit. Nothing that man did would surprise me."

Jefferson left his last shot half-drunk on the bar, and staggered out, muttering, "They can't do this to me."

He went home and shot his wife and three teenaged daughters as the last flakes of the last storm of the long, long winter drifted earthward. He reloaded his shotgun and blew away the couple next door, along with their mangy dog. He reloaded again and sat quietly on the snow-covered lawn, sucking both barrels until his colleagues arrived. Then he squeezed the trigger.

The Zenith tabloids played with the "Psycho Cop" for a week, until a twelve-year-old girl distracted them by burying her newborn baby in a snowdrift. She said she did it because it made so much noise she was afraid her aunt would find out. The discovery that the baby's fourteen-year-old father rode around in a chauffeured limousine and ran a half-dozen drug houses for the Wrecking Crew, occupied another week's worth of headlines, followed by revelations that the kid's uncle was Mayor Jeremiah Brown. The "Psycho Cop" didn't get back to page one until the day the Zenith Police Department's Internal Affairs division cleared Sergeant Jefferson of all charges. Except for the murders of his wife and daughters, and the neighbors, of course.

* * *

Narrows missed the first barrage of "Psycho Cop" reporting, being caught up in the throes of his own personal drama. He wasn't the type to waste time perusing the tabloids, or watching TV news for that matter, but even if he were, he wouldn't have been able to concentrate. Not for the forty-eight hours following his lunchtime confrontation with Patterson. He'd thrown his hat into a far more perilous kind of ring when he bearded the lion in his den, and he wasn't sure he was up to it. Patterson wasn't your run of the mill merciless bastard. As the hours wore on without any hint of action, Narrows began to suspect he'd be lucky if all he lost was his investment.

Friday afternoon Ted Jr. called from Tucson, Arizona. "That you, Burton?" the old man barked.

"Sure is, Ted. I'm glad to hear from you."

"You sure as hell shouldn't be, and you'll be even less glad to see me come Tuesday."

"What's up?"

"I'm coming out there to rip your fucking head off!"

Narrows smiled in spite of the threat. "Been talking to Patterson, eh?"

"Yeah, I—how'd you know?"

"I always feel like ripping someone's head off after talking to him.

Ted laughed, but only briefly before the rage swept back into his voice. "He says you're dealing behind my back."

"Yeah, what if I am?" Narrows tried to inject a little heat into his side of the conversation. "All that'd mean was I was playing according to Patterson's rules."

"Start making sense, boy," growled the Arizonan. "You tell me what kind of deal you cut with the DNR."

"What kind of deal? Come on, be reasonable, Ted. Even if they were interested, what could I do? I don't own the property. I'm not your agent. Besides, even if I could cut a deal, what good would that do me? I'm trying to put a development together."

"You mean you never talked to them?"

"Of course I did. That's the first place I checked."

"Then Patterson was right—"

"If they had the slightest interest, no way would I touch it. I can't fight you, Patterson, a truckload of investors, and the entire state government."

"Yeah, but Patterson said—"

"I was trying to get him off center. Jesus, Ted. This has gone on for six months. I can't afford it, and neither can you. I've got Curtis Gentry breathing down my neck. He's talking about pulling out, and if he quits, the rest won't be far behind."

"You lied to Patterson, eh?" Ted wasn't following very well. He couldn't get over that first hurdle. Nobody lied to Patterson. Not if they valued their livelihood, or maybe their knees.

"I can't play his game, Ted. I don't know where you stand on Oak Grove anymore, but all I can tell you is either you come on board now, without Patterson, or I take my losses and go home. You can cut any kind of deal you want with him, but watch your ass, or you'll have to get his permission before you can wipe it."

Ted was silent for a long minute, during which Narrows kissed his dream goodbye. He kissed his hundred thousand goodbye, the five million he stood to gain, and the fantasy he'd entertained of playing with the big boys. Then Ted said, "Alright, let's do it. Hell, it's what Dad wanted anyhow." Narrows could hear him rustling papers at his desk. "Listen, I already booked a flight next Tuesday. Why don't we meet at the property Wednesday 'bout noon, just you and me, and wrap this up?"

"You sure you aren't luring out there so you can rip my head off?"

Ted laughed garrulously. "Tell you what, I got me some whiskey that might just do that."

Chapter Four

On the day of Narrows' meeting, winter finally released its grip on the city. Having held on too long, the effect was like that of an overstretched rubber band. The temperature soared thirty-five degrees above Tuesday's high of fifty. The day dawned bright and warm, not a cloud in the sky. Spring was forgotten, summer sprang full bloom. All over Zenith people celebrated the return of the sun. Businessmen shucked their overcoats, and their jackets. They paraded downtown in rolled-up shirtsleeves, their ties loosened, winter no more than a bad memory. Businesswomen peeled off their efficient jackets, letting cream colored blouses celebrate their liberation from seasonal oppression. Secretaries broke out their summer dresses and took extra-long lunches, sunning themselves on the plaza. The homeless saw their portfolios rise as everyone had spare change for once, and relinquished it willingly.

All over the state, farmers, having sat on the sidelines too long, stormed their fields, hoping to salvage a season's crop. Working bare-chested, savoring the sweat on their backs, they tried to recoup a lost month's plowing in a single day. Pushing themselves and their machinery beyond the customary bounds of caution, they found their tractors mired to their axles in black, gummy mud. A similar frenzy gripped household gardeners. They rousted the winter blanket of leaves from their beds. They worked the soil and nursed their sun-starved plants back to health.

It was a day for cancellations and shattered traditions. Among those less significant was Narrows' broken squash date with Denny. Others bore greater consequences. As the day grew steadily warmer, and his beloved garden cried for attention, Robert Rollins Jr. faced a moral dilemma. He had never called in sick before, not in thirty years. It had been a matter of pride with him, but after a moment he decided he had no choice. He couldn't let his garden languish any longer. He wasn't alone. Throughout Greater Zenith men and women who'd remained faithful through the sickness and depression of the long winter, succumbed to euphoria and stayed away from their jobs.

* * *

At 11:30 Narrows left his office in Athens to drive twenty miles to a 1,500 acre plot of undeveloped land surrounded by Zenith's northeastern suburbs. He avoided the congested freeway, which once had funneled commuters into the city, but now more frequently served as an escape route for the steady stream of urban refugees. It was one of the oldest freeways in the country, but the pride with which Zenith's boosters had pointed to that fact had soon turned to sorrow. The ease of access had unleashed the city's energies on the unsuspecting countryside. It had paved the way for the hell of Zenith's exodus.

Narrows followed Wellington Boulevard past the glistening mid-rise towers and campuslike headquarters of Athens' burgeoning crop of corporate residents. He noted the brash modernity of the Winston Brewing Company building, an array of tinted blue glass and naked steel infrastructure concocted into a bizarre trapezoid. The design, by John Phillipson, (a Zenithite profiled in "Time" as a leading member of "The Midwest's Cadre of Hyper-Modern Structuralists"), had been awarded a blue ribbon last year by the American Architectural Society's Design Council. The public relations firm of Anderson, Alcott and Zest, (whose pink granite horizontal wedge was being thrown up just down the hill from Winston), had generated such a storm of publicity for the award that the coincident closure of Winton's last Zenith brewery had passed almost unnoticed. Except within the families of the 800 employees who lost their jobs.

Beyond the strip of office buildings, Wellington Boulevard narrowed from six to four lanes and limped through the Burroughs Bottleneck. Narrows downshifted and contemplated good intentions gone awry. As early as 1953 the Burroughs City Council had passed anti-development ordinances. Determined to retain its identity as a small community with character, instead it found itself betrayed by frenzied development. Since it refused to be part of the future, Burroughs was consigned to the scrap heap of the past. As once all roads led to Rome, in Zenith all roads led through Burroughs. Because no developers had vested interests there, the State Department of Transportation rerouted the freeway through West Burroughs. The expansion of County Road 16 into the Meridith Parkway, a major east-west thoroughfare, cut another piece out of the heart of the mile-square community. If the city did manage to prevent the widening of Wellington Boulevard, it was a pyrrhic victory. The resultant congestion made curbside parking so hazardous that it was ultimately banned. Rather than stand the expense of building off-street parking, Burroughs' Wellington Boulevard merchants decamped en masse for surrounding shopping malls.

Now Narrows crept past porn shops, topless bars, and adult theaters. Down side streets lined with rusted hulks of automobiles he could see burned-out shells of vacant houses and dozens of idle men and youths congregating on the ramshackle porches of the remaining inhabitable dwellings. "Urban comfort in a suburban setting," he mused, in mockery of the ill-fated slogan with which Winston had attempted to lease space in Brewery Park. As a sop to the troubled city of Zenith, the company had redeveloped its abandoned brewery into a low-rise office park. Narrows was the only commercial real estate specialist who still serviced the development. After two years of unstinting labor it remained only twenty percent occupied. Somehow, "Suburban Comfort in an Urban Setting" hadn't wowed 'em the way the whiz kids at A2Z had expected.

The only good thing about Burroughs was its ability to make the town next door look good. Regal Heights was neither. Situated at the base of Burroughs Hill, Regal Heights was given over to small tool and die shops and light industrial parks. The boulevard was lined by chainlink-fence-enclosed graveled yards in which semis were backed up to loading docks. A thin layer of soot hovered over the city, the inevitable by-product of the kind of concentrated industrial activity which gave Regal Heights one of the highest tax bases in the state. Because the city had so few residents, it also boasted the state's lowest tax rate. This, combined with the municipality's lax environmental standards, resulted in a waiting list of small industrial firms longing to move in.

The Burroughs City Council cast hungry eyes at their neighbor. They implored the courts, the legislature, and the good, if cancerous, citizens of Regal Heights to allow a municipal merger. It seemed a match made in heaven. Regal Heights had all that money with no one to spend it on; Burroughs had all those people with no money to spend. Just the other day Burroughs City Councilwoman Carmelita Williams had hauled out the shopworn terminology of racism to explain not only the established powers' reluctance to allow the marriage, but the origins of the city's problems as well.

Narrows wasn't about to claim that racism didn't exist in Zenith. To the contrary, he believed the economic, social and geographical stratification of black and white put the city on a par with pre-Mandela South Africa. But this Williams woman was way off base. Burroughs' problems were obviously the result of strategic blunders by its planners, coupled with a burst of regional growth far beyond anyone's expectations. One thing it wasn't was racially motivated. Burroughs hadn't even had any Black residents until after it hit bottom. It would be funny if it weren't so damned aggravating. Still it wasn't uncommon for a Black leader to cite racism as the cause of every problem his constituency faced. Williams probably figured it was easier to blame whitey than to actually try to solve the problems, and was a much safer road to reelection than suggesting that Blacks might actually have some responsibility for their own plight.

Narrows shook his head and accelerated up the hill towards the marginally more appealing town of Merrydale. A sign at the border said Merrydale's official flower was the petunia, which told him all he needed to know about the place. A suburb of some 100,000 souls, it had sprung up almost overnight in the mid-sixties when, in the aftermath of the race riots, the retreat from Zenith became headlong flight. Merrydale and the neighboring city of East Zenith were populated by former Zenithites harboring an almost pathological hatred of their hometown. East Zenith went so far as to mount biennial campaigns to change its name to Wellington Heights, East Merrydale, or some other label enabling its citizens to scrub their origins from the history books.

Both cities consisted of three-bedroom ranch style, two-story mock-colonial, or split-level stucco houses lining meandering streets called Pheasant Lane, Oak Glen and Goose Lake Road. Their fanciful names paid backhanded tribute to the hardwood forests, rolling grasslands and placid lakes which had been clear cut, bulldozed and filled in by developers unwilling to spare a square inch of land for something as unprofitable as park-land or recreation areas.

Wellington Boulevard, which had swelled to eight lanes by the time it entered Merrydale, was jammed with minivans and SUV's racing from Taco Bell to Target to the Merryvale Mall. The mall was the perfect cultural center for the smug, ethnocentric citizens of Merryvale. As he continued up the broad corridor along which every fast food chain and big box retailer had erected an outpost, Narrows wondered again why he stayed in this dying city choked by stillborn suburbs. As usual, he told himself it wasn't any better anywhere else, that Zenith was unfortunately a microcosm of America. Besides, he was about to transform the esthetic landscape of the city with a tasteful, environmentally compatible development of his own.

That reminder of where he was heading and why, shook Narrows out of his lethargy. He accelerated. With the sentinels of corporate America flashing past, he allowed himself the first giddy anticipation of success. It was almost in the bag. A handshake deal with Ted and he'd be on his way. He turned left on Mettler Road, bypassing Wellington Lakes, where he'd spent three years of married indifference. In his eagerness to get to Oak Grove, he denied himself the pleasure of cruising slowly past Wellington Lakes' stately Tudor and French Renaissance homes fronted by broad, immaculately kept lawns and shaded by elegant, soaring elms. Once he pulled off this deal he could buy one of his own if he wished. He sped along the narrow road basking in the contemplation of Narrows Burton, multi-millionaire before the age of forty.

* * *

Seneca Doane sat at his usual window table in the Philbert Club, atop the Second National Tower, nursing his scotch and soda and staring moodily down at the sun-drenched city. There was no way around it, he decided. He'd misjudged her. He'd made a mistake. His hand tightened on the icy glass. A mistake. God, how he hated that word. He was Seneca Doane III. He didn't make mistakes.

He glared at the untouched cup of coffee and the soggy, crumpled napkins in front of the empty chair. It had been a hell of a week. Things had moved so quickly, everything falling into place. It couldn't have worked better if he had scripted it. His investigator, Phil Chandler, had exceeded even his usual high standards. First finding the dead girl's mother, and when that didn't work out, really putting his nose to the ground.

Snooping around Police Plaza, Chandler came up with scuttlebutt that there was no way Jefferson had been bought. "He was a good cop," Chandler had reported. "And this Kong was a real burr under his saddle. He wanted him. He was obsessed with him. On the other hand, this Peters, the one he accidentally shot? Everybody says he was bent. Smart money says he was in the Wrecking Crew's pocket."

"So if Jefferson didn't do it—"

"Then he got screwed."

Doane had kicked that one around for awhile. Suing the city on behalf of "The Psycho Cop." That would be worth some publicity. Even "The New York Times" would give this one ink. "Court TV" would cover the trial. Hell, Greta Van Susteren might make an appearance. It sounded tempting, but how to get there from here? "I'm not seeing it, Phil. Sure, he got screwed, but I'd say his family and his neighbors got screwed worse."

"Don't forget about the dog," Chandler had noted.

Doane had chuckled. "Yeah, mustn't forget about the dog." He tapped his desk with a pencil. "But how does it work? Who's gonna feel sorry for the 'Psycho Cop'?"

"Oh, that's the good part. His sister, Celia Jefferson Wilson. A regular saint. Sweetest woman in the world. And she's good. I mean the media will eat her up."

"So I sue on her behalf. A good woman whose life is torn apart, all because the City destroyed a good cop to avoid looking bad. We got cover up on this Peters. Make it look like they knew all along. How high up did this go? Who else is in Kong's pocket? No wonder they couldn't stop them. Yeah, I can see how this would work. Throw enough mud and some of it will stick."

Doane had decided it was worth a go. No way he'd take it to trial, but make some noise, and the City would bend over backwards to settle. At least that had been the plan.

He took another sip of his scotch and replayed the morning. The press conference had gone well enough. The tabloids and local TV stations were out in force, even if the stodgy "News" hadn't deemed him worthy of its consideration. He had put on a show, his thin, red face quivering, the tears welling in his eyes as he catalogued the blunders which had pushed a good man over the edge. "Even today the police refuse to admit they accused the wrong man," he concluded.

Celia had been even better than Chandler had promised. Her voice had trembled when she spoke of what a good Christian man her brother had been, a devoted husband and father. Maybe his marriage was falling apart, but whose fault was that? He had spent his entire life trying to put people like the Wrecking Crew behind bars, and the police department never backed him up. They betrayed him at every turn, and beat him down, and destroyed him. It was the police who wrecked his marriage. The police who broke him down until that terrible night when he lost his mind, and his wife and—"

Doane had to admit it had been a stroke of genius to hold the PC outside the conference room where the city attorneys had arranged to make their stand. They'd arrived in the middle of it, totally unprepared for the sight of Celia breaking into anguished sobs. The media had assaulted them as only the media can.

"No comment," the lawyers had cried. "We have nothing to say. Now let us through!"

They'd scurried to safety behind the door and cowered there while

Doane brought the press conference to a leisurely conclusion. He'd stressed the damages sought, shouting the figure to make sure the shysters could hear him in the next room. It was a lucky thing they'd had to run that gauntlet, Doane recalled, because they'd come to the meeting ready to stonewall. No deals were on the table. They tried to stick to their game plan at first. "The mayor's pissed," they declared. "He says this guy's a fucking mass murderer, and no way he's gonna pay. Not one red cent."

But they'd left their balls out in the hallway, and they lost what little nerve they had left when Celia began to cry again. Softly at first, her sobs rose in volume and intensity. The lawyers were silenced by her masterful performance, and their guts turned to mush when Doane cast a few lures their way. Doane was good. He was fishing, he knew it, but he also knew he could read people better than anyone he'd ever met. He could tell when he got a nibble by the look in their eyes.

They were up against it. They knew what Celia's tears would do to a jury, and even though they didn't know how much Doane knew, they knew how well he could use what little he did. Throwing the rules out the window, they skipped stage one and went straight to the million dollar offer. Smiling, Doane reached for a pen to sign the settlement. Then, Celia's sniffles continuing behind him, he hesitated. That was when he made his mistake. He got greedy. "A piddling million bucks for my final case?" he thought. "No, how 'bout I take down City Hall? How 'bout I see Jeremiah Brown hauled off in handcuffs? How 'bout Chief Slaughter doing hard time?"

He shook his head. "Not good enough," he said, flipping the pen across the desk at the stunned attorneys. Then, his arm around the distraught plaintiff's shoulders, he walked into the strobelight of flashing cameras. The media had been riveted by the sound of Celia's bawling. Their diligence was rewarded by a shot of such pathos it was a cinch to make the front page of all four papers. The shot, and Doane's righteous indignation, his defiant announcement that "our silence can't be bought. We demand justice, and nothing less."

On the way back to his office Doane had interpreted Celia's shrug as assent to his suggestion that they have a celebratory lunch. He should have realized something was wrong when she vetoed his offer of a bottle of Taittinger, but he was too caught up in his own good fortune to notice her lifeless tone. He settled for scotch, and a cup of coffee for her. She started crying again when he held up his glass and toasted the very rich woman she was about to become. She wept softly, snuffling so delicately into a napkin that only those at the immediately surrounding tables noticed anything amiss.

"Hey, come on. It'll be alright," he said gently, approximating genuine concern for a fellow human being. He was startled by the hostility on her face.

She shook her head. "I can't do it." He could barely hear her, as though her words were being washed away by the tears now flowing freely down her cheeks.

He glanced uneasily at the other diners. "Take it easy," he said, handing her another napkin. "Save some of those tears for the trial."

"I can't do it," she repeated more forcefully. "I can't go through with this."

"What do you mean you can't go through with it?" All shreds of the solicitous solicitor had vanished. "We're talking about ten million bucks, lady."

She placed her napkin on the table with a daintiness which betrayed her struggle for control. "There won't be any trial."

"So we'll take the million. I'll call them right now." He refused to acknowledge the growing pain in the pit of his stomach. Could she be for real?

She shook her head again. "It isn't right."

"Damn straight it isn't right. They destroyed him. They destroyed your brother. We can't let them get away with this." He reached for her hand and patted it gently. "Listen, Celia. I know what you're going through right now, but hear me out." He shook his head sadly. "This isn't about the money. I know that. No amount of money can bring back your brother, and his family. They can't write a check big enough to fill the hole in your heart." He slapped the table. "But we can't let them get away with this. We've got to stop them. You and I, we have to make sure that the next Dunnington Jefferson doesn't get hurt. Don't you see?"

When she looked at him, he was shocked to see the contempt in her eyes. "There will not be a trial," she repeated. "It isn't right."

Doane took a deep breath and exhaled slowly, clenching and unclenching his fist under the table. "Now you listen to me," he said. "This isn't a fucking game. We've started it, and we're damn well going to finish it."

"It's wrong," she insisted. "Dunnington murdered all those people. I don't deserve anything."

Doane leaned across the table and gripped Celia's wrist. She squirmed but he wouldn't let go. "Let's put our cards on the table," he said in a low, vicious voice. "I don't give a good goddam about what you do or don't deserve. You're right, Jefferson was a piece of shit. Who cares? He's dead." Celia's face began to tremble again, but Doane couldn't stop. "This isn't a moral issue. We've got the city by the balls. They're begging us to take the money."

"But I don't want it," she squeaked.

"I don't care what you want. I want my share."

That was when she started crying in earnest. Great, heart-wrenching sobs poured out. The hapless attorney shrank in his chair as every head in the crowded room swivelled in his direction. Giles, the Philbert Club's masterful steward, glided silently over. "Is everything all right, Mr. Doane?"

He choked on a laugh. Did everything look all right? He jutted his chin at his pathetic companion. "Get her out of here. Now."

As Giles led her away, Doane grinned and raised his glass at the gawping faces. He took a sip and leaned back, hands folded behind his head as if he hadn't a care in the world. A few minutes later, Giles returned to inform him that he'd put her in a cab for her hotel. Doane nodded his approval and said, "I think I'll have the King Crab. Oh, and freshen this up, will you?"

Doane ate his lunch slowly, giving the impression of an epicure savoring every bite. In fact, he barely tasted it. Behind his relaxed facade he analyzed every move, trying to figure out where things had gone wrong. How could he have prevented it?

Aside from the obvious fact that he shouldn't have turned down the million when that was what he wanted, he concluded there was nothing else he could have done. Celia Wilson was a good, decent woman who had been tempted by a quick ten million. In the end she had remained true to her faith. For the first time since his days as a civil rights attorney, Seneca Doane's faith in humanity had been shaken.

* * *

At the Hotel Thornleigh, Denny Redmond was enjoying a much more successful lunch. Auburn haired, with small expressive green eyes, a pug nose and a Lauren Bacall mouth, Cindy Herringbone possessed a unique, piquant beauty. Her green silk dress swirled around her hips as she walked with Denny to their table beneath the vaulted, skylit ceiling of the Imperial Room. He enjoyed watching other men watching the way she moved. He enjoyed the way she projected an air of indifference about her appearance. Denny knew she was well aware of the way they stared, and admired her for never letting on.

It was customary for them to split a bottle of champagne before ordering. It was customary to follow that with a bottle of red wine during lunch. It was customary for Denny to follow Cindy out to the Wellington Lakes Country Club afterwards for a swim, or a round of golf if the weather was nice. Then came more drinks and dinner, still more drinks, and a friendly night in bed with one of the bevy of divorcees, or wives who no longer cared, which made the club its base of operations. The wear and tear of this tradition, which was as inviolable as Denny's rule of never threatening a friendship by ending the night with Cindy, was the only reason he was reluctant to lunch with her more than once a month.

He raised his glass. "Welcome back. How was France?"

"Oh, the usual," she shrugged. "Actually, the skiing was awful. You wouldn't believe how naked the slopes were—just like the Rockies. Deb and I had to go up to the glaciers, which was great, but so primitive. We gave up after a week and went to Paris."

"Did you see Kevin at all?"

She shook her head, and held out her glass for a refill. "He was off in, um, Nepal, I think, searching for some unspoiled village." She broke off to sip the sparkling wine, and sighed her pleasure. "Good luck," she continued. "Between the trekkers and the rebels, I hear the Himalayas are hell on earth."

"Sometimes I wonder what he's running away from."

"That's easy. Daddy."

"How is the old guy?"

"Oh, his usual self," she sighed. "Chasing all over acting important. You know how he is."

Denny nodded.

"His latest thing is funding some new department at ZU," Cindy was saying.

"Yeah, I heard about that. The Zenith University Transportation Safety Research Lab."

"The Herringbone Transportation Safety Research Lab," she corrected. "Oh, he's so silly sometimes. He gets an idea—"

"Or somebody gives him one," Denny noted.

She laughed. "That is so true." She paused for another sip. "Anyway, it just consumes him. Like he's spent his whole life working for it. Now all he can talk about is this Industrial Ecology course."

"Industrial Ecology?"

"It's the brainchild of Harry Bachman—do you know him? He's the head of Grassland Alliance? Anyway, he had daddy pull some strings and now he's teaching this course. It's all about sustainable economics. How can we maintain our economic system without destroying the planet? Daddy's become a huge environmentalist." She laughed out loud. "It is so funny! All he talks about is global warming this, and species diversity that. He's even started a compost heap in our backyard! The great thing is, he drives to all his environmental meetings in his Hummer."

"So he's in thick with this Bachman guy?"

"I guess you could say that. He's the one who got him to pony up the money for the department. Well, him and his wife—Mya. Do you know her? The poet?" Cindy leaned forward and whispered conspiratorially. "Personally, I think he's got a crush on Mya."

"Well, at least it keeps him out of the house."

"But I wonder if it keeps him out of trouble? I mean, isn't it time he grew up?"

Denny laughed sadly. Ken Herringbone Jr. had never quite gotten over being maneuvered out of control of Herringbone Motors. He'd inherited the firm at the age of twenty-two, after his parents drowned during a freak storm up on Lake Superior. Aware of his inadequacy, Ken had gone out and hired the best management team money could buy. Their response had been to take the company public. A complicated deal, it had left Ken with a lot of money and Herringbone stock, but no real power. Once he'd figured out what had happened, he quit. The money allowed him to survive a series of bungled investments. They were grandiose undertakings, each of which was supposed to be his vindication. Denny had long since given up trying to advise the buffoon. The man's credulity was exceeded only by the size of his ego.

"And now he might sell Herringbone," Cindy was saying.

That brought him back in a hurry. "Who is, Ken?"

She nodded and went on to discuss Peg Patterson's growing disenchantment with her marriage. "I think she's going to be at the club tonight," she announced impishly.

Denny searched for a way to turn the conversation back to Cindy's father without arousing her suspicions. If this meant what he thought it might...

"Peg's got a lot to be disenchanted with," he quipped.

Cindy giggled. "Rob is so disgustingly huge. It wouldn't be so bad if he were jolly, the way fat men are supposed to be."

"He isn't very pleasant," Denny conceded. "Still he's got a tremendous amount of discipline—or did when he was in rehab."

"Well, he doesn't now," she sniffed.

Denny refilled their glasses with the last of the champagne, and signaled the waiter with a fluid motion. Then he made a stab at it. "Rob reminds me a bit of your dad."

Cindy sat forward on her chair, a skeptical grin on playing on her face. "How so?"

"They both have tremendous talents—"

"Daddy?" It was as close as a woman like Cindy could come to snorting.

"Sure. It takes talent to control the kind of assets he has."

"Well, I wouldn't know," she replied sweetly. "That's what I have you for—by the way, how am I doing?"

Denny proceeded to give her a rundown on current and expected earnings through the end of the year. "Of course, it all depends on Herringbone," he added purposefully. "You still have a large chunk of it in your portfolio. The stock is undervalued, plus they're holding large cash reserves and—" Denny resisted a smile as Cindy's eyes glazed over. He asked, as if it were an afterthought, "You say Ken's thinking of selling out?"

"He's been talking about it ever since he started hanging out with the Grasslands Alliance people. How it's wrong to profit from the destruction of the planet. Then yesterday I overheard him talking on the phone. Some guy named Harriman or something."

Denny forgot about subtlety. "Could it have been Harrelman? Meyer Harrelman?"

Cindy's eyes brightened. "Yes, that's it! Do you know him?"

"Of him." The waiter chose that moment to interrupt with a bottle of Saddleback Cabernet Sauvignon. "'98?" Denny said. "The wine list says '97."

The waiter shifted his eyes uneasily. "I, uh, think we're out."

"Well, why don't you go find out for sure," he said abruptly. "And if you can't find a '97, you'd better bring me a Bordeaux. Ask Phillipe. He knows what I like."

The waiter scurried off with a terrified, "Yes sir."

"You can be such an ass," Cindy crooned. "But a lovable ass," she added, patting his wrist.

Conversation drifted aimlessly until Phillipe appeared with a '97 and his heartfelt apologies. Letting the wine breathe in the glasses, they attacked the lobster bisque, agreeing that it wasn't quite up to the Imperial Room's usual standards. Denny despaired of ever getting back to Harrelman. Then Cindy surprised him. "Tell me about this Harrelman person. Who is he? Should I have heard of him?"

"Maybe, if you took more interest in your affairs."

"Denny," she said, running a fingertip down his arm, from his elbow to his wrist, and trailing it tantalizingly across the back of his hand. "I'll have you know I take a great deal of interest in my affairs." She laughed as his face reddened in frustration. "I know I should, dear. It's just that I see what paying attention has done to Daddy, and Kevin, and oh, those other two…"

"Jenny and Rina?" Denny offered.

"Yes, that's it." She shook her hair back with a luxuriant motion. "Well, they're quite a bit younger after all."

"But they're your sisters."

She laughed again, a bit louder as the wine began to work its magic. "Denny Redmond, sometimes you can be so thick! I know who they are." She frowned, then continued in a serious tone. "They make me so sick with their three-piece suits and their market weighted analyses and their little junkets down to Houston to look at property. Honestly, they're just little feminine versions of Daddy."

She fell silent until the flush of anger drained from her cheeks. They concentrated on their lunch awhile, then she resumed in a more conciliatory tone. "I know I should pay more attention, Denny, and I do try. Honestly, I do. But all those figures, and those interminable financial reports—you know what I think whenever I read one of them? I think somebody had to write it. Then I think the poor guy probably wanted to be a great American novelist, and look what he ended up doing." Denny didn't smile. He kept his gaze stern and cool and focused on her glittering green eyes. "All right," she pouted. "I'll try harder." Holding her glass out for more wine, she added, "Let's start now. Tell me about Meyer Harrelman."

"Meyer Harrelman is probably the most successful investor in the past fifty years. His Windermere Fund is famous for uncovering value. He buys companies and holds them, for the most part, though occasionally he'll break them up. The important thing is, he's so big, he could buy out your dad before lunch and it probably wouldn't be his biggest deal of the morning."

"Then he's like Warren Buffet, then." Her face took on the gleam of a school girl about to impress her favorite teacher. "Berkshire Hathaway, right? Like the Carlyle Group. See, Denny. I do read."

"Headlines, at least," he murmured.

"Oh, you are so cruel!" she cried in that mock petulance he loved to provoke. "So if he's so big, why haven't I heard of him?"

"Because he likes to fly beneath the radar. While a guy like Donald Trump has a whole army of PR men trying to keep his name in the papers, he keeps one just as big busy keeping his name out."

"And he's talking to Daddy?" She went silent on that one.

Denny asked, "Did Ken mention a price?"

"I heard him say 45 was rock bottom."

Denny whistled. "It closed at 30 yesterday," he said, more to himself than to Cindy. "You could stand to make a lot of money off this."

"But it would mean selling Herringbone Trucking."

"Does that matter?"

She frowned. "I don't know. Narrows always talked about a company's obligation to its hometown. I remember how upset he got when I told him how they shut down all those factories in Zenith."

Denny shrugged. "It was a sound business move. Herringbone couldn't compete with Detroit. They had to get out of cars. Besides, that doesn't concern you. You had nothing to do with it."

"But Narrows said it was wrong to lay off 16,000 workers just like that. Sometimes I think it is my responsibility. After all, it's my name on the letterhead."

Denny smiled indulgently. "I never knew you had a social conscience, Cindy."

She hesitated. Social conscience wasn't a popular term in Wellington Lakes, where the word "charity" remained in vogue. The social calendar revolved around a series of benefit dinners and dances for the St. Francis Community Center, Operation Hope, Save the Children, and a dozen other socially acceptable causes. Many admired the round of parties because they raised large sums of money for worthwhile programs. Others considered the events to be attempts by the rich to assuage the guilt which often accompanies inherited wealth. Only the most perceptive, or cynical, saw it for what it was, a scam enabling a certain class of people to get tax breaks for throwing parties.

"Whatever social conscience I have is left over from Narrows," she said with a touch of sadness. "How is he, anyway? I haven't seen him in months."

Denny said he'd been awfully busy trying to wrap up his big real estate deal. "I guess he figured out a way of sidestepping Rob."

"I wonder if that's why he's been an even bigger ass than usual," Cindy mused. "At least, that's what I hear from Peg. She says she thinks he's losing his mind."

"I don't know. Burt's been pretty vague about it. He's meeting with Ted Jr. right now."

"Oh, I'm so happy for him," she said with genuine joy. "Now maybe he'll start coming out to the club again."

Denny was doubtful. "I think the work's just beginning for him now. Besides he—" He paused. Maybe he should leave that to Burt.

"He what?"

"Nothing, really. He just has his hands full right now."

"I don't understand why he wants to live downtown anyway," she went on, not really changing the subject, just approaching it from a different direction.

"You really don't, do you."

She started pouting again. "I miss him, Denny. I really do. Sometimes I think our marriage was better than either of us thought. He was a lot of fun, or could be when he wasn't all depressed."

"Leave him alone," warned Denny. "Please."

She started to reply, but thought better of it. She leaned back in her chair, stretching luxuriously. With her head thrown back, her auburn hair draped halfway down the chair. Her breasts pushed against the silk cloth of her dress, and all the remaining diners stared. Then she flashed one of her impish grins and said, "I feel like a swim." She grabbed her purse and walked out, leaving Denny to pay the check and follow.

* * *

Harry Bachman jumped up from the corner table when the big man walked into the Cobra Deli. "Rob, I'm so glad you could join us," he said, enthusiastically shaking the lawyer's hand. "Sit down, everybody's here. I think you already know Ken."

"How could one not know Ken Herringbone, Jr.?" Patterson rumbled amiably. "The man is a legend."

Herringbone chortled appreciatively. "To be called a legend by a man of your substance is an honor indeed," he said in his surprisingly high-pitched voice.

"And this is Chelsea Collins and Dave Brown, two of our key student coordinators," Harry continued, indicating a thin, pale woman with limp blonde hair, and a chubby young man with bad skin, thick glasses and unruly brown hair.

Patterson turned on the charm, engulfing their each of their hands in turn in his meaty paws. "You kids are doing a great thing here. I hope you realize that," he intoned.

They grinned their thanks, with Chelsea adding, "We couldn't do it without your support, Mr. Patterson."

"Call me Rob," the attorney said, patting her gently on her shoulder as he took the open seat next to her. A hint of a frown crossed Harry's face when Patterson scooted his chair closer to the girl. He wouldn't be hitting on the girl, would he? Before he could act on that thought, or even explore it, Patterson grabbed one of the menus. "So what's good to eat here?"

"Try the Lamb Vindaloo Wrap," Chelsea said, pointing it out on the glossy card. "If you like hot stuff, that is."

"I love it hot," he leered. "But what kind of creature is a Vindaloo Wrap?"

"The Cobra Deli is a unique blend of the finest Indian cuisine and the convenience and affordability of a corner deli," Ken read from his menu. "I've never been here before, but these kids swear by it."

"It's close to the University," Harry added. He glanced at his watch. "We'll have to make this pretty quick. I've got another class in forty-five minutes."

"You mean we don't get to eat?" Rob moped. "I came all this way for a discussion?"

"No, you go ahead," Harry urged. "I'll just grab something and run.

But don't feel you need to—" His explanation was cut short by the big man's hearty laugh.

"Just kidding, Harry." He swept his hand over his belly. "I could probably afford to miss a meal or two." He winked at Chelsea when she let out a little laugh. "So, what's on the agenda?" he continued.

"Right now, we're focusing on the Spring Fling," Harry replied. "On Earth Day, when the University turns the Quad into an environmental forum. This year, we're listed as one of the official sponsors. Why don't you fill us in on what we've got going, Dave."

Dave rummaged through his shoulder bag, and pulled out a crumpled sheet of paper. "Okay, we have four booths, one promoting Grasslands Alliance, of course. Big posters outlining our mission statement, lots of photos, and a sign up sheet. We hope to double our membership, and really get things moving. Also, we've put together a solid display on adaptive reuse, how we can salvage some of the abandoned warehouses and office buildings in Zenith, rather than just continuing to expand further outward." He glanced at Patterson, "I know you've done a lot of work on this in the past. It's really a great idea. Why should corporations be allowed to just abandon the city? I mean, everything's here already. Infrastructure, roads and whatever. Let's rebuild the core. Like when A2Z wanted to move out to Athens."

"We lost that one," Patterson muttered.

"That's because some people wouldn't let us take the gloves off," Chelsea said, glaring at Harry.

Harry said, "We don't work that way, Chelsea."

"Well, maybe we should start. I mean, you always talk about getting along, but how many times do we have to lose before—"

"Don't worry, kiddo," Patterson said, patting her hand. "We'll win the next one." Turning to Dave, he asked what was going in the other two booths.

"The new one is the Industrial Ecology display. Harry's just been great," he said, glancing his admiration at the group leader. "His course is just awesome. The stuff we're learning about sustainability, it just blows me away. I mean, there's stuff out there you wouldn't believe. Like these African villages where women are getting these loans and starting like, knitting businesses and stuff. 'Course they got to, because our agricultural subsidies are starving them. Well, wait 'til you see it."

"And we couldn't have done it without your support, Ken," Harry added, always knowing when to stroke the older man's ego.

"Glad to help, Harry. It's important stuff, and I always say, we've got to give back a little something, eh Rob?"

"That's why I've adopted this group. Again, you kids are doing amazing things."

"Thanks, Mr. Patterson," Dave replied. "One thing I've learned this year, it's not just about the environment, or I guess what I mean is, the economic system we're all working under has this huge impact on the environment. You can't save the environment until you do something about the system. Like globalization."

"Why don't you tell Mr. Patterson about the fourth booth," Harry suggested.

"Oh, right. We're working with the DNR and the Nature Conservancy to show how individuals can help preserve our threatened prairie ecosystem. I was just talking with the Nature Conservancy people before I came over here. They've got this kickass DVD that'll blow those industrialists out of the water."

"How confrontational are you looking to be on this?" Rob interrupted.

"How confrontational do you want us to be?" Chelsea replied to general laughter.

Harry jumped in, as he always did, to restrain the young activist's enthusiasm. "Grasslands Alliance has always considered it more effective to work with and within the system to effect meaningful change. That's why we've paired the DNR with the Nature Conservancy. We want to get two messages across, one that the prairie ecosystem is endangered by rampant development, and two, to show how individuals, through even small monetary contributions, can help take critical acreage off the development map."

Patterson hunched forward in his chair, his bulk overwhelming the small table. "That's the kind of thing I'm talking about," he said with a burst of enthusiasm. "It ties in with adaptive reuse, and it is only growing more important with each passing day. Just take a look at our city. Do you realize Greater Zenith covers more land than London, England? Even though London has four times as many people. That's got to stop."

He grabbed his attache case and set it on the table. Snapping the locks, he continued, "Let's put this in perspective." Removing and unfolding a map of the metropolitan area, he spread it across the table, the others scrambling to clear water glasses and cups of tea from the tidal wave of his zeal. "Look at this. In the whole vast suburban sprawl the one thing you don't see is green space. It's all been filled in with subdivisions and shopping malls. Hell, when I was your age, most of these towns didn't even exist."

"What's this area?" Chelsea asked, pointing to a white square to the west of Wellington Lakes.

"That, my dear, is the last remaining piece of undeveloped land in metropolitan Zenith," Patterson answered. "Wouldn't it be a shame if that got eaten up, too?"

"They wouldn't—they couldn't." Chelsea's face betrayed her horror. Her pale cheeks bloomed pink. "Doesn't anybody ever stop to think?"

"Sure they do," Dave put in. "They think about money, about profits. Who cares about the environment when there's a buck to be made?"

"Are you suggesting that somebody's going to build out that site?" demanded Harry.

Patterson shrugged. "I hear rumors." He glanced at his watch. "Listen, I've got to go, as do you, I believe, professor. Come on, I'll walk you out."

* * *

Narrows gazed through a rising mist at a landscape of brown, rolling grasslands mottled with scraps of unmelted snow, and dotted with clumps of oak and hickory. It was the last piece of undeveloped land in three thousand square miles of suburban sprawl. He felt a momentary twinge of guilt for the upheaval to be wrought upon it. Then he overruled his environmental conscience. He'd put too much into this, and besides, if he didn't develop it, someone else would, and that someone might not bring the same sensitivity and esthetic commitment to the project.

"It's hot," he announced with a laugh. He took off his jacket and tossed it on the front seat through the open car window. Then he tipped back Ted's bottle of whiskey and clinched the deal.

* * *

After months of freezing temperatures, eighty-five degrees felt much hotter than it would have in mid-July. Rollins was sweating profusely as he bagged the last of the wet, sticky leaves he'd raked from the beds. He was grateful when Monica brought him a glass of iced tea. He leaned on his rake and gulped it greedily. All around him pale green tulip and daffodil shoots lay in varying states of exhaustion. They were barely half the height they should have been, and almost devoid of color from having languished so long beneath their winter coats. The damp, black earth was starkly beautiful and marked with narrow grooves from the tines of his rake.

He held out his glass for more, and gasped, "It sure is hot."

His wife frowned. "Better not overdo it, dear. You have all summer."

He laughed and bent to pick up his hoe. "The flowers are crying out to me, Monie. There's no time to lose."

"Well, maybe you should rest awhile. The kids will be home soon. They can help."

He paused. Maybe he should wait. He wasn't as young as he used to be. Then he remembered Robbie had track on Wednesdays, and Tina would be afraid of breaking a nail. He walked stiffly back to the flower bed, avoiding his wife's disapproving glance. "I'll just do the iris and peonies. They need the most help."

"Well, all right," she said reluctantly. She watched him labor awhile, then retreated inside. Rollins broke up the soil around the tender shoots, then shoveled in some peat and fresh topsoil. He knelt to work it in with a trowel. All this bending and kneeling was taking its toll on his knees. He thought of his father's arthritis, which had forced him to spend his last few years in a wheelchair. He closed his eyes a moment in prayerful remembrance of the man who'd given him the strength to face the bewildering changes in this world. There was something to be said for the stoic.

He moved to the iris bed. They were awfully thick, he decided. He reached for the trowel. He'd better divide them now, or none of them would bloom. He thought about his own two kids while he gently separated the bulbs. Robbie was a senior in high school, and there was a chance of a scholarship, if he could shave a couple seconds off his time in the half-mile. The scholarship would help, but it wasn't essential. Rollins had made a point of that. He had enjoyed his place at the helm, at the Club, and at the Parisienne before that, but he'd decided long ago that he wanted something better for his boy. And Robbie was up to it. Robbie was going to do his father proud.

The last of the iris divided, he considered going in. He could plant them over the weekend maybe. But Rollins got greedy. He couldn't wait to see them bloom, and they wouldn't start until they were in the ground. He stood up slowly. His joints were giving him a lot of trouble today. Probably the heat. He looked around for a good place for the flowers. There, over by the side fence, among the tulips and daffodils. He'd always been dissatisfied with the lack of color there. The tulips faded so quickly, and then there was nothing until the mums came in late summer.

He trudged over and began to plant. But the soil was too hard. He had to work it with the hoe. While he chopped and raked he thought about Tina. He could never figure out how a frivolous thing like that got into his family. Always running around, dancing half the night away. Sometimes he worried she was growing up too fast. After all, she was only fifteen. But she was a good girl. She was active in the church. She sang in the choir. In fact, she was to sing her first solo this Sunday morning.

After the last of the iris was planted, Rollins picked up his tools and headed inside. On the way past the peonies he saw some more weed sprouts in the soft, broken dirt. He stopped to pull them out. He buried his hands deep in the soil to track a root to its source. It didn't do any good to lop them off at the surface. You had to get them way down underground.

This one went on quite a ways. He pulled up a portion. Thick, white and smooth. Morning Glory. He groaned at the recognition. He'd hoped this year it wouldn't be back. What was it? Two years ago? What a battle that had been. For awhile he'd been afraid he would lose the entire garden. But he stuck with it, and in the end, he won. Or at least had kept it at bay. He resolved not to let this one get away. Leaning over on his knees, he pried the soil loose with his left hand while gently tugging on the root with his right, and soon uncovered over a foot of the hated root.

This might be the vanguard of another assault, he thought, falling into the martial jargon with which he tended to characterize his campaign for horticultural supremacy. As he reached a little further, he felt a chill. Strange, in this heat. He paused, then the world started closing in around him. The air went tight against his head and his arms, and his chest. With a sickly, sinking feeling, he struggled to his feet. He gasped as a sudden jolt of pain ripped through his body, it felt like his throat was filled with sand, like his left arm had been ripped from the socket. Another wave of pain, and the air turned thick and hazy.

Rollins' lips curled into a curious smile as the pain gradually released its grip. "I shouldn't have called in sick," he thought as he pitched face first into the rich, freshly worked garden bed.

Chapter Five

The next day, Narrows was relieved to see that neither of the attorneys Ted brought with him to the closing weighed more than 180 pounds. There were no last minute hitches. Ted was quite happy with the terms. Ten thousand dollars an acre, and a ten percent equity stake in the development meant he stood to make as much as twenty-five million dollars on the deal.

Ted walked over to the scale model of Oak Grove which had been sitting in Narrows' office for over two years. It had played an important role in interesting investors in the project. Narrows saw the older man's interest, and moved over to him. Ted tapped the centerpiece, an undulating blue and green plaster slab. "According to Patterson, this four-hundred acre park is costing me over three million."

"Yeah, that's what makes Oak Grove unique," Narrows remarked. "This is the first Zenith suburb designed on a human scale, with recreation, education and shopping facilities built into the plan, not slapped on as an afterthought. Sure, we could have made the park smaller, or cut it out altogether. It would have meant a hell of a lot more money in the short run, but this is a community built to last. It's the same with the houses. We're taking a smaller profit so we can build in more quality. Your grandchildren will be able to visit Oak Grove and be proud that you played a part in it."

Ted laughed garrulously. "Save the spiel, Burt. I already signed."

Narrows grinned. "I can't help it, Ted. You don't know what this means to me. It makes me sick to look at the vast suburban wasteland that America's becoming. Now I've got a chance to change things. Oak Grove isn't another disposable town, it's a statement of how things can and should be." He gazed down at the model. "When it looked like it was about to fall through, those words would run through my mind." He shook his head. "It was hell. To have come so close and think it wasn't going to happen." His voice trailed off.

"Well, it's going to happen now," Ted assured him. He glanced at his watch. "My flight doesn't leave 'til three. Let me buy you lunch."

Narrows insisted he should do the buying.

"Nonsense. You just made me a much wealthier man." After gaining Narrows' grudging assent, he said, "So, is Mario's still around?"

Mario's occupied the basement of a dilapidated, sooty brick, turn-of-the-century office block in the warehouse district along the Ontanagon River. In the twenties Mario's had been one of the Midwest's central distribution points for prohibition booze. Though it retained much of the illicit ambience of those days, a sense accentuated by the journey along deserted, potholed streets between vacant, crumbling warehouses, the old roadhouse selection of spaghetti and veal parmigiana had given way to gourmet Italian food.

Over Fegato alla Veneziana and Timballo di Crespelle, Narrows continued to crow about Oak Grove until Ted cut him off. "What I want to know, Burt, is are you trying to con me, or are you really that naive?"

Narrows stared at the older man's weathered face. "What are you getting at?"

"You act like you just solved all the world's problems."

"Well, no, of course not. But I think Oak Grove will be a positive contribution."

"You do, eh?" He took another bite of liver, chewed it thoughtfully, then washed it down with a swallow of crisp Chianti Classico. "Well, I don't see it. No, no, wait," he insisted over Narrows' protests. "Oak Grove is everything you say it is. I just don't think another subdivision, no matter how attractive and environmentally sound, will make things any better."

"Why not?"

"Oak Grove is like getting a facelift when you've got lung cancer. It may make you look better on the outside, but you're still dying."

"You're talking about Zenith, then."

"Damn right, I am," Ted snarled. "Every time I come back here the city looks worse. Makes me sick if you want to know."

"Yet you left." Narrows' soft reply made the indictment all the more effective.

Ted didn't try to defend himself. "I did. I didn't want to. It doesn't make a man proud to walk away from his home."

"Why, then?"

"'Cause I got kids. Come on, you read the papers. The whites are all but gone, and the blacks are breeding like flies. Zenith's poor and getting poorer. It's falling apart at the seams."

"I don't think the color of a man's skin has any bearing on the matter," said Narrows, bristling at Ted's racism.

"You don't eh? Well, name me one good thing Hizzoner the Mayor Jeremiah Brown's done for Zenith since he got elected."

"Well, there's the Wilkinson Center."

"A bunch of crap," Ted sputtered. "Prefab concrete, looks like something out of Soviet Russia. Ten years from now it'll be falling down."

Narrows nodded reluctantly. It was so easy to get caught up in the any-development-is-good-development-if-it-happens-in-the-city mentality. The Wilkinson Center had meant jobs, a much-needed boost to the tax base, and a new face in a stagnant skyline. He had been one of the first tenants in the apartment tower. His eighteenth floor apartment presented a great view of the city: from the sparkling white facade of the Thompson Building and the soaring limestone dignity of the Second National Tower on the east; past the art deco whimsey of the Sentinel Building, to the squat, stuffy Hotel Thornleigh on the west; with the meandering blue ribbon of the Ontanagon beyond. But Ted was right. The Wilkinson Center was barely three years old and already it was showing signs of decay. The carpet had come loose in one corner of the lobby, and the wallpaper curled away from the walls in spots. One of the elevators was chronically out of order, and a hairline crack was snaking across his dining room ceiling.

"Okay, you've got a point," he admitted. "But what's the solution? Should everyone move to Tucson?"

"God, no," Ted cried. "We've got the same problems." He slapped the table for emphasis. "We're supposed to be so smart and we're making the same goddam mistakes. Inner city's crime-ridden, downtown's all but gone, all the growth is in the suburbs. Hell, we don't even have freeways." Then, continuing in a more sober vein, "I like how you put it back at the office, about disposable towns. Only it's not just suburbs, we've done the same thing with our cities." He gestured helplessly with his left hand. "You know, I was in Europe when Dad died—Maura and me'd split up and, hell, I was tired of throwing up houses—seeing all that desert land bulldozed like that. So I just took off. Always wanted to see Europe. Don't know if I'd of ever come back if it weren't for—" He stopped, rested his hands on either side of his plate, and stared at the uneaten slices of liver languishing in their brown sauce.

Narrows wondered if Ted's grief was genuine. He knew he'd had to work to produce remorse when his own father died. It wasn't like he'd hated the old man. They weren't close, but he had still loved him, loved him like a father. But when he died, all he felt was empty. Empty and cold. Sometimes he wondered if he was actually that coldly rational, or was his lack of feeling some sort of defense mechanism?

Ted pushed the food around on his plate and reached for his glass. Then he continued wistfully. "I was in Paris. It was raining. I must have walked for miles along narrow, empty streets. When I got back to the hotel there was a wire from Maura. You wouldn't believe how much contempt you can squeeze into a simple telegram. Anyhow, I caught the next plane home." A pause, then, "Paris was unlike any other European city I'd seen, but it has one thing in common with the rest of 'em. It radiates from the heart,"

"Radiates from the heart?"

"I mean the core of the city is the most vital part. The first place you go in any European city is the City Center. That's where you make your base. That's where you find out what you need to know."

Narrows nodded. That had certainly been his experience in London. "But what's your point, Ted?"

The older man scowled. "Where's the heart of Zenith?"

Narrows thought a moment, then shrugged. Zenith had no heart.

"Exactly. Same with Tucson, and not just Tucson, all American cities anymore. Maybe the airport. You fly in, rent a car or hop the shuttle to the hotel." He raised his arms in an almost pleading gesture. "Your hotel's your base, and pretty often it's a damn lonely one. We're letting our cities die from the inside out." He shrugged. "Disposable cities."

"And Europe's different?" Narrows prompted. With his cowboy boots, turquoise jewelry and folksy manner, Ted had seemed almost a caricature of a Westerner. His conversation had hitherto run to garrulous quips and hackneyed colloquialisms. Narrows was intrigued by the man's serious side. He wanted to draw out more of his surprisingly impassioned thoughts about the city.

"All those European cities are a thousand years old," Ted observed. "We've got nothing to match 'em."

"Well, of course we don't. We aren't old enough."

"We never will be," he said flatly. "Look at Zenith. Hell, it's been around 250 years. What's the oldest building in Zenith?"

"I haven't the slightest," replied Narrows. "I've never thought about it."

"Well, I have, and this time I found it. There's a little brick building next to the old Herringbone Number 3 Plant, that's out Worsted Way in case you didn't know. It's 150 years old, used to be a fur trading center. Trappers'd come from all over the region with beaver, fox, even bearskins. Now it's just a shed, stuffed with scrap metal and old tires, windows busted out, roof half-stove in. That's Zenith's history."

Narrows wanted to argue, to cite places like Boston and New York, cities with history. Then he realized they were just the same. Their historical districts were only tourist attractions. They weren't alive. They weren't used, except as museums, or to house fast food shops and T-shirt vendors. "In London people live in centuries-old buildings," he remarked by way of agreement.

Ted jumped on the point. "That's right. They don't throw their past away. Their cities have—" he groped for the word—"continuity. Obviously our cities will never be as old as European cities. The point is, our cities will never be older than they are today. We keep tearing them down, tearing them down, putting up new ones until we get bored with 'em. Then we just tear them down and walk away. Or just walk away and let them fall down." He drained his glass. "You know where out history lies? Old photographs." He tossed some bills on the table. "Now, if you'll excuse me, I got me a plane to catch."

"Let me give you a lift, Ted."

"Sure, might as well. Never could catch a cab in this town."

* * *

Up on the twelfth floor of the Sentinel Building, Denny sat at his desk with the phone wedged against his shoulder. He drummed his fingers on the desktop, and watched a storm march across the plains on the other side of the Ontanagon River. He winced at the glaring jangle of the other phones, the whoops and shouts of brokers who'd guessed right on Amgen or the dollar. Here it was, two in the afternoon, and he still felt sick. Damn that Cindy. She seemed to take a perverse delight in torturing people who had to work for a living. He took a deep breath, and sent the drum and bugle corps in his head into another march.

Oh well, you have to admit, it was a good night, he told himself while listening to the Muzak over the phone. He hated those systems which couldn't just let you wait. It was okay for the gas company, most of whose callers were irate neanderthals whose breasts needed soothing, but an investment firm for Chrissake? Then he grinned as the Living Strings segued from "Having My Baby" to "Suicide is Painless." Who put these things together, anyway?

Outside, the wind picked up. Whitecaps scuttled across the Ontanagon's current and Denny resorted to memories of the night before to soothe the tempest in his head. After a hazy drive up the freeway, he and Cindy had taken their swim. She was right, Peg did make an appearance. She joined them in the otherwise empty pool, and dove and splashed with such enthusiasm that her breasts threatened to spill out of her swimsuit. She shared some coke with him in the anteroom to the sauna, to which they retired when Cindy went to dress for dinner. Peg's breasts did spill out of her suit in the sauna, along with the rest of her nicely tanned, and toned, body, albeit with a little help from Denny. She drew inordinate pleasure from his attentions, and he was too far gone to care that her husband was his best client, and the worst enemy a businessman could have.

She peeled off his speedos with a casual skill he found surprising in light of her constant reference to her lack of practice the past two years…

"Sorry to keep you waiting, Den," the voice breezed. "Babysitting a high roller on the other line. You know how it is." He waited for Denny to assure him that he certainly did know how it was, then asked, "So, how are things out there in the rust belt?"

"Oh, the usual. We keep making 'em, and you keep buying 'em."

"Dream on factory boy." The voice was vaguely restless. "Saw a nice piece on Sixty Minutes the other night, on Zenith's drug wars. Couldn't help but—"

"Listen, Ron," Denny butted in. "I've got something you might be interested in."

"I'm all ears, Den."

"Herringbone Trucking."

"Trucks, shopping malls, trading around 25-30, dividend flat," Ron recited. "What's the poop?"

"Meyer Harrelman."

"Harrelman? Harrelman's buying?" There was a pause. "Numbers, give me numbers, boy."

"Forty-five minimum. He could go as high as sixty and still beat break up."

Ron was silent for a moment, then he said, very seriously, "How good is this?"

"Solid gold."

"Who's your source?"

"A twenty percent shareholder. He's selling next week."

"Who else have you told?"

"Nobody."

"Are you in?"

"Can't. Got a Herringbone in my stable."

Ron gave a low whistle. "This is good. This is real fucking good, buddy." He went silent, and Denny could hear a clicking keyboard. He knew what Ron would see because he had it up on his own screen. "Down fifty cents today, low volume. Looks like I'm moving to the Upper East Side." "Ron chuckled. "You never talked to me, right? And you'll never mention this in an email."

"Yeah, sure Ron. Listen, I—" Denny faltered. How did these deals work?

"Thanks a lot, pal. I owe you, but big."

* * *

By the time Narrows got back to the office, all the elation had been drained out of his system. To say it hadn't been a pleasant trip, was beyond understatement. On the way to the airport, Ted had been unrelenting in his pessimism. He went on about visiting his grandfather's house and seeing the blight creeping up the hill. "Mark my words, Burt. In five years, Floral Heights'll be a slum."

The sad thing was, he couldn't argue. The Arizonan's bleak outlook affected him, and the return trip did nothing to improve his outlook. After deciding to see for himself, Narrows left the Belham Expressway at Zenith's eastern boundary and cut across the city on surface streets. At first it didn't look so bad. Perryman Avenue was lined with shops and offices, and restaurants doing a good midday business. There were plenty of late model cars on the street, driven by middle class whites and blacks. Down side streets he could see well-maintained brick bungalows and stucco split-level ranches. Maybe Ted had been overly bleak.

Then Narrows noticed the profusion of For Sale signs. He detoured down a side street. There were four or five to a block, and even more disturbing, about three-quarters of them read, "For Sale By Owner." A bad sign indeed. Now, it could have meant nothing more than a lot of frugal homeowners seeking to avoid paying commissions, but such a preponderance usually was a sign that Realtors either couldn't, or wouldn't, move them.

On closer inspection some of the houses showed telltale signs of neglect. Paint peeling under the eaves, cracked windows taped instead of replaced, porch railings out of plumb, the occasional sagging roof. It wasn't every house, not even a majority, and none of those for sale, but it meant a neighborhood in transition.

When Narrows returned to Perryman Avenue, he noticed the iron accordion gates, the broken parking meters and the garbage piling up alongside the stores. Now there was a preponderance of liquor stores and convenience shops, many of whose windows were covered with plywood painted a garish orange or yellow. Fast food chains had replaced family restaurants, major grocery store chains were nonexistent, and churches occupied abandoned bank branches. Small businesses, service, legal and medical practices stood vacant. There were fewer cars, and those parked at the curb were older, with dents, broken tail lights, or rust-eaten fenders.

Where Perryman jogged southwest towards downtown, Narrows continued west along Douglass. Now he was entering unfamiliar territory. Douglass wasn't as wide as Perryman, and was primarily residential, or had been in happier days. Now at least every third house was missing, replaced by a rubble-strewn lot. Some blocks were completely gutted. Virtually all the remaining houses were in a state of disrepair. Porches had either collapsed or were supported by precariously tilted posts. Most houses had broken windows. They were covered with plywood or plastic, or simply ignored, their jagged edges revealing darkened interiors.

The wind began to blow harder as Narrows drove along. It pushed old newspapers, McDonalds wrappers and dead leaves down broken gutters and through gaps in the rows of houses. He passed skeletons without windows and doors, and burned-out shells. Their roofs were gone, their walls sagged. They were collapsing in on themselves like black holes, sucking light and life from the city.

An occasional solid, well-maintained home shone like a distant beacon. But when he got closer he saw a homestead cowering behind a chainlink fence. Windows and doors were barricaded, and Rottweilers hurled themselves at the fence as he passed.

A chilly rain began to fall, as if the city had already used up its quota of decent weather. People clustered around tire- and windowless cars at the curb. Others gathered on decrepit porches, or tortured mangy dogs in the lots. They stared at him as he passed, and Narrows wasn't seeing a lot of love.

They didn't notice the rain. They continued to loiter on the sidewalks, tipping back bottles of Thunderbird or Colt 45. Toddlers, and infants clad only in diapers, whose whiteness stood in sharp contrast to their skin, knelt or squatted on hillocks containing rubble from the house which once had stood there. They were strangely silent as they played in the dirt and the mud puddles, crouching next to blackened mounds of unmelted snow.

Narrows felt very tired, worn out, old. He kept repeating, "This is America." As he approached a black Cadillac Escalade, his mirror began vibrating from the bass throbbing from its radio. He stared at it, wondering how they could stand the noise. A door opened, a kid stepped out, hands buried in the pouch of his hoodie. He glared at Narrows and stepped in front of the car. Narrows hit the brakes, and stopped inches from the boy. The other doors popped open on the Escalade, pouring other youths onto the street. Narrows slammed the car into reverse and raced back to the corner, expecting a hail of bullets to shatter his windshield. He slithered around the corner, then put it in drive and sped away.

Two blocks further on he turned left, and hurried down the potholed street, his car's suspension shrieking in horror at the abuse. After a few blocks, he turned left again, hoping to get back to Douglass, and to make his way back to civilization. But the street deadended in the middle of the block, in front of a rusted chain link fence surrounding what once had been a grassy expanse. There was a building there. It looked like a hospital, but it was empty, abandoned like everything else in this godforsaken corner of the nation. Windows were broken. The siding had torn loose in spots, and hung like giant sheets of fabric from the skeletal remains. Narrows made a u-turn and headed back to the nameless street. He drove on, hoping to find a major road which would speed him out of this Third World nation which had mysteriously been planted in the middle of his city. Up ahead was a traffic light. He peered at the sign but didn't recognize the name.

Narrows knew Zenith better than most native Zenithites of his acquaintance, so it came as a shock to realize he was lost, to realize that he'd never really seen the city before. He'd spent twelve years here island hopping, darting from one enclave to another. The poverty had been a blur zipping past the freeway at sixty miles an hour, or glimpsed briefly in the Metro pages of "The Zenith News." Now he was lost in Zenith, and he realized he would be, even if he knew where he was.

After another mile or two the houses gave way to several acres of empty land. There was a gridwork of streets, and he could see sidewalks between the dead, dry stalks of weeds and tall brown grass. There were streetlamps and fire hydrants, and here and there a driveway, but there were no houses. It reminded him of a failed development he'd seen outside San Francisco once. The developers had put in all the capital improvements before running out of money, leaving a network of winding lanes and sidewalks sprawled across a hillside in the golden summer grass. The difference here was there had actually been houses once. He saw an occasional pile of broken bricks or fire-scarred lumber. Other than that, nothing. Was this one of Mayor Brown's grandiose schemes which Rob Patterson had scuttled, or had years of neglect consumed an entire neighborhood, leaving only the broken skeleton behind?

Further along he came to a series of dingy brick towers surrounded by sprawling two-story apartment blocks. This must be the Douglass Projects. It was the kind of place you read about but never saw. You had no reason to go there. They'd been built in the late forties as temporary housing for the thousands of returning soldiers. Over the years they had become a sort of municipal landmark because of the stream of boxers, football players and entertainers who'd grown up there. In each case, the Douglass Projects loomed large in their bios, feel good stories about a talented kid beating the odds and escaping to make a success of things. And it was true. True and tragic, because for every talented kid who climbed out there were dozens, or hundreds who couldn't find a rung. Those were the ones whose only hope of getting their names in the papers were in the reports of the sensational murders, rapes and drug-related shootouts which occurred there.

Narrows was startled to think these buildings were only fifty years old. They looked like they'd been around at least as long as Ted's fur trading center, and had been neglected nearly that long. All up and down the towers were black streaks where fire had gutted a flat. In one tower it looked like the top five floors were vacant. Hundreds of windows were boarded up throughout the projects. There were swing sets without swings and rusted monkey bars; basketball courts without hoops, with weeds sprouting in the cracked asphalt. There were parking lots without cars, benches without seats, apartments without light; a ghostly presence without a future.

Beyond the projects was more emptiness, then a half-dozen blocks studded with fieldstone mansions. They had slate-covered mansard roofs, ornate stonework around the chimneys, doors and windows, gingerbread wrought iron trim on the eaves and along the eight-foot high fences and gates. They were massive homes, still in good structural condition despite their age and neglect. They were without exception, empty and unowned.

Narrows drove past the haunted relics into a block of abandoned grocery stores, and restaurants in the shape of pagodas. It was Zenith's Chinatown. He'd never even known the city had had one. His treasured travel books made frequent mention of the ubiquitous Chinese merchants and hoteliers. The intrepid traveler emerged on foot from the jungles of Borneo, the deserts of Africa, or the rugged, barren mountains of South America, to find a village consisting of a half-dozen primitive huts, a handful of chickens scratching in the dust, a solitary pig sprawled in the shade, and a Chinese man tending bar or minding the shop. They ran businesses in the most godforsaken corners of the earth, yet even the Chinese had abandoned Zenith.

It was with relief that Narrows finally reached Wellington Boulevard. He fled north past empty warehouses, past the tenacious pioneering spirit around Zenith University, the tired elegance of the Cultural Center, the hard-bitten, disease-ridden whores along the Strip, the overgrown greenery of Willard Park, the armed-camp vigilance of Percy Woods Estates. The other side of Percy Woods, Narrows crossed Grayson Way, and burst into the serenity and security of Crystal Heights. Never had the suburbs looked so good, and that thought, even more than anything he'd seen, depressed him.

Finding a message from his ex-wife on his desk didn't help his mood. He checked his watch. 3:15. The drive had only taken forty-five minutes, yet he felt he'd aged fifteen years. He felt he would never be the same. It was as if he'd been wearing blinders all this time. Only today had he seen his city, seen his world, as it actually existed. The phrase he had repeated during his tour came back now: This is America. Three simple words, they were an indictment of everything he stood for, of everything he'd accomplished. Ted was right. Against the backdrop of Zenith, Oak Grove was nothing more than a band-aid. It didn't change a thing.

Narrows slumped in his chair, his eyes closed, his head cocked to one side. He held his hands in front of his chest, as if to ward off the insight, or perhaps to push away his suddenly unpalatable achievement. This is America. Land of the free, home of the brave. He'd always been a believer. Maybe the CIA did run amok from time to time. Maybe National Defense was more about preserving a small industrial and military elite than the security of the nation. Maybe the vast bulk of elected officials were small-minded, money-grubbing worms. Maybe the war on terror was blurring the lines between justice and torture. But, and it was an all-important but, the qualifier which had made him an unabashed patriot; but America was in fact the land of the free, home of the brave. It was the Shining City on the Hill, the focus of the world's downtrodden. To deny it was to deny the essence of America. To deny it was the only logical reaction to what he'd just seen.

He picked up Cindy's message. What did she want now? To Narrows, Cindy was the apotheosis of the American Dream. She always had been, and when she agreed to marry him, it had been as if he'd crossed a threshold into a realm where all things were possible. It wasn't her money—Narrows could pay his own way, and did—it was her attitude, her benign acceptance of all good things which came her way. They were expected. It was her right. He had been flattered to be accepted with the same aplomb. It meant he was one of the good things she'd been groomed to receive. He struggled to live up to her acquiescence. He joined her clubs, ran with her crowd. He let her dress him in the fashions of the moment. He mouthed her catchwords and opinions, and squired her to the requisite number of charity balls and dinners. When it proved too much, when he realized he'd lost track of who he was or should have been, she agreed with him that it wasn't working. They put an end to it without attorneys, without wrangling, without rancor.

They each took back what they'd brought to the union, and Narrows went off to search for what he'd lost. If they ran into each other on occasion, unavoidably owing to mutual friends, not least of whom was Denny, it was with no greater discomfort than that in which they'd spent the last year of their marriage.

In the end he decided to return her call, before heading over to the ZAC, where he hoped to drown, in sweat or drink, the awful vision of America which he feared would never leave him.

Chapter Six

As the ZAC Business Manager, Russ Devonshire was unaccustomed to working behind the bar, but when your Chief Steward has the temerity to die without giving notice, everybody has to do a little bit more. He rummaged behind the Men's Grill bar for the appropriate ingredients with which to fill the trickle of orders drifting his way. He didn't know how Rollins had done it, and couldn't have done it himself without the help of the steward's well-trained crew. Grimacing at the chaos behind the bar, Russ wondered if he should select Rollins' replacement from the existing staff, or try to pirate one from one of the other clubs. At least he had another day to decide. The lunch rush was over, leaving only the usual handful of midday drinkers hiding from the office, killing time until returning home became imperative, throwing down drinks until returning home became tolerable.

Rob bellied up to the bar, flourishing a pair of tumblers in one hand. "Two more, Russ."

The manager smiled apologetically. "I'm sorry, Mr. Patterson. What were you drinking again?"

The attorney exhaled a blast of warm, pungent breath. "Russ," he rumbled. "I hope to hell you do a better job on the books than you do behind the bar." He mollified the implicit threat with a grin. "Chivas."

Russ squinted at the line of bottles, hesitated, then grabbed the right one. It was empty. He knelt behind the bar, muttering as he clinked bottles and shoved boxes of napkins and utensils out of the way. Finally, he reappeared. He thrust the bottle across the counter. "Why don't you just take this—make it easier for the both of us. Bring back what's left and we'll settle up."

The ex-athlete limped back to the table where his companion nudged a bishop diagonally forward with a long, thin forefinger. Rob poured two generous drinks and scoffed, "Sicilian Defense again? You'll never learn, will you Red Man?" He downed half his glass in a gulp. "Maybe losing Rollins won't be such a bad thing if Russ keeps serving bottles instead of glasses." He guffawed and ran his own bishop out to threaten the black king. "Check."

Doane stared at his friend through sharp blue eyes which dominated his thin, red face. His skin was pockmarked from a battle with acne which had raged well into his twenties. In times of stress his face was subject to renewed hostilities, evidenced now by the re-emergence of pustules alongside his nose. He ran his hands through his shock of fiery red, unruly hair. "Rollins was a good man," he said softly.

"He must have been. You treated him like shit." He watched Doane advance a pawn and flashed a vulturish smile. The move blocked his thrust all right, but it took Doane out of his defense. The game was as good as over. "Have you contacted the family yet?"

"No, why should I?"

"I'd think you'd want the case."

"What case?" Doane asked with a touch of impatience. He was tired of it, truly tired of being treated, even by those he was close to, as nothing but a legal machine. "Rollins had a heart attack."

Rob pushed his rook pawn forward. "A man died. Surely you can figure out someone to sue."

Doane tipped over his king.

"That's the first smart move you've made today, Red Man," Rob laughed. "Hey, where you going?" he called as Doane marched unsteadily across the room. He watched the thin figure disappear through the door, then he shrugged and helped himself to another drink. Somebody'd be along soon. He had half a bottle.

Narrows was surprised when Doane brushed past him without a word. He didn't mind. Having to make conversation with weasels like Doane was one of the drawbacks to membership in the ZAC. Doane always had something to say, some comment to let you know he was one of the players. Today he only stared dully at him. Narrows watched him stagger down the steps to the porter's station, then headed for the Men's Grill. Maybe Rolllins would know what was up.

Doane told the porter to summon his car. For once he was glad to have a driver. He'd been drinking since eleven, and wouldn't have trusted himself behind the wheel, though what he had to lose he didn't know. The Wilson case would be front page news by now. The yellow bastards would crucify him. They'd laugh him out of court from now on, that is, assuming he could muster the energy to return there. "So this is how my career ends, not with a bang, but with a whimper," he muttered ruefully to himself.

He told Jake to take him to the Art Institute, and rode out Wellington Boulevard through a chilly rain which made the city look even more forlorn than usual. People on the street wore bleak overcoats and grim expressions. Such a contrast to yesterday's sun-splashed euphoria. Once inside the museum, however, he succumbed to a familiar sense of anticipation and drifted towards the Great Hall. He wandered down hushed corridors past the men he loved most: Monet, Gaughin, Rembrandt, Turner. Their very presence here in Zenith was a tribute to the fortunes amassed during the century in which the city exploded from a riverside trading post to a metropolis of a million souls. The names of the galleries, Breckenridge, Wellington, Perryman, Philbert and Meade, encapsulated the great history of the city.

More compelling than the grandeur and history of the museum were the paintings themselves. Each merited an hour's contemplation. If he could only spare a couple of minutes, each stop helped restore a sense of peace. The experience was, as always, soothing and revitalizing. Back on an even keel, Doane abandoned self-pity and his gnawing hatred of that sanctimonious Wilson woman. He moved down the corridor to the Great Hall which housed the American Landscape Gallery, where he drew solace from the dark, brooding depictions of raw, unspoiled countryside.

He loved the formula so many of them followed. Dominating the left side was a mountain peak or giant outcrop of rock which dwarfed a man or group of men camped at its base, usually huddled around a fire, often with freshly killed game lying nearby. One of the men stood with his back to the viewer, in the lower center of the painting, where the mountain sloped down to a ridge, gazing out across a valley or vast plain stretching to the horizon. Often painted at dusk, with mist rising from the ground, or the sunset colors reflecting in the myriad streams snaking their way across the valley floor, the paintings gave the attorney an aching desire to step into that long lost world. He stood beside the adventurer at the edge of a precipice. The world unfolded at his feet, waiting, waiting for a man courageous enough to carve a life from its untamed wilds.

Doane drifted from one landscape to another until he reached a particular painting. This one, no better or worse than the others, always held his attention. For him it was the center of the display because on the card next to the frame were the words: From the Collection of Seneca Doane.

Doane remembered how surprised people had been when it was revealed that his grandfather had been an art collector. Some of the museum's leading patrons had threatened to rescind their support if the Art Institute accepted this gift from their lifelong enemy. In his own way, the collector had been even more deeply mired in controversy than his grandson. An apostate corporate attorney, he had embarked on a career of offending the sensibilities of the city's gentry by defending labor organizers, indigent laborers and feminists. No knee jerk malcontent, his radicalism had been honest, sincere, born of a desire to temper Zenith's burgeoning industrial and financial might with a sense of humanity. The state of the city today illustrated how utterly his grandfather had failed.

His efforts had earned him the scorn of Zenith's bankers, Realtors and clergy. He had suffered humiliation, ostracism and imprisonment. He had slaved away for the common man, and pursued his passion for artwork in the same quiet, unassuming manner. He had married late, raised a son, and died with little more than a dozen or so paintings to his name.

Years before his death however, his wife gave up on his crusading, and his only child, Seneca Doane Jr., dealt him the ultimate rejection by taking a job as Zenith Steel Corporation's in-house counsel. Because of the unbridgeable gap between father and son, Doane had almost reached adulthood before he met his grandfather. By then the old man was blind and nearly deaf, wracked with emphysema. Still, he would never forget the power of his grandfather's words. He spoke in little more than a whisper, interrupted every few minutes by a painful, burbling cough, about his thankless labors on behalf of the downtrodden. They spent many hours together in the last six months of the old man's life. On their last day together, as if he had an inkling of his demise, his grandfather had ended their session with the words: "You've been given a great gift, Seneca. Use your mind well, and remember to give something back before you're through."

It was because of his grandfather that Doane became a lawyer. If was because of him that he joined the Civil Rights Movement. The hard work had already been done. The freedom riders were history, but he had met some of them, and heard their tales of braving police dogs, gunshots, and firebombs hurled from speeding cars in the dead of night. He tried to adopt the spirit of the activists, to build on their work.

He failed, as miserably as his grandfather had. The system bent but didn't yield. The movement had changed from a fight for justice to a fight for power, and no one's motives were pure. He saw his grandfather's ideals once again shattered and trampled in the name of progress and profits. He realized how helpless he was, how weak, and in spite of his love and admiration for the old man, he decided he'd given enough. Now it was time to take. He lost his respect for society, and its law, and used the law to make his fortune at the expense of justice.

Now he stood before his grandfather's painting, gazed across the littered landscape of his own paltry existence, and wondered if he'd given up too soon. He'd made a lot of money, a lot of enemies, but not a hell of a lot of friends. Maybe it was time to give a little back again. Maybe that Tuscan villa could wait awhile

* * *

Narrows had accepted Cindy's offer of a celebratory dinner, and suggested a couple of places downtown. She'd held out for the Country Club. He couldn't imagine a place he'd like less to dine, and in the end they compromised on La Petite Auberge, a nouveau French place overlooking Wellington Lake. At first, her acquiescence was encouraging. The old Cindy would have rescinded her offer before giving in. Once at the restaurant, however, Narrows realized he'd been had. Though only three months old, La Petite Auberge had supplanted the Wellington Grill as the mecca for the aging youth of Wellington Lakes. He had to endure the very gauntlet of bemused greetings and perfunctory japes he'd hoped to avoid by steering clear of the Country Club. There were few things he considered more tiresome than rehashing the good old days with people he'd never liked.

Cindy smirked and wrinkled her pretty little nose in triumph. These were her people, her crowd. Gazing at her through the cluster of Karens and Barrys and Mimis and Kurts, Narrows was struck once more by her beautifully expressive face, the long, slender legs she crossed and uncrossed as she swivelled in her chair to retain everyone's attention, the eyes sparkling as the pace of the banter escalated, the cheeks which flushed as the gin began to work; he could love her again if it weren't for her friends.

When their table was ready, they escaped the crowded bar and picked over the bones of fitful conversation. This was the first time they'd been alone together since their divorce. They dispensed with family and gossip in short order, and clinging to Narrows' work, sought to avoid the shoals of shattered intimacy. He tried to muster enthusiasm for Oak Grove. She was perplexed by his failure. He tried to explain, which left her even more confused.

Outside, under the sky which had cleared following the afternoon storm, they went for a midnight stroll. They watched the winkling lights studding the shore, and the dull orange glow of Zenith to the southeast. The water lapped gently against the fieldstone seawall. The breeze soughed through the pines. Somewhere along the shore a kildeer cried, a bullfrog bellowed, and the sound of a late-night cruiser guttered across the open water. Before Narrows could find the words to tell her how beautiful she looked in the moonlight, Cindy returned to the conversation he'd hoped the change of venue had ended forever.

"I still don't know why you're getting all worked up about Zenith."

Her voice sounded unnaturally loud in the still night air. "It's like you don't think you deserve happiness." She gave her head a toss. "I don't know why you should feel guilty when you've never, ever, done a single thing wrong."

How could she make that sound like such an indictment? What should have I done wrong, and would you still love me if I had? Would I want that? He shook his head free of that web, and said, "You've never seen it, have you? You've never seen that side of Zenith."

"No, and neither should you." She turned and grasped both his hands, peering intently into his face. "What's wrong with you, Narrows? Why risk your life going into places you're not wanted just to see things that don't concern you?"

"But they do concern me," he insisted. "I keep thinking, 'This is America.' I can't shake loose from it."

"It's not your fault!"

"Maybe it is," he murmured.

"Narrows Burton, you are so—" She stopped short, grabbed his face, and kissed him fiercely. Then she groaned. "Oh God." She turned and walked briskly towards the parking lot, leaving him standing alone beside the water. She turned back. "Well, are you coming?" she demanded.

Moonlight through the bedroom window cast her skin a milky glow. Cindy straddled Narrows' hips, toying with his nipples. Her hair straggled across her damp shoulders. "This doesn't mean anything," she warned. Then she grinned, the little lopsided grin he'd only seen after lovemaking. "I don't even know why, exactly, except I wanted to."

"That's always been sufficient reason for you."

She leaned forward to kiss his forehead and his arms went around her. Her skin felt cool under his hands so he pulled the blankets up to her shoulders. She snuggled against him. "You can stay all night if you want. I'll let you."

Narrows gave a sad laugh. That was what she said the first time, was it seven years ago now? It had been his first visit to Wellington Lakes. Denny had invited him for the Mixed Doubles Finals at the Country Club's annual tennis tournament. Narrows found himself staring at Denny's partner. He loved the way her thick auburn hair bounced when she performed a little hip-hop jog while waiting for a serve, the way the muscles rippled up her legs. She was slender and trim with a surprisingly firm backhand. Her laughter was genuine. She was having fun.

Narrows decided he had to meet her, but before he had a chance to figure out an effective strategy, Denny rendered the issue moot by presenting her to him. He presented her, then abandoned them to their own devices.

He didn't mind when she laughed at his name, though he was sensitive about it. He told her he preferred to go by "Burt." Naturally she became the only person to insist on calling him Narrows. She asked him how he got the name, and laughed when he blamed it on his mother, who'd thought it sounded sophisticated.

He congratulated her on her victory, and she laughed. He praised her game, and she laughed. It wasn't self-effacing or bubble-headed. It was genuine pleasure. It was the way she looked at life. Emboldened by her laughter, Narrows told her exactly how he'd watched her play, how good she'd looked and what he'd thought about her, until the blush crept under her tan. She laughed again and said she had to shower. He asked her to have dinner with him. She didn't laugh then. She nodded gravely, as if she knew how things would turn out.

He bought her drinks until he was drunk and she drove him home. She laughed when he fumbled with the clasps and buttons of her clothes, and laughed again when she came. Then she said, "You can stay all night if you want. I'll let you," in such a little girl voice that he laughed.

Narrows nuzzled her hair. He listened to her gentle, steady breathing, and remembering everything, he fell asleep. In the morning he made breakfast. She cooed when she came downstairs, and kissed him and said, "Your omelets. That's what I miss most of all." He knew it was true. She wouldn't say something like that just to hurt him.

The day was warm and pleasant. They sipped their coffee and watched the cardinals at the feeder and the squirrels playing tag in the trees. Narrows told her about Rollins. "When I asked Russ what he was doing behind the bar, he said Rollins had died. I asked him if he'd suffered. Then I asked about his family, when the funeral is going to be, if the club is going to do anything special for his family. I talked with him for about five minutes. Then Rob called me over for a drink and I talked about Rollins some more—I can't believe he wished me luck on Oak Grove, but that's another story."

He refilled his coffee cup and laughed when Cindy pretended to yawn. "What I'm getting at, Cindy, is this. All the way out here I reviewed my conversation with Russ to make sure I'd shown the right amount of sorrow and the right amount of concern. And I realized it was all a sham. I didn't care."

"Well, of course you didn't," she said abruptly. "He was only a steward."

"No, you're wrong," he said firmly. "I liked Rollins. I always enjoyed talking with him. It wasn't like a stranger had died. But it might as well have been. Don't you see? My first reaction was, 'Oh God, I've got to pretend I care.' But I don't care. I don't care about him or anyone, and that bothers me a hell of a lot."

Cindy smiled sweetly and put out her cigaret. She walked over and sat on his lap, and said, "Narrows Burton, you are the strangest man I have ever known."

She kissed him until he slipped his hand beneath her robe. "Why don't you skip the office today?" she said. "You can take all day showing me how much you don't care."

Chapter Seven

A soft tap on his office door rescued Reverend John H. Peabody from his meditations. "Come in," he rumbled. The door opened to admit the gaunt figure of Brother Cleve Clifford. At thirty-one, he could have passed for fifty.

"Everybody's been seated, Reverend," he announced deferentially. Peabody clambered to his feet, nodding approvingly as the younger man helped drape the cerulean robe over his two-hundred-fifty pound frame.

Peabody met Cleve six months ago in unpropitious circumstances. Returning late from a Zenith City Council meeting, where he'd led a vocal delegation from the Perryman Park Neighborhood Council demanding additional police protection, he ran into Cleve backing out his front door with his arms around his television.

"Here, let me help you with that, son," he said cheerfully, wrapping his arms around the set, and Cleve. "This way," he urged, moving back inside the house.

Cleve cast a jittery grin over his shoulder at the preacher. "Is this your house, man? I didn't know."

Peabody responded by hugging the set more tightly to his chest, squeezing the breath out of the skinny thief in the process.

He invited Cleve to sit on the sofa, after first searching him for weapons. Then he sat down next to him and clamped a solid hand over his knee.

"Now, what have we here?" he asked. "Another enterprising young man trying to start a TV repair business?"

Cleve nodded enthusiastically, then convulsed when Peabody squeezed his leg just above the knee. "But my set's not broken," he said in a low, harsh voice.

Cleve begged him to stop. "You're breaking my leg!"

The minister relaxed the pressure and watched the pain dissipate from the haggard face. The dingy brown skin, marked with nicks and scars from a lifetime of street fights and scrapes with the pavement, seemed to contract into a death mask. His eyes, black circles in sallow pools shot through with streaks of red, were devoid of feeling. Cleve became a puppet. Peabody could have marched him around the room, or down the street. He could have tied him to a stake and used him as a scarecrow in his vegetable garden. He could have broken him over his knee and used him for kindling. It was all the same to Cleve, who was all used up.

"What you want to go running after that crack for, boy? Don't you know it'll kill you?" Cleve shrugged listlessly.

Just another human disaster area, Peabody thought. Just another zombie prowling the vacant lots and littered sidewalks for another nickel to score another five minute rush, another milestone on the road to destruction. Peabody studied his prisoner. If he called the police he'd be doing Cleve a favor. At least he'd have a place to sleep tonight. Or he could give him fifty bucks and let him buy a fatal dose. That would be another favor. He sighed. No, it was time for another project.

Ever since his wife died he'd taken on these reclamation projects. He chose his subjects at random, or rather they chose him by trying to rob him, hitting him up for spare change, or simply hanging around the church waiting for a crust of bread. He adopted them. He put them up in his home. He fed, bathed and clothed them. He nursed them back to health.

In fifteen years he'd had a half-dozen successes and five times as many failures. They all cleaned up, they were all gratefully sycophantic at first, for periods lasting from two weeks to several months. The longer they clung to him the more likely they were to fail. The good ones got jobs. The failures cleaned him out, or worse, cleaned out the church. His failures cost him more than money, they cost him prestige; they cost him his church.

When Elvie died, John Peabody had headed the largest church in the city. His rich, resonant voice made him a spellbinding orator. None of this prancing and dancing around the stage for him, he was a sober, distinguished speaker, cut more from the Martin Luther King Jr. cloth than from that of Al Sharpton. His sermons were thoughtful interpretations of the Scriptures, and his congregation consisted of the most successful and respected elements of the community.

They were concerned when he began his first reclamation project. They were relieved by its success, but grew increasingly disturbed with each subsequent endeavor. A delegation of lay leaders confronted him in his office one afternoon. It wasn't proper, they maintained, for a man of God to associate with drug addicts and prostitutes. He was giving the church a bad name.

The preacher laughed and opened his Bible. He read a few passages from the life of Jesus, and the delegation left with a problem on their hands. The problem became a crisis when Peabody's latest project absconded with the Sunday evening offering. Since stealing their money is the greatest sin respectable Christians can imagine, the good people of the First Baptist Church of Zenith decided Pastor Peabody needed a little vacation. They selected his replacement while he was away.

It hadn't been hard to find another church. If it lacked the size and status of his previous post, it was still respectable, certainly more so than his third church, which was better than his fourth. By the time he reached his seventh church in the past fifteen years, the papers had long since ceased mentioning the name of the Reverend John H. Peabody in their biennial speculations as to Mayor Jeremiah Brown's successor.

If Reverend Peabody had fallen from the lofty heights of respectability, he still stood head and shoulders above the likes of the Reverend Hezekiah Justice of the Salvation Temple of Jesus Christ the Savior. There was nothing self-aggrandizing about Peabody's conduct, nothing deceitful about his message. He didn't drive a gold-trimmed Escalade or drape his body in golden chains. He didn't christen his female parishioners Sister Purity or Sister Merciful and baptize them in his own holy fluids during special, private ceremonies conducted in a luxurious suite adjoining his office.

When he came to Perryman Park Baptist a year ago, he found a community in disarray. White flight had long since passed into history, an exodus which had left only a handful of diehards behind: senior citizens too stubborn, sentimental or poor to abandon the homes in which they'd raised their families; and young addicts who preferred to live within a short commute of their drug of choice. Crime was on the rise, property values continued to plummet, and the Black Middle Class was bailing out as quickly as the whites had.

Peabody's congregation was no longer community based. The membership hailed from all over the city. They would soon opt for something closer to home unless the new preacher could hold them together. Peabody accepted the challenge with aplomb. Galvanizing an audience had never been his problem. Here he found the ideal setting for his brand of Christianity.

The people of Perryman Park Baptist couldn't deny the existence of the world of which their pastor spoke. They witnessed it each time they came to hear him preach. Standing on the front steps of the church, they could see eight vacant lots, four burned-out shells, three abandoned houses awaiting the arsonist's touch, five decrepit tenements, and one neat, clean, structurally sound home—their preacher's own. It wasn't just that one block, the blight went on for several in every direction.

Once Peabody had stopped his congregation from running away, he began reaching out to the community. Bars on the windows and a new security system weren't the answer, he insisted. "We shouldn't try to keep these people out, we should encourage them to come in."

That was his rationale for instituting a soup kitchen, a health clinic, and a day care center on the church premises. Opening the church doors was easy. Opening the hearts of the parishioners took a little more effort, but after a year, a quarter of the congregation was actively involved in at least one of Peabody's initiatives. These were people who cared, who gave, not just money, but their time, a part of their lives, to the work. They'd stopped the bleeding. Perryman Park was still wracked with crime and poverty, but it wasn't getting any worse, and in a city like Zenith, that was saying a lot. A nucleus of a community had formed around his church, and it was his church. The Reverend John H. Peabody had finally found a home.

He thanked Cleve for his assistance, and said, "I guess it's time." Cleve left him then. As he moved to his seat near the pulpit, he nodded at the organist who began to coax melancholy chords from the aging instrument. Peabody appeared through the door on the front left side of the starkly white, unadorned sanctuary. He made his way to the pulpit with the stiff, sluggish steps of an aging warrior. He gazed down at the assembled mourners while the grim tones of the processional plodded to their conclusion.

He was pleased to note that the church was packed, with every seat filled, and some dozens standing along the walls. There were a smattering of white faces in the crowd. Not as many as Peabody had expected. After all for twenty years Rollins had been one of the most influential men in town, white, black, whatever. Then again, for most of the city, Peabody supposed, Rollins' influence had been primarily negative. He was the gate keeper. It didn't make sense for them to come pay tribute to the man whose presence they'd spent the past ten years trying to forget.

Still, it was a large crowd, the largest ever gathered, at least during his tenure, at Perryman Park Baptist. It was a fitting tribute to Robert Rollins, Jr. This was a man who had lived according to the Scriptures. He was gentle, kind, yet possessed of a pride which forced the world to treat him as a man. Peabody knew that Robert had chafed at the indignities he'd suffered at the Zenith Athletic Club, when those he'd scorned at the Parisienne had exacted their vengeance with slights of their own, harsh commands, and muttered insults he couldn't help but hear. He had confided his shame, his bitterness, and his anger which threatened to metastasize into hatred, and the preacher had counseled him to remain true to his own sense of integrity.

"If you find the job is wearing you down, then leave it," he had told him. "Your soul is more important than your title."

But no, Rollins refused to give in, to those small-minded men, or to the temptations of hatred. The job was a tool, a stepping stone to a better life for his children.

Peabody glanced at the front pew where Monica, Robbie and Tina sat. The women's faces were wet with tears. Robbie sat between them, holding their hands and murmuring words of comfort. He stared straight ahead at nothing. The preacher's heart went out to the boy. It seemed like he would never smile again.

When the last notes died away, Peabody began to speak in a low, steady voice, of the fine man it had been his honor to know. He spoke with an urgency and sincerity those gathered found particularly moving. He spoke from the heart, directly to Robert's family. This wasn't one of those distasteful ceremonies in which he had to gloss over a man's shortcomings, to select his least repulsive traits and recycle them as strengths. It was easy to praise this man, and at the same time, the hardest thing in the world. For he had loved him. He summoned every ounce of his ability to deliver an eloquent, moving, even celebratory eulogy; he sought a message worthy of the man.

* * *

Toward the back of the sanctuary, Narrows was wedged between two fat, black, sweating matrons. He was cramped in the crowded pew, uncomfortable with the effusive, yet obviously heartfelt praise for a man he realized he'd only flattered himself into believing he knew. Worst of all, he wrestled with his racism.

He hadn't detected the slightest indication of incipient racism in his thoughts or behavior until, after a long weekend of pondering his cold, hard heart, he decided to exorcize it by attending Rollins' funeral. The uneasiness returned as he drove down the mean streets to the church. It was a bright, sunny day. Flowers were blooming and leaves had begun to bud, but the neighborhoods looked as forbidding as they had in the cold, gray rain.

At first he didn't attribute his discomfort to racism. Instead he wrote it off as compassion. It was a reprise of "This is America." Recognition didn't set in until he got to the church, until he parked and locked his car in the congested lot, entered the building, and found himself submerged in a sea of black faces. They stared at him with what he felt was undisguised hostility. He couldn't think of anything to say to anyone, and mumbled meaningless phrases when addressed. He was ashamed to admit his connection, though he was certain they were all aware of it.

Even then he didn't correctly identify the source of his behavior. He chalked it up to his inveterate abhorrence of the rituals surrounding death. It was only when he caught himself searching desperately for another white face that the truth hit him. That dismaying realization was exacerbated by the fact that the first white face he saw belonged to Seneca Doane.

What could that worm want here? After the Wilson fiasco, Narrows was surprised that even an armadillo like Doane would have the gall to show his face in public. But he envied the ease with which the attorney moved through the crowd, stopping here and there to answer somebody's questions. Of course, someone like that would be unable to resist the opportunity to spread his name around. You never knew when it might come in handy. Narrows half expected the vulture to start pressing his business cards on the other mourners.

What really galled him was the way Doane so aptly mimicked the others' sorrowful expressions. He acted as if he were truly grieving. The bastard. His very presence was an insult, a mockery of the man. It was just last month, at the club's annual Spring Stag, when Doane got drunk and regaled the other guests with his repertoire of off-color jokes. Then, as the champagne continued to flow, and encouraged by the laughter of his peers, Doane turned vile. "I'm thirsty," he shouted. "Let's get a nigger over here."

Narrows had looked around at three hundred white men in black tie being served by a dozen black men in white jackets, and he was ashamed. He saw Rollins at his station, studying a watermark on the surface of the bar. When Doane repeated his demand, Narrows went up to him and said, "Shut up, you asshole."

His remark was met with stunned silence. He had offended the arcane standards of club decorum. Doane's behavior, while beyond the pale, was nothing compared to Narrows' offense. Stunned to find himself on the other side of a barrier he'd never known existed, he turned and walked out. He stopped at the bar to extend his profound apologies. Rollins gazed into his face with unblinking innocence.

"For what?" he asked in his usual soft voice. "I didn't hear anything."

Now Narrows stared across the crowded lobby at his nemesis until Doane's eyes met his own. Then he looked away and darted inside. Once the service began he forgot about the attorney. He was enveloped by the massaging cadence of the preacher's voice, immersed in the dichotomy of his inability to grieve the death of a man he had respected. He viewed the surrounding mass of black faces through the filter of his uncomfortable ghetto tourism. Was the city really dying, or was it just turning black? He needed to explore that question in greater depth. Cindy's petulant question came back to him: "Why risk your life going into places you're not wanted just to see things that don't concern you?"

"Well, they do concern me," he answered her, in his head and three days late. "I need to see these things. If this is America, I need to understand it."

Peabody's ringing conclusion stirred him from his reverie. Maybe he has some answers for me, Narrows thought.

* * *

Doane was as surprised to see Narrows there as Narrows was to see him. He had always interpreted Burt's self-conscious friendliness to Rollins as a kind of backhanded noblesse oblige, a patronizing kindness characteristic of those unaccustomed to dealing with servants. It was an embarrassing manifestation of guilt, of class-consciousness which was actually insulting to the servant. It was better not to notice him that to be constantly apologizing for his denigration. The ultimate absurdity of that attitude was an attempt at friendship, a blurring of the lines which always ended badly. Coming to the funeral was consistent with that mentality, but he hadn't thought Burt had the sand to do it.

Doane wasn't sure what his own reasons were for coming, beyond the certainty that it was what his grandfather would have done. He'd found himself thinking more and more about the old guy over the weekend. That Wilson woman had agreed to interviews with the local papers and television stations after the city announced that she'd dropped her suit.

She claimed Doane had coerced her into legal action. She blamed it all on him, as if her own greed hadn't dragged her out like a sow with a ring through her nose. The tabloids looked like they planned to run with the story until Christmas, plastering their pages with interviews, rerunning photos of the Psycho Cop's bloodbath, and penning scathing, self-righteous editorials. The state bar was threatening an investigation, and rumor had it Doane was facing suspension or possibly disbarment.

In a way it was only proper for the tabloids to make such a fuss over his humiliation. After all, they'd made him a litigatory icon with lavish front page accounts of the more outlandish awards he'd coaxed from unwitting jurors. It was hypocritical of them to turn on their creation, but it wasn't out of character.

Doane had stuck to his schedule all weekend, attending all the social functions on his calendar, brazening out the uproar. He laughed it off, giving the impression that it didn't matter, but inside he was hurt, and worse than that, he was ashamed. The experience did help strengthen his conviction that he was through with the law. He wasn't certain where he was headed, but the old man was right, it was time to give something back.

Then Doane, too, was caught up in the preacher's message. He was impressed with the man's voice and his deliberate eloquence. This guy would have made one hell of a trial attorney, he thought, giving Peabody his highest accolade. Sooner or later the words got through, and Doane began to regret his treatment of the steward. I must have made his life hell, he thought. He listened to the description of the man who worked in the soup kitchen on his days off, who delivered Sunday evening homilies in that very church, and wondered how much of it was eulogistic hyperbole. Then he considered the size of the crowd and the obvious sincerity and grief of the speaker. This man is no actor, he realized. He means every word.

For the first time he regretted his cruelty, and regretted his inability to make it up to the man. Looking around at the somber mass of men and women, he realized he didn't belong there. What he mourned was not a dead man, but his own ignoble life. He slipped out of the sanctuary unnoticed, walked out of the hushed building and into the glare of the noonday sun.

It was strangely quiet, all the bustle of the city spending itself in other sectors. Here the streets were empty and still. Birds flitted soundlessly between clumps of tall grass and overgrown shrubbery in the vacant lots. The jagged remains of a broken window stared at him from an abandoned house the other side of the parking lot.

Doane got into his car and drove quickly away. He wasn't sure where he was going yet, but an inkling of his destination began to form in a dusty corner of his mind.

* * *

To reach the Copper Kettle from the State Capitol Building you walked down the seventy-three marble steps from the west entrance. You crossed Quentin Carson Boulevard and ducked down a nameless alley. Halfway down the narrow passage a battered oak door stood beneath a sooty representation of an antique tea kettle. Inside, a dozen creaking wooden stairs, lit by a naked forty watt bulb, led down to a series of dusky caverns. They were arranged in a semicircle around the bar, behind which stood a ruddy-faced man with burly arms and a handlebar mustache. He looked like a relic from the nineteenth century, even down to the black garters with red roses which held the rolled-up sleeves of his crisp white shirt.

The Copper Kettle wasn't on any tourist maps. It wasn't taught in any civics classes, yet it was the true heart of state government. It was where lobbyists met representatives, and senators plotted against the governor; where selected reporters were given exclusives in exchange for a solemn oath never to mention the Copper Kettle in print. It was the place where Family Values candidates could meet their mistresses, and where once prohibition Senators had downed a couple stiff ones before delivering diatribes against Demon Rum on the Senate floor. It was the place where Rob Patterson arranged to meet Darren McCafferty.

McCafferty was one of those shadowy figures without whom very little business would be accomplished. A little more than a lobbyist, a little less than a criminal, he was a fixer, a man who arranged things: meetings, bribes, elections, the running of a certain story, the killing of another. If he rarely broke any laws himself, he'd made countless crimes possible during his career.

McCafferty was a little man with elfin features: round, red cheeks and chin, bright little eyes and bushy red hair surrounding a crescent of baldness. He stood five-feet-six, with tiny hands and feet, and dressed in navy blue Brooks Brothers suits. He was a laughable contrast to the enormous bulk of the real estate attorney with whom he shared a booth, but he matched him scotch for scotch as they discussed their business.

"You're talking about the Babbitt property then," McCafferty affirmed in his light Irish brogue. Whether it was authentic or cultivated, whether he'd ever seen the green, green hills of Ireland, was the subject of frequent, if surreptitious speculation, for Darren McCafferty was as much as fixture in the public lore as the Copper Kettle itself.

"What I want to know is, does the Department of Natural Resources have any interest?"

The little man stroked his dimpled chin. "The DNR always has an interest. The DNR doesn't have any money."

"Don't worry about the money," Patterson said dismissively. "If I can turn the public against it, the money'll take care of itself. But can a case be made?"

"A case can always be made."

The lawyer laughed. "So true, so true. I've already planted a seed with Harry Bachman. Told him and his little crew of sob sisters how the developers are going to rape the last piece of open land. I'm sure the Grassland Alliance will run with it, get all the other environmentalists out in force, get the media in on it—" He interrupted himself to light a cigar, and said, "Kid stuff," between vigorous puffs. "But I've got to have something on the state level."

McCafferty nodded. "I can handle that. No problem. The guv's still feeling the heat from the Ontanagon River Nuclear Plant. He's dying to get the whale huggers back on board before the election." His eyes crinkled in impish delight. "Be nice if you could come up with an endangered species."

Patterson grinned. "I like it, and with 1500 acres, there's got to be some kind of bird, plant or insect out there." He chuckled. "The Zenith

Midge. That'd kill 'em."

The little Irishman joined the laughter briefly, then got down to business. "How long and how much?"

Patterson said they had to move quickly. "The sale's already gone through."

McCafferty frowned. "I didn't know that." he drummed his fingers on the table while he worked it out. "We can still do it, but it won't be easy. You should've moved on this before."

"No, no. I like it better this way."

"This is personal, eh?" He frowned. "Double fee, plus expenses."

"Twenty grand?" Patterson sputtered. "Why, I could do it myself, but—"

"So do it," McCafferty snapped. "I don't do vendettas for nothing."

Mustering his professional glare, Patterson tried to stare the fixer down. Then he grinned. "All right. But I want something in a week." Summoning all his gravity, he added, "I don't need to tell you how sensitive—"

"I'll keep your name out of it," McCafferty said wearily. He hopped off his chair and extended his hand. "A pleasure, as always."

Chapter Eight

These long nights in Wellington Lakes aren't doing much for my game, Narrows thought between throbs of pain. He flailed after Denny's precise shots, and failed more miserably than usual to stand up to his onslaught. He gave up after just five games and limped off to the locker room alone, leaving his disgruntled friend smacking forehand rails off the front wall, "So at least I can work up a sweat."

It was wearing him out, running around with Cindy almost every night. He felt himself falling—not back in love—back into the same routine he'd run away from three years before. She neither asked for nor offered commitment. She just demanded his presence, his body. She was still the same girl who got her way, but after three years of doing without her, Narrows thought he could put up with it for awhile. Still, nights like last night gave him doubts. During dinner he let slip that he'd started working in the soup kitchen at Perryman Park Baptist Church.

She howled with laughter. "Oh God, Narrows. Next thing you're going to tell me you've joined the Peace Corps." Then she added mirthlessly, "Kennedy's been dead for decades, you know."

"Yeah, and Carter's a public joke. But people are still starving. Here. In America."

That launched another argument. They'd been frequent over the past couple of weeks, revolving around his nascent concern for the city. He couldn't leave it alone. He couldn't shake the shame he felt that Americans should exist in such squalor. He saw it as an indictment of the system by which he was profiting. She saw it as a none-too-thinly-veiled attack on her lifestyle. Maybe it was a good thing, he thought, all that passion. They hadn't been able to muster the interest before. When Cindy angrily accused him of throwing his life away on a whim, maybe she was actually showing him how much she cared for him.

"I still don't know why you should have such a guilty conscience," she insisted. "If you have to help the poor dears, fine. I guess I can't stop you. But why don't you just write some checks, like I do. You can certainly afford it now, and that way you don't have to get your hands dirty."

Narrows mulled over her words as he padded back from the showers. He almost shouted when his half-hearted toss actually found the towel bin. Naturally, the locker room was empty. He tried to sort it through as he dressed. Why did he have to get personally involved? There were plenty of lah-di-dah do-gooders out there willing to ladle out macaroni and cheese to a bunch of indigents. It didn't have to be him. Lord knows, he didn't enjoy doing it, and he wasn't really accomplishing anything. Then why? He groaned with frustration at his inability to understand his sudden compunction to get his hands dirty, to use Cindy's phrase. Only, he wasn't dirtying his hands. He was cleansing them. And he was writing checks, too. The actual cost of running the operation was so small compared to the numbers he was used to dealing with, that he had offered to cover each month's shortfall. It was such a small thing. One day a week, for a couple of hours at midday. He skipped lunch to feed others; it was good for him.

When Denny finally joined him in the now sparsely attended Men's Grill, Narrows was halfway through his diet plate. He hailed him with a glass of sparkling water. "'Bout time, Den." He ducked when Denny feigned a punch. "Just weighed myself—down eight pounds from last month."

"Well, it hasn't shown up in your game," Denny observed ruefully.

Narrows apologized. "Cindy had to drag me to that new Cajun place out on Mettler Road, then we stayed up late talking."

Denny raised a skeptical eyebrow. "Talking?"

"Well, arguing."

"And drinking, obviously."

"So, when'd you join AA?"

Denny glared at him. "What the hell are you doing, Burt?"

"Is there something special you want to say, or are you just in a lousy mood?"

"I'm talking about your fucking life, buddy. I mean, look at yourself. You're all over the map. Either you're a lousy social worker of you're a goddam jet setter. You can't have it both ways."

Narrows had been waiting for him to bring it up. "I'm not a jet setter," he replied. "I don't know what's happening with me and Cindy. We just kind of fell into it, it guess. But it doesn't mean anything." He hesitated, unnerved by his friend's unwavering glare. "It's nothing I can't handle."

"Don't think I don't believe you, Burt, but I'm not going to bail you out this time. You'll have to find some other shoulder to cry on."

Narrows waved away the challenge. "As for the soup kitchen, I—"

"Yeah, yeah, I know. You're trying to figure out how we as Americans can tolerate such abject poverty in our midst. You can save the speech, Burt. I've already heard it." Denny broke off to shovel a bite of cottage cheese into his mouth. "Everybody's heard it," he added, flourishing his hand at the nearly empty room. "Everybody's heard it, and frankly, we're all getting a little sick of it."

"Did they select you to represent them, or are you just freelancing?" He'd never been angry with Denny before, but at that moment Narrows was ready to throw away twelve years of friendship. Then Denny grinned.

"Sorry, Burt. I guess you have to do what you have to do." He punched him playfully on the arm. "But you've got to admit your conversion to liberalism was awfully sudden."

"I'll admit it was sudden," Narrows conceded after a moment's deliberation. "Sudden but understandable. If you'd just go with me once, it would change your thinking, too."

"I don't want to see it."

Narrows shrugged. "Suit yourself. Anyway, I don't think of myself as a liberal. It's not liberal to say that welfare is the cause of our problems, not the solution. It's not liberal to say urban policy is a national disgrace, that it's a drain on the economy. You can build a hell of an argument for social change from a market-oriented philosophy."

"Yeah, and Karl Marx was just a humble shopkeeper."

"No, I'm serious, Denny. Fifteen percent of the population is outside the economic mainstream. They don't show up in the unemployment figures. They're what the real liberals, those class conscious elitists, call the underclass. I hate that term. It implies a permanence to urban poverty. The problem with that is it isn't static. The underclass is growing much faster than the rest of the population. And as it grows, it places a greater burden on the economy. I say we should try to eliminate the underclass. We should provide jobs, real jobs, not busy work. Don't you see? That fifteen percent is a huge untapped market. If they had disposable income, the federal budget deficit would be history."

"So you want to bring back CETA?" Denny scoffed.

"No, it's got to be private sector employment, or if it's public sector, it's got to be legitimate work. I wouldn't mind seeing the government get involved in industries which the private sector finds unprofitable: making televisions, DVD players, hell, making cars the way things are going."

"But how are you going to get these people to work? That's the main thing."

"That's easy. Motivation."

"Oh, great," Denny laughed. "Just tell a bunch of homeless drug addicts to get motivated. I'm amazed nobody's ever thought of that. I mean, when you're done saving America, you can go over to Africa and solve the hunger problem. Just tell people to eat!"

"I can see I'm wasting my time here," Narrows muttered. "But I have to tell someone. I think I'm on to something. It's got to do with housing, something John Peabody and I have been discussing. A way to clean up the city, provide decent housing, provide employment training, jobs and—motivation—all in one package."

"Hey, good luck—I mean it." Denny flashed his best salesman's smile. "Listen, not to change the subject—ever think about that phrase? Not to change the subject? It's a flat out lie."

Narrows chuckled. "Yeah, I know what you mean. The other night at the club—"

"The club?" Denny widened his eyes in disbelief. "Are you referring to the Wellington Lakes Country Club by any chance?"

"Oh God. I did say 'the club,' didn't I. Maybe Cindy's rubbing off on me after all."

"Again."

"Yeah, again." He nodded gravely.

"So what happened at 'the club'?" Denny put in quickly, to rescue him from imminent gloom.

Narrows smiled. "You know Beth Andrews? Well, Cindy and I were getting a drink at the bar when Beth came barging up. 'Sorry, I don't mean to cut in front of you,' she said as she stepped to the bar. So I said, 'But that's exactly what you mean to do.'"

Denny laughed. "What'd she do?"

"She flashed one of those if-looks-could-kill glares at Cindy and marched off without her drink. Cindy thought it was hilarious, though she told Jake to send one over to Beth, on me."

"In true Herringbone fashion," Denny said.

After a moment's silent contemplation of the true Herringbone fashion, each man in his own fashion, Narrows said, "So. What didn't you mean to change the subject to?"

"Oh, right. Big stuff." Denny slipped easily into his professional mode. "Hot tip. Carlisle Medical Technologies. Trading at 60 right now. I think you should go in big."

"How big?"

"At least two thousand shares."

"But that's a hundred-twenty grand. I haven't got that much."

"You've got exactly that much," Denny countered. "I checked before leaving the office."

"Yeah, but it's all tied up in long term stuff." Narrows was perplexed. Denny had never been a plunger. "I should be getting my Oak Grove commission in a couple of weeks. We can take it out of that if you still think it's a good idea."

"Two weeks'll be too late," Denny said with a bit more urgency than he'd intended.

"What are you up to, Den?"

"It's a good tip," was all he'd say.

"Is this inside information?"

"Well, not really," the stockbroker temporized. "It's nothing illegal. I overheard a couple of brokers talking about Carlisle the other day, so I looked into it. I did the research, Burt. It's my baby and I'm offering it to you."

Narrows had known Denny long enough to tell when he was lying. On the other hand, he was his oldest friend. He wouldn't bring him into something illegal, even if he did break the law himself."

"If you don't get in on this, you'll regret it," said Denny.

Narrows searched for a clue in his friend's eyes. "It's that iron clad, is it?"

"Look, the market's changed recently. Companies are flush with cash right now, and the market's still oversold. Definitely in certain sectors. Techs haven't come back the way they should. As a result, M & A is once again the hottest game in town."

"M & A?"

"Mergers and Acquisition. I mean, the numbers are astounding. It's been like a stealth movement. Nobody really knows what's going on, but big companies are snapping up little ones, especially in the medtech sector. So you look at Carlisle Medical Technologies. They have two divisions, biotech and medical devices. They've got this colo-rectal cancer treatment that's in the third stage, and the scuttlebutt is that the FDA's gonna approve it. Plus they've got an external monitor that's supposed to speed up diagnosis of intestinal disorders. It's going to go huge. Johnson and Johnson, Zimmer and maybe even GE are looking to buy." That much was true at least, and speculators had driven Carlisle's price up from 45 over the past two months. Denny figured Narrows didn't need to know about Ron's call this morning, telling him that Johnson and Johnson was going to announce a bid at $90 a share.

"Look," he continued when Narrows failed to respond. "Carlisle makes sense on just the fundamentals, but with the M & A trend, it's as close to a sure thing as I've ever seen."

"Alright, let's do it," Narrows decided. "You've never let me down before."

Denny moved on quickly to Oak Grove, before Narrows could dwell too long on the mechanics of the deal. "So, you decided to go with the commission after all?"

Narrows nodded. "Yeah, I couldn't resist it. Five hundred thousand is a hell of a lot of money."

"It's peanuts compared to what you stood to make off it."

He shook his head. "Too many intangibles. Too many things might go wrong."

"Like what? This Grasslands Alliance thing? It'll blow over." Denny scowled. "Bunch of earth first idiots. What do they want us to do? Go back to living in grass huts? No, that wouldn't satisfy them—think of the millions of innocent stalks of grass that would be slaughtered."

Narrows didn't laugh. "I'm not so sure, Den—but that's not why I went with the commission. It seemed to be what they wanted me to do. I was afraid of an end around—I mean, do you know Curtis Gentry? Well, he's a greedy bastard, and about as ethical as Patterson." He shrugged. "So in the end I decided to go with the sure thing."

"You know what I think? I think old Reverend Peabrain has turned you off capitalism altogether."

"Hardly," Narrows grinned. "I held out for a consultancy."

"Terms?"

"Two hundred bucks an hour, twenty hours a week, minimum. One year. I got a contract."

"So you keep your hand in, then." Denny nodded his grudging approval. "Maybe you can have it both ways." He waved Jerome over.

A stocky, solemn man of forty-five, whose prematurely gray hair contrasted sharply with his smooth, unlined face, Jerome had spent the past five years tending bar part-time at the Wellington Lakes Country Club and working private parties to bring in extra cash. Until Russ Devonshire called, he had just about given up hope of ever regaining the status he'd enjoyed as Steward of the now defunct Union Club.

"Yes sir, Mr. Redmond?"

"A couple of scotches, Jerome," Denny said easily. "We've got some celebrating to do."

"That right?" His genuine enthusiasm was expressed in a soft Mississippi accent. "Well, congratulations, then." He returned to the bar without the slightest idea of what was to be celebrated, without the slightest expectation of being informed.

While Denny was phoning in his friend's order, Narrows pondered the Grasslands Alliance's demonstration against Oak Grove. He didn't share

Denny's confidence that it would soon blow over. He suffered a nagging suspicion that he'd blundered in not getting approval from the county earlier. At first he'd been too busy lining up investors. He couldn't go public with his plan until he had his financing in place or some other, better-heeled developer would have snatched it out from under him. After that he was too busy wrangling with Patterson.

"You know, the Grasslands Alliance does have a point," Narrows said when Denny returned. "It really is a beautiful piece of land."

"So, have you already joined them? Or do you have to pass some sort of test first, like killing a logger or something?"

"I wouldn't laugh, Den. They aren't all crackpots."

Denny shrugged. "I suppose not—they've got to have something upstairs to run a scam like that."

"What do you mean, 'run a scam?'"

"You don't think they really give a shit about the environment, do you?"

Narrows laughed. "Of course. Why else would they work so hard?"

Denny rubbed his thumb and forefinger together. "It's all a fund raising gimmick. Have you seen their offices? Marble floors, oak-paneled walls—a hell of a lot nicer than yours or mine."

"And a hell of a lot cheaper, too," snapped Narrows. "They're in the Thompson Building—where my office used to be. You're damn right they're nice, and you know what they pay? Five bucks a foot. That's one of the most beautiful buildings in the city, and we can't give the space away. Nobody wants to be downtown anymore."

"You ought to know about that, Burt. What's the line you real estate always rattle off? The three most important things to consider are location, location and location?"

"The place is in the heart of the biggest city in the state, overlooking a park—"

"Filled with crackheads, muggers and bums."

"Yeah, well, maybe that's why I'm becoming a 'goddam social worker,'" Narrows said softly. "We can't let this city die."

Chapter Nine

Seneca Doane lurched out of an overstuffed armchair and wandered to the living room window. His apartment was in the Zenith Tower, the westernmost of a half-dozen twenty-story spires strung along the river like dusty jewels east of downtown. They were built in the thirties, during the decade-long Golden Age of American architecture, when Zenith was a city with a limitless future. He had picked up his apartment for a song in the early eighties, when a past was all Zenith had left. The apartment had two bedrooms, a spacious kitchen, a full dining room, a study, and a thirty-foot-long living room. All the rooms had twelve-foot ceilings edged with intricate plaster work, cherry kick molding, chair rails and paneling. A balcony ran the length of the living room accessed by floor-to-ceiling sliding glass doors. In the distance, downtown Zenith sparkled in the late afternoon sun, a series of white, yellow and reddish-brown towers of brick, limestone and terra cotta. There were no glass and steel boxes in downtown Zenith. Like the Zenith Tower, it was a period piece.

When the city's last great boom ended with the start of the Korean War, Zenith had enough new office space to last until the sixties. In fact, demand never did catch up with supply. From his apartment, Doane could see three twenty-five-story buildings which had never been more than half-occupied. All three were completely vacant now. The owners got tired of losing money and finally let them go. Now they were falling down, brick by brick.

"Like the whole fucking city," he muttered. Lighting another cigaret,

109

he rambled back to his chair, and the nearly empty bottle of scotch on the coffee table littered with newspaper clippings. Doane was going through his scrapbooks, reliving the glory days of a scoundrel. He gazed down at the collection of banner headlines trumpeting every shocking triumph. He hadn't minded that the stories were a cynical pandering to the voyeuristic sensibilities of the readers, because prominently displayed in each headline was the amount of the award. One million, three million, five million dollars; that was what grabbed the public's eye. That was what brought them running to him every time they caught a cold.

Doane drank his scotch and reviewed his greatest hits. There was the alcoholic who broke his neck falling down a flight of stairs in the Douglass Projects. That was worth a million because the city hadn't put slip guards on the steps. It didn't matter that the victim's blood alcohol level was one one hundredth of a percentage point higher than the point marked "death" on the charts. Doane had produced a three-month-old work order for the slip guards: a classic case of criminal neglect, and in those days the city still had deep pockets.

Then there was the lady whose children died when her house burned down. She'd left the coffee maker on while she ran down to the bar for a pack of cigarettes. She stayed for drinks with some friends—it was only for a few hours. That was good for two million because Doane showed the jury pictures of three charred little bodies. The grieving Mom (she was basically a good mother, her surviving neighbors testified) received one-and-a-half million from the coffee maker manufacturer, and four-hundred thousand from the corporation which owned the apartment building because they hadn't replaced the batteries in the smoke alarm, and they had deep pockets.

Doane lit another cigaret and rummaged through the pile for his favorite case. That was the one in which three families split five million after their eleven-year-old sons were electrocuted at Zenith Edison's Regal Heights Electrical Generating Facility. Doane had only been fishing when he went to Zenith Edison, hoping for fifty grand each because they had very deep pockets. The company flatly refused to settle. They had an ironclad case. The boys had scaled three eight-foot high chainlink fences, one topped with barbed wire, each plastered with huge black-on-orange signs blaring: DANGER: NO TRESPASSING. After getting past the fences, they had picked a lock to gain access to the building where they got fried. There was no way anyone, even Seneca Doane, could prove neglect.

Or so they thought. That case got national publicity. That case had put him on the map. It wasn't that the company refused to settle, that was part of the game. It was the way they did it. Those smug little bastards laughed at him. They insulted him, and he got mad. It wasn't three little future inmates he was fighting for any longer. It was revenge. He filed for twenty-five million and argued that, boys being boys, chainlink fences and no trespassing signs were far from being deterrents. They were, in fact, irresistible challenges. He cited as precedents any number of cases in which an "attractive nuisance" was judged reasonable grounds for liability.

What really made the case was an extraordinary piece of luck. Doane had gone into court feeling he'd gone too far on this one. He was steeling himself for the public ridicule such a defeat would earn him. Then, the day before the trial, Zenith Edison announced a ten percent rate hike to offset expenses incurred by its troubled Ontanagon River Nuclear Power Plant. As a result, the victims had little bearing on the case. Zenith Edison's management policies were on trial. The jury didn't find for the plaintiffs as much as they got revenge for their higher electric bills. After that, Zenith Edison always settled with Doane, no matter how ludicrous his claim.

He stumbled back to the window to watch the sunset. As the light began to change, high cirrus clouds drew strips of pink, silver and gray across the robin's egg blue sky. Daylight receded and lights flickered on across the city, but none of that could touch the darkness he felt inside.

In the two weeks since Rollins' funeral, Doane had been to his office three times. He'd returned a few calls, answered some letters, and declined a half-dozen cases, including a wrongful death suit against the Winston Brewing Company by the widow of an alcoholic. A month ago he would have jumped at that one, not least because Jerry Winston III had twice vetoed his application to the Union Club. (Well, he'd already gotten even for that. Three years ago, during the club's annual staff picnic, the son of a part-time waiter broke his neck playing tackle football. Nothing like unsupervised contact sports under the aegis of a white, racist organization to get a Zenith jury going. The Union Club settled for two hundred grand, but the insurance company wouldn't pay, and the club went under).

Though nobody knew it yet, Seneca Doane had retired from the vulture business. He was tired of not being able to look at himself in the mirror. Lately all that scotch had rendered the task impossible, but he knew that was only a short term solution. No way was he going to drink himself to death. Not yet, anyway. He wasn't the kind of man to run out on a debt, and he owed a big one. It was like Gramps had said, "Give something back."

Gazing out at his city, Doane knew what it was he wanted to do. He wanted to save Zenith, great Zenith, Zenith the city dying literally at his feet.

But how could he save Zenith? He could spend every cent he had and not make a dent, unless he had a plan. He could work in a soup kitchen like that goddam idiot Burton, but what good would that do? Burt already held title to laughing stock of the ZAC. They didn't need another one.

Doane shook his head. What had come over the man? One minute he was hustling to break into the big time developer game—and doing a damn good job of it, too—and the next he was out there playing Mother Teresa, as Patterson had put it. There had to be a better way of working off a little guilt, if that was what it was. Burt certainly talked a good fight, ranting about the scandal of American poverty until everyone in the club had the speech memorized. Doane secretly applauded Burt's statement that Zenith was the symptom, not the disease. It was a point well taken, but what the hell did slopping beans and rice on some flea-bitten crack whore's tray have to do with solving anything?"

If Burt really cared, why didn't he use some of his talent to make a real difference? And he did have talent, too. You didn't get the drop on Rob Patterson without having something on the ball. Of course, Doane mused, if you were really smart, you wouldn't get the fat bastard mad at you. And Rob was plenty pissed at Burt. It was all he could talk about these days. Burt this and Burt that. "Look at the little shit suck up to the new steward. Look at him nibble his lettuce like a goddam rabbit." Rob could mimic Burt's spiel about the African-American crisis with hysterical precision. He had been the leading contributor to the scorn with which Burt was regarded by almost everyone these days.

Doane suspected the ridicule was just the first step in a larger plan. He knew Rob well enough to know when he had something on the burner. He didn't know what it was—the big man was being strangely secretive about it—but he knew Burt was going to get hurt. If he liked the guy a little more he might even consider warning him, but right now he was too busy trying to work out his own salvation. Though Rob had an ulterior motive for mocking Burt, he also had a genuine horror of all manner of social activism. As soon as Doane figured out what he was going to do, it would mean crossing Rob, and that scared him.

He turned back to the window, contemplating the twin horrors of the night time city awakening from its slumber, and the unlikely prospect of Burt becoming his ally. He shrugged. Maybe it was time to talk to this Peabody. Maybe he had some ideas.

* * *

The Thompson Building was supposed to have been the glittering jewel of downtown Zenith. It was completed in 1949, the last big construction project in the city until the Wilkinson Center, nearly forty years later. Its fifteen-story edifice was sheathed in white-enameled terra cotta, and its lobby featured a sky-lit atrium surrounded by five marble-clad levels of retail space. The design had been daring in its day, the most innovative and ambitious undertaking in the history of the Thompson Real Estate Company. It remained the company's greatest blunder, one which almost destroyed it. The company never came close to leasing it, and finally gave up hope in the early eighties, when it changed its name to Thompson Properties and relocated to the suburban office center it was developing in Athens. Now the building housed a handful of medicare doctors and dentists, a half-dozen foundations and public interest groups, and a small weekly newspaper. The building's services were minimal, its maintenance budget barely sufficient to keep it habitable, and its profitability nonexistent. The company would have unloaded its white elephant long ago, but there were no takers in downtown Zenith at any price. So the company continued to lose money on the building year after year, and would continue to do so as long as a Thompson remained at the head of the firm. A proud family, the Thompsons couldn't bear to see a building bearing their name standing empty and abandoned, even if most of those around it were already falling down.

Up on the eleventh floor, Harry Bachman stood at the window and watched the rush hour traffic creep up Wellington Boulevard. The boulevard bisected the two-block wide expanse of Philbert Park, where the grass was finally growing. It was time to mow it, and someone should plant some flowers, and maybe pick up the moraine of litter left behind by the retreating snow pack. Harry made a note of it on his calendar. It would be nice if the city would take care of these things, though he knew the money wasn't there.

But why not? Just think if they made a major investment in urban esthetics, he mused. Hiring a hundred men would take a hundred men off the welfare rolls, and they would make the city that much more attractive. Oh, he knew it would never work. The city council would insist the new hires be union members, and their pay scales were way out of whack with the job description. But the unions would make sure of it, and they had the clout to do it. Better the parks remained eyesores than they surrender one shred of power, or the opportunity to gain one more dues paying member. Harry shrugged. Sometimes he got sick of the people he had to think of as allies.

Harry Bachman, ensconced in the three-room suite of the Grasslands Alliance headquarters, stared out the window and pondered the urban environment. Unlike most of the developers he fought, Harry gave more than lip service to the city of Zenith. He lived in it for one thing. He and Mya shared an old brownstone near the University. They put up with crime, junkies, and the city's ineradicable rat population because they believed in the city. They loved its pace, the accessibility of services, amenities and humanity. Harry was a native Zenithite, and at thirty-eight, had been witness to the city's steady decline. So many of his peers had emigrated to the suburbs, but he couldn't imagine a worse fate than a lifetime spent in sterile, sprawling subdivisions jammed with crackerjack houses and interchangeable shopping malls. If life in Zenith was a constant battle for safety, if not survival, at least the battle was fought amidst the vestiges of character.

Harry liked nice things. He liked the esthetics of leaded glass windows, carved oak lining the staircase, detailed plaster work on the ceilings; he liked the feel of solid stone walls, the gleam of polished hardwood floors, the charm of gas-lit chandeliers and street lamps. As far as he was concerned, he lived in paradise. On his salary as Director of the Grasslands Alliance, and the little bit that Mya brought in with her poetry, there was no way they could afford a comparable place in Wellington Lakes, or even Percy Woods. But close to downtown, near the intellectual stimulus of the University, and the compelling genius of the Art Institute, he and Mya lived in a palace for less than they'd pay for a plywood and stucco ranch in Crystal Heights.

The irony of it. The irony of sitting around this empty office waiting for a phone call, when he should be at the Zenith Bizarre, sipping a Guinness and waiting for Mya's latest poetry reading to begin. He checked his watch and rifled through a stack of correspondence which he'd been putting off for weeks. He selected the most pressing and began composing a reply while awaiting his instructions for Round Two of the fight against Oak Grove.

Oak Grove. The very name set his teeth on edge. He considered the destruction of the last bit of open land in the entire Zenith Valley to be a personal affront. It was as if he'd wasted the last ten years trying to educate the public about their environmental heritage. Didn't anybody care? How could they be content to watch the last natural preserve be bulldozed and paved into history?

Harry didn't fit the environmentalist profile. He wasn't obsessed with global warming or frothing at the mouth over animal rights. He wore blue jeans and loafers, with a white shirt and a tweed jacket. His black hair was cut short and he kept his beard neatly trimmed. His thick-lensed glasses had rugged black frames which proclaimed his immunity to fashion. He was of medium height, slightly built, but with a wiry strength enabling him to carry a fifty-pound pack twenty miles a day in the Canadian Rockies.

He saw nature as a legacy, one to be preserved and passed on in at least as good condition as that in which he'd inherited it. His motto was, "Environmentalists are like misers. They aren't easy to live with, but they make good ancestors."

He recognized the inevitability of a certain amount of development, unlike his more radical colleagues, who brought a heavy dose of ideology to their environmental concern. He wouldn't stand in the way of necessary development, but he demanded at least a nodding recognition of its surroundings. He tried to look at both sides, except for projects like Oak Grove. It just wasn't necessary. There were three thousand square miles of concrete and houses in Greater Zenith already. They didn't need another subdivision. The only reason for developing that piece of land was simple, unadulterated greed. If they really wanted to build houses, why didn't they do it in Zenith? There were thousands of acres lying empty, abandoned; plenty of room for houses and shops, and the infrastructure was already in place.

Harry was grateful to Rob Patterson for bringing Oak Grove to his attention. Though he prided himself on his attention to detail, this one had slipped past. Patterson said that was because the developers had intentionally kept it quiet. They didn't plan to go public until the bulldozers were already at work.

Patterson wasn't the easiest guy to work with, but he was a friend of the cause. His legal counsel was invaluable, and he worked for next to nothing. Harry knew the man helped other, less conscientious organizations, who believed that the wholesale dismantling of the construction industry would help usher in a new era of peaceful interaction with the land. Harry just couldn't buy into the dogma of eco-feminists and earth-firsters. He couldn't muster much enthusiasm for the idea that interest of human beings should be subjugated to the interests of rats and fleas. He didn't know what Patterson believed, or why he represented such groups, but as far as the Grasslands Alliance was concerned, the attorney was a great asset.

When the phone rang at 6:15, Harry thought he just might make Mya's reading on time.

Patterson didn't waste time on small talk; saying hello was about as social as he ever got on the phone. "Listen Bachman, how many bodies can you round up by a week from tomorrow? S'gotta be at least two hundred if we're going to have an impact."

"I can get the people, but what's the deal?" As usual, Harry resented the lawyer's officious tone.

"County Building, 2 p.m. Planning Commission's looking into Oak Grove. S'posed to be hush hush. Your little protest has got them scared."

"Thanks to you." All Harry had done was spread the word around the campus of Zenith University. It had given them the unifying theme they had been looking for to make the Spring Fling a truly vitalizing event. Patterson had rounded up the media, and it just snowballed from there.

"Thanks to me, nothing," Patterson blustered. "We're fighting the same battle, Harry. We've got to keep them away from this land—it's all we've got left."

"So you want the usual banners and chants. Do we need a permit?"

"Nope. Got it." There was a pause, then Patterson resumed in a rasping whisper. "But I want you inside. They're trying to make it a closed meeting."

"But that's illegal," Harry protested.

"Damn right, it is. But like I told you, these are real sleazy bastards. You saw that list of Oak Grove investors I faxed you, right?"

"Yeah, a lot of muscle." The list included just about every influential name in town. Harry had recognized all of them except the developer, Narrows Burton. But he worked for Thompson Properties, the company which had done more to destroy Zenith than anything else through its full scale development of Athens. That was reason enough for Harry to hate him.

"It's muscle all right, but behind-the-scenes muscle. They don't like to work in the light of day. If we keep this on the front page, they'll scatter like the cockroaches they are."

"I don't know how to thank you, Rob."

He laughed and said, "No, I owe you, Harry." He hung up and turned at the sound of his wife's voice.

"Who's that?"

"Business, just business," he replied in the brusque voice to which he had been resorting more frequently of late. Then he noticed her outfit. Black and white silk dress and white sable coat; pearls and diamonds: a ten thousand dollar package. "Where are you going? Another battered wives benefit?"

"I just thought I'd run over to the club for dinner," she announced casually, inspecting her short blonde hair in the gilt-framed mirror. It dominated the wall opposite the spiral staircase in the two-story, marble-lined foyer.

"What about my dinner?"

She flashed her eyes at him in the mirror. "Juanita's already gone, but I think there's some roast beef in the fridge. I don't know." She brushed a wayward strand back into place and added, "Besides, I thought you were in Chicago."

"I finished early," he said, watching her touch up her mascara. She was an artist with blush and powder, and the hell of it was, she didn't need it. She looked great unadorned. Completely unadorned, he thought, imagining the shape of her body beneath that coat. "Maybe I should go with you," he offered. "I haven't been to the club in months." Noticing the sudden tension around her eyes, his stab at tenderness dissolved in a sneer. "Unless," he challenged, "You've got other plans."

"Oh, no. just the usual crowd," she assured him with a game attempt at breeziness.

* * *

Denny sipped his scotch and gazed appreciatively as Cindy crossed her legs in the low-slung chair opposite him in the Country Club's Member's Lounge. "Where's Burt?"

Cindy rolled her eyes. "He had some lousy meeting to go to."

"Oak Grove?"

"No, with that Black preacher." She opened a gold case and removed a long, slim cigaret with long, slim fingers. Flashing her most confident smile, she waited for Denny to produce the desired flame. She touched his hand to draw the fire to her tip, acknowledging him with her eyes, and exhaled with finality. "What are we going to do with him, Denny?"

He laughed and held up his hands as if to ward off a blow. "I think the question ought to be, what are you going to do, or are you doing?"

She made a face. "I'm not doing anything that ought to concern you."

"But it does concern me. He's my best friend."

"Oh look, there's Peg."

Denny sprang out of his chair, then froze when she added mischievously, "And she's got Rob with her. Isn't he just too grotesque?"

Denny tossed off the rest of his drink and headed back to the bar, grimacing when he heard Cindy calling them over. She sounded so happy to see them, it was hard to believe she found Rob despicable. Denny ordered a double, gearing up for a performance, dead certain that Cindy was going to insist the Pattersons join them for dinner. He couldn't help admiring the way her improvisation had cemented his plans. He half-believed he'd actually intended to dine with Cindy tonight. Her impishness was instinctive. She couldn't know that he and Peg had arranged to meet tonight. She couldn't know that he'd taken a room at the club, and that Rob was supposed to be in Chicago. She couldn't know, but she could guess, and she could have her fun. He braced himself for an evening of innuendo, wondering if Cindy knew how dangerous Rob was, and if she cared, and just how many people she was willing to hurt for an evening's entertainment.

He returned with two scotches. He greeted the couple with an appropriate amount of pleasure and handed one of the drinks to his as yet unsuspecting rival. "Sorry, Peg. I didn't know what you wanted."

"I bet you could have guessed," Cindy said sweetly. Denny laughed a bit too heartily and offered a weak parry. "But I didn't know if she'd like a Planter's Punch."

"Oh, that sounds like fun," said Peg.

"Jake, four Planter's Punches," Cindy called across the lounge. "I feel like having fun tonight," she announced. "Don't you?"

Peg and Denny exchanged rueful glances while Patterson covered one of Cindy's knees with his hand and said he was up for a little fun.

After another round they opened a bottle of red wine while perusing the menu and discussing area chefs. Their orders placed, they opened another bottle while waiting for their table. The steak was tender, skillfully if unimaginatively prepared. Rob continued to run through the wine list, ordering different varietals from different lands, and what had begun as forced amusement for at least half the foursome became sincere. The banter was fulsome and unrelenting. Denny gave as good as he got, while trying to ignore Peg's bare toes pinching his calf.

Then Patterson shattered the mood. "So, Denny, what do you hear from Mother Teresa?"

Denny took his time chewing his mouthful of steak, hoping someone would pick up the dangling conversation and move it elsewhere.

"Isn't she dead?"

"I think he means Burt, Peg."

"Yeah, God's gift to the downtrodden." Patterson chuckled. He leaned back in his chair. His jacket hung down on either side of a massive belly encased in a freshly starched tent. His left hand rested proprietorially on the back of Cindy's chair. She pretended not to notice, and tried to shift the subject to what New York had to offer in the way of summer fashions. Still suffering from her whimsical treachery, Denny sought revenge by ridiculing his friend. "He told me over lunch today that he doesn't think soup kitchens are the answer."

Patterson snickered. "Oh, he doesn't? Did he happen to tell you what the solution might be? An anxious nation awaits."

"He said he isn't sure of the mechanics, but there has to be some way 'to break the downward spiral of poverty and social dependency.'"

"How about putting the lazy fuckers to work?" Patterson reached for the bottle, and finding it empty, signaled for the waiter.

"How do you do that?" Cindy wondered. "How do you put people to work when there aren't any jobs? Narrows says they're—"

Patterson leaned over and grabbed her hand. "My dear, I don't give a good goddam what 'Narrows' has to say about this, or anything else."

Denny fought back the impulse to call him down. This was Cindy's battle. Her forehead was furrowed, as if to assimilate a spasm of pain, and her eyes were colder than he'd ever seen them. He doubted she had ever been addressed like that in her entire life. It would be enlightening to see how she handled it.

Cindy removed her hand from Patterson's paw, and fastidiously wiped it on her napkin. The others waited for her reply, each having his or her own hopes and expectations. She stared at the attorney, her mouth pursed as if to speak.

The waiter chose that moment to intervene, presenting the evening's fifth bottle with a flourish. He poured a taste into a fresh glass and offered it to Patterson with a surfeit of gravity and humble anticipation. Expertly swirling the ruby liquid beneath his nose, the bloated gourmand drank deeply of its aroma before introducing a tiny quantity into his mouth. He ferried the wine throughout the cavity with a skillful tongue, meting out a fair portion to each key reservoir of taste buds, while a frown of concentration contorted his face.

"Oh, do give us your judgement," Cindy said acidly. "Is it the oak of the barrel, the freshness of raspberries, or the scent of freshly mown hay which your scholarly palate detects? Do tell us quickly. As much as I would love to try it myself, I don't dare until you tell me how it should taste."

Patterson set down his glass and announced, "This wine is unsatisfactory. Bring me a different bottle."

The waiter was nonplused. Standard procedure called for him to taste the wine himself to be certain, but standard procedure had never confronted the likes of this porcine epicure. He scurried off in search of the chief steward. In his absence, Cindy grabbed the glass and took a sip. "There's nothing wrong with this wine."

"Rob…" Peg pronounced her husband's name with a voice mingling supplication and shame.

"The wine is bad," Patterson reiterated. "I had a '92 Chateau Palmer just last night—in Chicago. There is no comparison."

"Maybe the one you had last night was bad," Cindy suggested. Peg giggled. Patterson shifted his imperious glare from one to the other of possibly the only two people in the city immune to his power. Denny studied the intricate curlicues of the country club monogram on the plates, the glasses and cups, the silverware and the napkins, and hoped he wouldn't get caught in the crossfire.

Cindy offered Denny the glass. "You're a bit of a connoisseur, Denny. Why don't you give it a try?"

Denny gave a nervous laugh and scowled at her. He was reasonably certain the wine was okay, but after all, Rob was a client. He took his time, studying the color in the light, and swirling the glass. Where was that damn waiter?

A simple process followed the wine steward's arrival. After determining whose palate the wine had offended, he tried it himself, announced his agreement with the gentleman's judgement, and his personal chagrin that this "one in a million" misfortune should befall a man such as Mr. Patterson, and offered a replacement with his compliments. The crisis averted, the dinner limped to a limpid conclusion, with no further mention of Narrows or his beliefs.

The guests departed. Cindy followed Denny upstairs for a nightcap, and the Pattersons returned to their mausoleum, to retire to separate rooms, to hurl unspoken imprecations at each other through the walls; one party wishing she'd never signed that prenuptial agreement, the other dreaming unrequited dreams of the Football Hall of Fame.

When the last of the guests stumbled out the door, the waitstaff enjoyed an excellent, full-bodied Bordeaux at the height of its oenological powers. Their chatter drifted through an open window upstairs to form an amiable backdrop to a hushed, earnest discussion between two close friends concerning the sudden aberration of a third.

On the eighteenth floor of a downtown apartment tower, the aberrant third posed before his window watching the insomniac city toss and turn. Sirens ululated through the night while geysers of flame shot up from the black fabric of the neighborhoods. He thought about the people he'd met that night, about the words he'd heard, the dreams still deferred and starting to fester. He wondered, was it possible he'd stumbled upon a way out of the pit he'd dug for himself while mining the depths of Zenith's decline? Was this a way to douse the flames, stop the bleeding, to rehabilitate the American Dream?

In another house, the eighty-year-old mother of a senior vice president of the Winston Brewing Company, who'd refused her son's pleas to leave the house she'd been born in, awoke to the sound of breaking glass. "Oh God, not again, please," she whispered through her terror. Her eyes squeezed shut, she listened to assailants unknown make a shambles of her living room and kitchen, and she prayed they would go away. She prayed long and she prayed hard. She prayed until the beam of a flashlight stabbed her in the eyes. And she screamed. She pounded her tiny, frail fists against the solid hands and arms which seized her. She screamed and bit and cried until her heart gave out and she never knew the things they did to her body.

And in another house, in another part of the city, a teenaged boy and a thirty-year-old whore rolled around on the floor and giggled at her three-year-old son bouncing off the walls and floor and she crawled over to give him some more wine.

And in another house another teenaged boy, a track star, decided he had mourned his father long enough. He slipped out the back door and went running on the streets. A different kind of running this time, he ran with a pack and saw and did things he'd never dreamed of doing before.

And on Douglass Street the moonlighting cabbie dropped off the last fare of the last night before his wife and kids returned from visiting her mother in Ohio. He pocketed the tip which gave him enough to buy that flat screen TV for their anniversary next month. He put the car in gear and was about to drive away when he noticed the little boy outside his window. He couldn't of been more than eight. He rolled down the window and laughed when the kid said, "Check it in, Mister." He was still laughing when the kid brought out a nickel-plated thirty-two and shot him in the face.

Chapter Ten

The Perryman Park Housing Corporation needed a board of directors. Rev. Peabody nominated Narrows for Chairman, but he insisted it should be someone from the community, preferably a man.

"Why a man?" demanded Althea Williams, a heavyset woman with milk chocolate skin and wide, brown eyes. "Why not a woman?"

"Because—can I be blunt?" Narrows asked, a little uneasily.

"You better be, or I can't work with you."

Narrows grinned. "Okay, I'll give it a shot. We need a black man because there aren't a hell of a lot of them around." The statement earned hearty assent from the eight women and two men in the room. "See, we aren't just building houses here, we're building a community. Communities need families, and families need men."

"And my boy Darrel needs a man he can look up to," said Angela Duggins.

"Exactly. So, are there any prospects in the community?"

Cleve Clifford raised a tentative hand. "I'd like to try."

"Are you sure you're ready, Cleve?"

"I got to do something, Rev'rent. I can't keep holding onto you."

Peabody beamed. He'd been waiting and hoping for some show of independence. Never had he seen as dramatic a change as that in Cleve's life over the past seven months. He was clean and sober and he truly believed. Now he was stepping forward. He prayed that Cleve was ready. He hoped he could grow into the job.

It was agreed, then, that Cleve Clifford would be Chairman of the Perryman Park Housing Corporation. Narrows agreed to serve as a Director. "And I want each of you here to be on the board as well. Plus I'd like to hold a half-dozen seats for Zenith's corporate leaders."

"Why them? They aint done shit for us."

"Money, Althea. We're going to need a lot of money to get this project off the ground, and they're the ones who have it."

"Well, they never gave us any before."

"We never had a plan before," Peabody interjected.

"We don't have one yet," Narrows cautioned. "All we have is an idea. We need by-laws, a mission statement, eligibility requirements, a volunteer recruitment committee. We need offices, staff, supplies. We need a fund raising apparatus—"

"Hold on, hold on," Althea cried. "You're gonna talk us out of it before we even get started!"

"Yes, let's take it one step at a time," Peabody suggested. "Burt, why don't you handle the by-laws, you and Cleve. We can all work on the mission statement and eligibility requirements. Althea, you start recruiting volunteers."

"Why me?"

"Because I never saw anybody who could say no to you," he said to general laughter.

After they agreed to meet the following Thursday morning, Cleve performed his first official act as Chairman of Perryman Park Housing Corporation. He adjourned the meeting. Narrows lingered in the hall with Peabody, Cleve, Althea, and two other new board members, Krystal Williams and Darnella Jackson. Krystal had fine features and long, black hair. Her skin was the color to which summertime Wellington Lakes sunbathers aspired. She wore an efficient gray suit, a couple of thin gold chains and pumps. She told Narrows she was taking a long lunch from her job in the collections department at Zenith Edison.

I don't live in the neighborhood now," she explained. "But I grew up here, and I still attend the church. When Pastor John started talking about this project, I just had to get involved."

Narrows said he hoped one day it would be the kind of neighborhood she'd want to move back to, and asked her to find out the name of a contact person in her company's community action program.

"Do we have one?" asked Krystal, flashing a disarming smile.

"Most companies do—maybe not by that name. You might check with PR."

Just then Darnella's little boy let out a yelp. "I wanna go home," he wailed.

"You shut up or I'll slap you again," Darnella snapped. "I'm talking to the rev'rent." She was tall and lean, with tangled hair, dirty jeans and an old sweatshirt. Her skin was black as asphalt, with a hard, grainy veneer. Her eyes were menacing, and her lips were laced with a series of tiny scars.

Later, when the others had left, Peabody told Narrows that Darnella had only recently moved into the neighborhood. He'd located a house for her after he found her curled up with her son by the back door of the church. Her boyfriend had turned her west side flat into a crack house. When she complained, he beat her up and threw her out. She'd left all her belongings behind, but was afraid to go back and get them.

"Isn't there something we can do?" Narrows wondered.

Peabody smiled kindly and wrapped a fatherly arm around Narrows' shoulders. "First thing you have to learn, Burt, is you can't do everything. If you try, they'll eat you alive."

"But I can't just sit back and watch her suffer."

"She's not. She's got shelter now, and DHS will replace her belongings."

"DHS?"

"Department of Human Services. The Welfare people," Peabody explained disdainfully. "Darnella will have everything she needs to scrape by. The one who's going to suffer is her boy. The odds are better than even that he'll be dead or in jail by the time he's twenty."

"You don't sound very optimistic."

"I'm not. I'm an idealist at heart, but I don't have much hope," the preacher said bluntly. "I don't do these things because I think they'll work. I do them because I have to."

"You have to…"

"God won't leave me alone." His voice trailed off and his eyes with it, but he came back after a moment. "If you want to feel good about helping people, go home and write some checks. Stick around here and you'll get a hard heart and a thick skin. You'll learn how to say no, and mean it. You'll learn how to throw junkies out of your office." He stopped and stared meaningfully at him. "You'll learn, or you won't survive."

Narrows said he didn't know if he could do that. If he was going to act like a caring person, he had to get involved in people's live. "Aren't people the key to this project?" he argued. "There's a lot more to this than fixing up houses, you know. We can't turn the neighborhood around until we turn the people around."

Peabody smiled sadly. "Oh, to have your faith." Then he shrugged. "Talk to me in six months." As he ushered him to the door he said, "We're going to need legal advice, you know."

"We sure are. Know any lawyers that'll work for free?"

"Actually, one paid me a visit the other day. He said he wanted to give something back to society."

"Great. Let's get him on board before he changes his mind," Narrows said. "What's his name? Maybe I know him."

"Seneca Doane."

His smile faded. "You don't want him," he said flatly. "He's not a lawyer, he's a judicial terrorist. He has no conscience, no values. He's a racist, a liar, and a conniving bastard. The only reason he'd want to get involved is to make money off our dreams."

"I almost invited him to our meeting," Peabody said wistfully. "Are you sure he's so bad? He seemed pretty sincere."

It was Narrows' turn to smile knowingly. Peabody might know the streets, but this was his area of expertise. "He's a lawyer, John. It's his job to sound sincere."

Peabody shrugged. "I guess we'll have to keep looking."

Instead of heading directly back to his suburban office, Narrows drove up and down the six blocks comprising the target area. Skidmore, Wright and Merrill streets weren't as bad as some blocks he'd seen. They were about fifty-fifty. As he drove along, he identified those structures worth saving, and those which needed to be demolished. It's like cancer, he thought. The disease consumes a dwelling, then jumps to the next one.

What would happen if we destroyed all the diseased organisms, if we tore down all the houses already dying of neglect? Would it keep the others healthy?

Then he reminded himself that people lived in those wrecks. That was the problem, and that was the beauty of the preacher's dream. Repairing the dilapidated housing would enhance the neighborhood's appearance. If it looked like a better place to live, it might become a better place, especially if people helped fix up their own homes. In the process, maybe they would acquire a few marketable skills, and more important, a sense of accomplishment and the pride of ownership. If Peabody's right, welfare won't be good enough anymore. Welfare's great for just scraping by, but it's a lousy foundation for building dreams. If we can give them motivation, maybe they can...

"It's all blue smoke and mirrors as far as I can see," the other Narrows thought. "How can we get these people to fix up their houses when they're the ones who are letting them fall down in the first place? Where are they going to get the money? Do they think I'm going to bankroll the whole thing? No way. Even if I could, no way."

He drove on. Owings and Portman Streets were bad, but Stirling was the worst. On the whole long block there were only six houses still standing, and none of them for long by the looks of things. Scattered between the structures were heaps of rubble overgrown with weeds. It was the bleakest vista he'd yet encountered in his almost addictive meanderings along the mean streets of Zenith. It was worse than a battlefield. It was a graveyard, a forgotten, decaying cemetery.

He fought back a sense of futility until, halfway through his slow perusal of the block, his vision altered. Suddenly he saw it not as it was, but as it could be. He saw new houses. He saw a complex of townhouses, with landscaped common areas dotted with swing sets and benches, with off-street parking; a clean, well-lighted place. Stirling Street wasn't in the final stages of decay, it was in the first stage of a new, user-friendly housing development. Overcome with the force of the possible, for the first time Narrows applied his developer's mind to the opportunities, not the obstacles.

All those problems of financing, liability exposure, zoning laws, a hostile bureaucracy, a recalcitrant community, diminished before his resurgent confidence. "We can do it," he cried. "We can do it."

He stopped his car and walked across the street to one of the lots. He sat on a pile of crumbling bricks, lit a cigaret, and picked a stalk of grass. While winding it around his finger he watched a new city rise out of the detritus of the old. I'm the man to do it, he thought. Didn't I just pull off Oak Grove with little more than a good idea and a whole shitload of confidence?

If he could do that, and he had, though sometimes it was hard to believe, and he still couldn't shake the suspicion that something was about to go wrong—

"Hey man, you got a light?"

Narrows glanced up at a skinny, shave-headed kid wearing a bomber jacket. He said, "Sure," and tossed his lighter. The kid lit a Kool, and, pocketing the lighter, said, "You got any money?"

Narrows laughed and said, "How'd you like a house of your own?"

The kid scowled. "What kind of shit is that?"

"It's not shit. It's the real thing. You help fix up a house, and then you can buy it for almost nothing."

The kid shifted uneasily. He looked around at a block full of emptiness, then back at the strange man in the nice suit sitting on a pile of bricks. "C'mon, just gimme the money."

"What's your name?"

"Darrel," he answered without thinking, then with mounting suspicion, demanded, "What's goin' on? You a cop or somethng?"

Narrows took a shot at it. "Do you know Angela Duggins?"

Darrel's eyes widened. "Yeah, she's my Ma." He frowned, now completely bewildered. "You know her?"

Narrows stood up. He towered over the scrawny youth, and outweighed him by at least sixty pounds. Unless the kid had a gun, which was always a possibility, he wasn't in any danger. He took out his money clip and peeled off a five while Darrel gazed hungrily at the rest.

"You want some money? Here." He reached over and tucked the note in a pocket of Darrel's jacket. "My name's Burt," he said. "Ask your mother about me." He stepped around the kid, half expecting him to come after the rest, then stopped, turned, and said, "Oh yeah, can I have my lighter back?"

Darrel was too shocked to speak. He retrieved it from his pocket and tossed it to Narrows. "Thanks. See you around." As he got into his car he heard Darrel shout, "Hey, you crazy. You know that?"

Narrows waved and drove off, hands shaking on the steering wheel, thinking Darrel was probably right.

When Narrows got back to his office he found a stack of mail and a message to call Curtis Gentry. He began punching the number even before he sat down. Curtis Gentry held fifty percent of Oak Grove. He was a schemer and a hustler, a financial street fighter who didn't like to lose. Narrows didn't trust the man. He didn't like him and he didn't look forward to working with him. He suspected the feeling was mutual, which was the main reason he'd opted for the commission.

If Gentry wanted him to call, it must be important. He was pretty sure it wasn't a dinner invitation.

Gentry's secretary said she'd try to raise him on his boat. Typical, Narrows thought, and sorted through the rest of his mail. There were the usual if-you're-the-typical-busy-executive-earning-more-than-seventy-five-thousand-dollars-a-year-then-you'll-want-to offers, a renewal notice from the "Journal," various legal correspondence, and notification of the Onganaw County Planning Commission hearing on Oak Grove. June 22, next Thursday. But it wasn't until two, so he could still make the Perryman Park meeting.

"Burton? Listen up," Gentry snarled. He was one of those ostentatiously busy types who probably had a stenographer at his elbow, three attorneys holding contracts for him to sign, a half-dozen reports he was scanning, and a conference call on hold, as well as a video screen tuned to CNBC.

"I'm all ears, Curtis."

"Good. About this planning commission hearing."

"I just got the notice."

"What's the poop?"

"Just a routine hearing," Narrows said blithely.

"Routine hearing about what?"

"Approval."

"You mean you haven't even gotten a goddam go-ahead yet?" As Narrows settled down for a harangue he decided Gentry definitely had a boatful, and probably a couple of girlfriends as well. He wasn't the type to waste a tantrum.

"Don't worry, Curtis. The county needs Oak Grove. They need the revenue. Zenith is bleeding them dry."

"What about this Grassland Alliance bullshit?"

"No problem," Narrows assured him with a confidence he didn't quite feel. "They're just letting off steam. It'll blow over, if it hasn't already."

"Yeah? Is that so?" Gentry broke off for a whispered conversation with an aide, leaving Narrows to speculate about the nasty surprise Gentry obviously had in store for him. ("Just do it. Just do it. I don't give a rat's pecker what Halyard says, just get it done!") Narrows wondered if Gentry's performance were meant for his benefit. Then he wondered what the other four early warning signs of paranoia were. Gentry came back and said, "Have you seen 'The News' today? Well, get a copy, and then tell me how it'll blow over."

When Narrows asked what he should look for, Gentry simply said, "Just read it." Then he added, "If there's any trouble over this, Burton, your ass is grass."

"And a pleasure doing business with you, too," Narrows said to the resounding click. He pressed a button and asked his secretary to scrounge up a copy from someone. Before he could return the receiver the other line buzzed.

"Hello, stranger," Cindy replied to his gruff greeting. "Has the reverend got you serving dinners now, too?"

Narrows mumbled something about work, realizing for the fifteenth time in a month that Cindy was one complication too many at this point in his life. He begged off when she suggested dinner. "I don't feel like driving all the way out there tonight."

"I'll come downtown," she offered. "You can cook me your fantastic spaghetti and we can have a bottle or two of Chianti, just like old times."

It was tempting, it would be nice to just play, and to play with Cindy would be especially nice. It had been almost two weeks since they were last together, and he was starting to miss it.

"You know, I've never seen your apartment," she added, which was a close as Cindy Herringbone ever came to begging. That made it doubly difficult for Narrows to say no, but he had an almost physical need to be alone tonight.

"Can't we do it tomorrow?" he asked.

"No, I'm going to New York for the weekend." A pause, then, in a bright voice, "Why don't you come with me? It'll be fun."

Why not, he thought, then said it, with the qualifier, "You're sure I won't be in the way?"

"Of course not, silly. It'll save Rina having to scrape up another boring investment banker for me—we're going to the theater, you know, the new Harold Pinter play."

They arranged to meet at the airport at 4:30 tomorrow afternoon, though Narrows almost changed his mind when she said she'd already bought his ticket. Then Diana came in with the paper and he had to go. There was nothing in the business section that would have made Gentry gloat. Narrows paused in sports long enough to check the baseball standings, then returned to search the front section.

* * *

At just about that time, right after the closing bell at the New York Stock Exchange, at a well-attended press conference in the midtown headquarters of Kelso, Harper, a fast growing boutique investment bank, Charley Kelso announced that his firm was overseeing Johnson and Johnson's nine-billion dollar, ninety-dollar-a-share takeover bid for Carlisle MedTech. The reporters scribbled down the particulars, eager to get to their laptops and fill in the blanks of the story they'd been waiting to write for weeks. The JNJ buyout was one of the best-leaked stories ever sprung on Wall Street.

Arbitragers had been jerking Carlisle around on a peculative choke chain since the beginning of May. It wasn't a matter of if, but when. This was one late-breaking story they could file without missing happy hour.

Walt Simpson, a gaunt-faced man with a protruding Adam's apple and an ill-fitting suit, sat taking notes with the rest of them. Only for him, the press conference was the beginning of the story, not the end. His report would require a lot more work than the others', but his wasn't going to an editor. It was going to the chief of the Securities Fraud Division of the SEC. Simpson frowned at the glowing terms Kelso used to describe the deal. Numbers and earnings projections weren't of any use to him. He needed names and faces, hard cold facts and witnesses to back them up.

He was on the track of a different kind of insider. Not big money, high profile people like Martha Stewart, who went to jail just so a certain egomaniac prosecutor could mount her on his wall, but members of an extensive, highly organized network who kept to themselves, limited their profits, and got in and out with the stealth and speed of Taliban insurgents. They were harder to catch, and though he could hazard a guess at how many millions they'd already made on Carlisle MedTech, he didn't have one piece of evidence that would stand up in court.

Half the reporters in the room were suspects, and he realized that that and ten million dollars would get him into Trump Tower. But give him time. He'd find a crack somewhere, and when he did, he'd worm his way inside and blow the network out of the water.

* * *

If he had known that Denny's tip had just made him $60,000, Narrows might have felt a little better. As it was, he sat alone in a windowless office in Athens, his chin resting on his fists, brooding over the article dominating page three of the "The Zenith News":

Priceless Grasslands Threatened by Developers
by Stewart Cooper

An aging office building on the crumbling fringe of downtown Zenith might be the last place one would expect to stage a battle to preserve a piece of virgin prairie land, but according to Harry Bachman, it is an ideal location. "We're closer to the center of power here," says the slim, bespectacled Director of the Grasslands Alliance. "We can get the message out more effectively, plus the rent's a lot lower than it would be in a more glamorous location."

Glamorous is hardly a word which leaps to mind to describe the view from Bachman's eleventh floor office: a vista of abandoned office buildings and empty parking lots. Such a specter can actually be an advantage, Bachman says. "Whenever I get discouraged, all I have to do is look out the window. It helps remind me what I'm fighting against."

What Bachman is fighting for is 1,500 acres of rolling grassland and hardwood forest surrounded by Zenith's northeastern suburbs. "One hundred fifty years ago all of Onganaw County was like this," Bachman explained during a recent walking tour of the site. "Deer, elk, fox and bear, and hundreds of species of birds and small animals thrived here.

"Now, there's only this one little piece of our environmental heritage left, and they want to destroy that, too."

Environmental heritage is very important to the 38 year old activist. "I'm not a knee jerk opponent to development," he emphasizes. "After all, people have to live somewhere. But something like Oak Grove (the new community proposed by a development group headed by Narrows Burton, of Thompson Properties) is completely at odds with environmental reality. It's unnecessary. It's destructive, and I'll fight them every step of the way.

There was more, but Narrows didn't bother reading it. He closed his eyes and massaged his temples. It was worse than he could have imagined. It was a smear job. It defied belief that a Pulitzer Prize winning journalist like Stewart Cooper would write a story like that without even trying to hear the other side.

"Why, why, why?" Narrows repeated. "Why didn't he talk to me?" A story like this could galvanize the public against Oak Grove. It didn't matter that he had anticipated Bachman's reaction, that he actually shared the environmentalist's concern, and had designed a community which would preserve, in perpetuity, a slice of Zenith's environmental heritage. Narrows despaired of ever having the opportunity to tell his story to the public.

Even if his pitch to the planning committee were successful, they would probably postpone a decision until they saw which way the wind was blowing. "Damn him," he muttered "Damn the lousy bastard. Why didn't he talk to me?"

If Cooper wouldn't talk to him, Narrows decided he would talk to the reporter, and while the "News" voice mail computer gave him the run around, he speculated about Harry Bachman. He didn't blame the guy. He probably would have done the same thing in his position. Still, it was ironic that the man should view him as an enemy when they had so much in common. He toyed with the idea of calling—

Finally, the system found Cooper's phone. It rang four times, then the reporter's reporter's voice informed him that he was away from his desk, out sabotaging somebody's dream, doing a hatchet job, and not even giving the guy a chance to defend himself, but if the poor sucker wanted to leave a message, he'd probably check in later today. Maybe that wasn't a word-for-word transcript of Cooper's message, but that's how it sounded in Narrows' anguished mind.

He left a message, and asked him to give him a call. After he hung up, he decided to give it a shot. Maybe it wasn't too late to save Oak Grove. If he could just convince Bachman that development was inevitable—and it was, now that Ted Sr. was dead—then he would see that Oak Grove was the best way of preserving at least a part of the land. He had to know that the DNR's budget had been slashed. They couldn't buy the land even if they wanted to. Bachman had to understand that Narrows was on his side.

* * *

Harry wasn't in his office either. He was on the campus of Zenith University with a handful of students, coordinating next Thursday's demonstration. In addition to Dave and Chelsea there were the usual spectrum of left-of-center student movement representatives: Cathy

Farnsworth, from the Environmental Defense League; Richie Nichols, representing ANSWER; Debbie Rymoor, who headed the campus chapter of Greenpeace, and Camilla Hernandez, from Hispanic Women for Justice and Against Rape. Harry almost asked Camilla if she was in the wrong room, but she threw herself into the planning with a knowing demeanor. She was no stranger to demonstrations. None of these kids were. For some reason, suddenly it all seemed so juvenile, so useless, such a sham to be working out the logistics for yet another demo.

Harry wondered if he was becoming jaded, or maybe he was just tired, or maybe it was an allergic reaction to the other member of the session. Jack Rabinowski, Chelsea's latest love, was President of the Young Socialist Worker's Party, a splinter group formed when the Revolutionary Worker's Party imploded following the fall of Moscow. The Young Socialists' sole claim to fame was their habit of defacing freeway overpasses with incoherent and frequently misspelled slogans. Jack was the only true radical in the group, and Chelsea clutched the sleeve of his leather jacket as if she were afraid he would float away.

The others, though no less sincere in their beliefs, were nevertheless adherents to the larger status quo, seeking change within the system; in short, much like Harry himself.

"We want a high visibility, a high impact event," Harry emphasized. "The media will be there, so be sure to get your most articulate speakers in front of the cameras. Here, I've put together a list of talking points to help prepare you," he added, distributing a sheet of paper to each of them. "We'll review that next week. But for now, I want to stress that our most important objective is to get inside the room. It doesn't matter how effectively we come across on the street if they go ahead and push through their approval up on the third floor."

"Why don't you just go in yourself?" asked Cathy, a third-year med student who planned to open a practice in a small Wyoming town.

"Harry doesn't like to be confrontational," Chelsea explained cattily. Her chronic dissatisfaction with Harry's methods seemed to have grown more acute through interaction with the radical Jack.

"I plan to go in," Harry said pointedly. "But I don't want to go in alone. And not because I'm afraid," he added quickly before Chelsea could speak. "I don't want them to think I'm just some kind of crank. I'd like to have at least thirty well-behaved—and I can't stress that enough—people with me. If we outnumber the developers, we may have a chance of stopping them.

After discussing the best approach, they decided Harry should take his group through the Wellington Boulevard entrance of the County Building while the main demonstration took place in the plaza along Perryman Avenue.

"What if they try to break us up? Should we fight back?"

Harry laughed. "Sorry, Jack. I don't think there's much chance of that. We have a permit."

"But what if they do?"

"I tell you, they won't," he snapped. Then he grinned. "You'll just have to wait for another chance to start the revolution, Jack." After glancing at his watch, Harry announced, "Listen, I gotta run. Try to get as many people here as possible next Tuesday to make banners and go over logistics."

He grabbed a bus heading downtown, where he was supposed to meet Mya and a few other people for drinks at Bynam's a rustic jazz club in the warehouse district. As the bus wheezed past the Thompson Building, he considered checking in at the office. But no, it was already 5:30, the rest of the staff had probably already gone home, and he'd been on the go since six that morning. Besides, who knew when another bus might come along? Tomorrow would be soon enough.

Tomorrow was filled with meetings all over Greater Zenith, and interviews with all four local television stations. He didn't get back to the Grasslands Alliance office until after three. When he saw the message from Narrows, his first inclination was to throw it away. Probably wants to negotiate some sort of understanding, he thought. Typical big money MO. Buy me dinner at some fancy restaurant, coopt me with some vintage wine and a nice, thick steak, make me see his point of view. Harry wouldn't have to give in or anything, just keep an open mind, agree to hold off on the demonstrations until they worked out a compromise.

"No way," he decided, crumpling up the message. He tossed it at the can in the corner. A perfect shot: a two-wall bank and it rattled into the metal cylinder. Then, recalling last night at Bynam's, the way he and Mya had to scrape together enough money to afford a half-carafe of vinegary house wine, and then cadge off their companions for another, Harry thought how much he'd like to treat her to a nice evening. There was nothing that said he'd necessarily be corrupted, not if he went in with his eyes open.

He could take Mya with him. They could enjoy a nice dinner without having to decide whether to stiff the electric company or the phone company that month—a tough call since he'd like to stiff them both every month. After the bastard paid the check he could let him know what he really thought.

Harry retrieved the message slip and returned Narrow's call. But his secretary said he was out. When Harry pressed her, she said he was out of town until next Tuesday.

"Typical rich bastard," Harry decided. "Jetting off somewhere for a long weekend." He crumpled the paper again, and this time missed the can by a good two feet.

Chapter Eleven

June was already three weeks old. The temperature hovered at eighty degrees, the fifth consecutive dry, sunny day; something of a record given Zenith's notoriously changeable climate. After a weekend bobbing on the river in thirty-foot speedboats, or lolling around the house, basking in that most comfortable suburban symphony of guttering lawn mowers and whining weed trimmers, with the crackling aroma of barbecues wafting through the leafy trees, the august members of the ZAC had returned to their offices with their energy regenerated by the onset of summer, determined to make that deal, sign that contract, or fulfill the long-contemplated dream of finally jettisoning that profit-draining, stress-building, union sinecure of an engine plant on the south side. After just two days of noble endeavor, the best and the brightest were ready for an afternoon of frivolity around the Round Table.

In the midst of the usual hijinks and japery, the assemblage contemplated the dual mysteries of Seneca Doane's ongoing languor and Rob Patterson's ebullient good humor. They'd almost grown used to the former, having endured it for over a month. Doane was preoccupied, morose, unable to shake the lethargy which had reduced his sparkling wit to a fading memory. He failed to rise to the ethnic, sexist or racist bait, no matter how frequently it was dangled. Beyond a flashing of the eyes, he made no response even to their obligatory twitting over the Wilson fiasco. The corporate lions were concerned by his lassitude. They wondered if there was anything they could do to lighten the mood the attorney inflicted on the gathering; where could they find a suitable replacement for the jovial anchor Doane had been?

Equally perplexing, though more satisfying, was Patterson's sudden transformation. Jolliness was not an overstatement. Though no one would ever have accused him of lacking a sense of humor—no one would have dared—it had hitherto been manifested only in vicious barbs on which one or another of the guests found himself impaled. Now, with the exception of that capitalist apostate Narrows Burton, whom all the Round Tablers were happy to have as the focus of their cruellest jibes, Patterson's humor had no victim. He sparkled rather than stabbed, amused but did not wound. Even Doane, who in his vulnerability would have been sliced to ribbons under Patterson's prior tyranny, escaped the force of the big man's wit.

No, Patterson seemed almost at peace with himself, content in a way none would have thought possible. If they enjoyed his camaraderie, they sometimes missed the liveliness he had brought to the table, the alertness he had engendered in his companions. One or two of those whose wounds had taken longer to heal, went so far as to suspect this kinder, gentler Patterson was merely a subterfuge, a calculated move in a game none of them could fathom.

Though errant in thinking themselves potential victims, they weren't far off in their assumptions. For it was a game of deceit which had produced Patterson's geniality. He hadn't felt this good since that warm, sunny afternoon, just before his knee exploded under eight hundred pounds of offensive linemen. As he watched his scenario unfold, it produced a satisfaction akin to that he'd experienced when, with a right hip fake and an open left hand to the helmet, he'd dispatched the opposing guard and had a clear shot at a quarterback scanning the right sidelines, waiting for his primary receiver to clear.

He knew when the whistle blew on this play, Mr. Burton would be as dazed and broken as that quarterback had been moments after three-hundred pounds of solid muscle slammed into his back. And maybe, he continued with a mystic, serene smile on his lips, maybe this guy wouldn't get up either. Maybe they'd have to carry him off the field as they had had to carry, what was it, eight quarterbacks during his brief career.

"Look at him over there," he said to the gathering, indicating with a jerk of his head the table for two across the room where Narrows and Denny consumed their usual Wednesday lunch after a very successful squash match. "The king sits with his council, his courtiers, and all his loyal retainers—" He grinned at the chorus of snickers. "You notice he no longer speaks to we mere mortals," he continued. "Now that he's a major league developer and philanthropist." He opened last Thursday's "News." "He doesn't realize it yet, but he's about to be sent back to the minors."

Doane roused himself long enough to ask what was in store for Burt. Patterson chuckled. "Wait and see, Red Man. Wait and see."

"Why don't you let it drop?"

Patterson's eyes glinted within their surrounding folds of flesh. "Some of us are still in the game," he said cryptically. Doane stared wordlessly at the bloated creature he'd once considered to be a friend. He knew now that he hadn't known what a friend was. He didn't know yet beyond the certainty that he had none. Nor had he ever, with the possible exception of his grandfather. Nor would he until he climbed off this treadmill. Right about now a friend would come in handy. Just somebody to talk to, somebody who could help lead him out of the maze. Lately, mired in solitude, rejected even by a small potatoes housing group, he'd discovered the answer to his oft-posed query as to why a field as lucrative as his should be so devoid of competition.

It was the loneliness. A shark is a solitary creature. It lives alone. It swims alone. Its only contact with others comes in the form of violence. No one trusts sharks, not even other sharks. No one touches a worm. No one wants to get close to a weasel. No one wants to sleep with a snake.

Doane raised his piercing blue eyes at his rapacious colleague. "Some of us outgrew the game."

The other Round Tablers exchanged sly glances. Seneca Doane was speaking. More than speaking, he was locking horns with Patterson, in defense of another human being. In defense of Burt, of all people. This was a new Doane, a seemingly more compassionate one. Now, that was truly frightening.

"Outgrew the game?" snorted Patterson. "I'd say the game outgrew you. You got lazy, started believing your own press, and you took on a case nobody could win, not even the inimitable Seneca Doane."

"Leave that out of it," he snarled.

"What? Cut too close to the bone?" Patterson glanced at the others to make sure they were still with him. "You lost a big one. You got your hand slapped, by a nigger bitch, no less, and now you don't want to play anymore." He unleashed a burst of calculated laughter.

"She was right." Doane's statement was delivered in a quiet, almost reverent tone, but it cut through the racket. Patterson went quiet. He gazed at the narrow, pockmarked face which reflected nothing less than hatred.

When he spoke, it was in a hard voice, evoking pity and contempt. "You make one lousy fumble and now you want to quit. Well, that's fine. You run along home now. But don't you dare take the ball with you. I'm still playing. It's still my game."

"How can you call it a game? You're playing with people's lives here. Those aren't touchdowns you're putting up on the scoreboard. Those are dreams you've destroyed."

"You got religion," Patterson said with a pretense of astonishment. He looked at the others. "Red Man's gone soft on us. He wants us to start worrying about other people's feelings." he pursed his lips and raised his eyebrows at Ben Richards, a fleshy, middle-aged manufacturer's rep for Zenith Fasteners. "How 'bout it, Ben? Should we give up our immoral practices and start drinking ourselves into a stupor like a decent Christian would?"

Ben coughed into the drink he'd picked up for courage. He adjusted the round, wire-rimmed glasses on his pasty moon face, and said, "I didn't know it was wrong to make a buck. Isn't that what it's all about?"

"Well, Benny, that's where you're wrong," breezed the big attorney. He gave a friendly wink to Doane. "See, Red Man gave me the straight poop last night."

"You wouldn't dare," gasped Doane. "That was a private conversation." He shouldn't have done it. He'd known at the time it was foolish to confide in a man such as Patterson, but the weight of his solitude had grown intolerable.

Patterson laughed. "Anything you give me's mine to use, Red Man, and—Sit down!" he roared.

Denny glanced up and nudged Narrows. "Looks like a bad moon's rising over the knights of the Round Table." Doane stood trembling with rage. His face had turned such a shade of crimson that his normal complexion seemed pale by comparison. In spite of his wounded pride and his overarching longing to escape, Doane returned to his seat.

"I want to share with you the gospel according to Seneca Doane," Patterson announced to the other five men. They shifted uncomfortably. Fun was fun, but this was getting out of hand. They didn't know what was going on, but Doane's discomfort was almost physically painful to witness. Each had witnessed the others being carved up by the master swordsman, and had kept his tongue, grateful that he wasn't on the menu that day. But this went beyond swordplay. This was virtually murder.

"Is this, uh, necessary, Rob?" asked Ernie Jacobs, an institutional trader for Merrill Lynch.

"I only seek your edification," he replied with a look of such seraphic innocence that it was hard to keep from laughing. Then Patterson resumed in a sonorous voice. "In the beginning was the word, and the word was gold. Seneca Doane heard the word. He knew the word and all its value. He saw the word and said that it was good. Seneca Doane toiled long and hard for that word. He wanted, then he wanted not. He thirsted, until he drank from the cup of gold, and then he thirsted not. He toiled until there came another word. Seneca Doane knew that word also. That word was shit, and it was his name.

"Seneca Doane saw the word and said it was not good. He thirsted once more. He drank deeply. He drinks deeply still." Here Patterson paused to grace his colleagues with a knowing leer.

"But it shall not always be thus, gentlemen. One day Seneca Doane will thrust the cup aside. He will take the volume of words he has amassed—the former word, I mean, the word of gold—and he shall break it into pieces, and he shall distribute it to the hungry masses gathered at his feet. He shall divide the gold among them until there remain none who are without, and there shall be seven baskets of gold left over.

"And there shall be a new word, and that word shall be Doane, and the people shall know that word, and they shall say the word is good.

"Soon Seneca Doane will take his lips from the cup from which he drinks so deeply. He shall descend into the wilderness. He shall follow in the footsteps of his father's father. Little is known of his father's father. Though the scribe did write of him, that scribe is little read today. But Seneca Doane's father's father was a man of the people. He gave his life for the little people. He toiled long and he toiled hard, asking little in return and receiving less. Yea, I have heard these words from the mouth of Seneca Doane himself. Thereby am I assured of their veracity.

It was time for another theatrical pause, and Patterson was obliging. He gazed at each of his listeners. They shifted their eyes and remained silent. He gazed longest at Seneca Doane. Frozen by his humiliation, ashamed of his inability to get to his feet and walk away, Doane stared at the now watery drink sitting in front of him, and vowed not to finish it.

"Go ahead, you know you want it," urged Patterson. Doane shook his head. "Go ahead."

After Doane grabbed his glass and drained it, Patterson resumed his recitation. "Now is the time for Seneca Doane to go out into the world to seek and save that which was lost. He goes now to join Narrows Burton, to feed the hungry, to clothe the naked, and to give shelter to the homeless. Go now, Seneca Doane," he whispered. "Go now. Go now." He repeated the command, his voice increasing in volume with each repetition, until the little lawyer fled the room.

He would not run. He told himself he would not run, so he retreated in a crabbing, half-bent shuffle, brushing Narrows' shoulder as he passed the table for two.

"I wonder what that's all about?"

"The end of an error, I believe," Denny quipped. He raised his glass at Doane's retreating back. "I don't think we'll be seeing him anymore." His farewell toast was drowned by an uproarious burst of laughter from the remaining occupants of the Round Table.

"One down, one to go," Narrows murmured. "Wouldn't it be nice if all our enemies could be so easily dispatched?"

"Wouldn't it be nice if all your investments could appreciate fifty percent in a month?" Denny countered.

Narrows grinned. "So, what do I do now? Plow it back into blue chips?"

"Keep it liquid for the time being."

"Why liquid? Have you got another—"

"I'm researching one right now," Denny answered smoothly. "It's a form of roulette, I'll grant you, but these things have a certain logic. I think I've detected a pattern, and if I'm right, it'll make us both rich. I think the medical technology sector has legs, so it's just a matter of picking the right company. I'm betting on Ryan Systems."

"I never knew you were such a speculator," Narrows said warily.

"It's not risky, Burt. See, the same qualities which make companies good takeover targets—low book value, large cash reserves, a dominant product in a niche market—also make them legitimate investments. That's why the larger firms are snapping them up. They aren't into charity—unlike some people I know."

Narrows dodged the barb, but took the bait. "The whole thing's coming together, Den. There's enormous potential. I visited a similar project in the South Bronx while I was in—"

"Oh yeah, how was the Big Apple? I guess you and Cindy are back at it, huh?"

"Cindy and I are—" Narrows stopped. Are what? Going steady? "All I know is, it's working right now. For how long, I have no idea—and neither does she. But we're having a good time. There's no pressure. None. We've already done jealousy and possessiveness. Now we're just mutually selfish, trying to take as much as we can and having a great time doing it." He grinned. "Going around with your ex might be the best relationship there is."

"Now that you're a millionaire, I suppose the 'kept man' pressure has—" Noticing the grim mask Narrows assumed, Denny asked, "Is there a problem? You didn't turn your commission over to Reverend Peabrain, did you?"

Narrows scowled. "I don't know, there may be a problem. I assume you saw 'The News' article."

"Yeah, real nice puff piece."

"Real nice hatchet job, you mean. The SOB never even talked to me, and he won't return my calls, either."

"He's getting a lot of mileage out of it."

"Who? Bachman?" Narrows lit a cigaret. "Yeah, I guess so. He's been on the news almost every night."

"Still, it's no big deal. He's a charter member of the loony left."

"But that's just it, Den. He's not. He comes across as very gentle, caring, and above all, intelligent."

"Yeah, but he's still an environmentalist. Who's going to take him seriously?"

"Curtis Gentry, for one."

"You mean he—"

"Tomorrow's the big day," Narrows said flatly. "If anything goes wrong at the hearing, I may never see a penny."

"Surely you'll get your costs back."

"You don't know Gentry. He makes Patterson look like a Sunday School teacher."

"Son of a bitch," breathed Denny, unable to come up with anything more cogent. "I don't know why such a great idea—"

"It's gone wrong ever since that fat bastard got involved," said Narrows, staring at the Round Table. Patterson caught his eye, grinned, and raised his glass in a mocking salute.

* * *

Chief Ernest Slaughter wiped an already sodden handkerchief across his face as he limped out of the press conference. The little shits are on my trail again, he thought as he ducked back into his office. Another bad night, another of his boys shot dead. That made eighteen officers killed already this year, and there was no end in sight to the Zenith Drug War. Everybody wanted to know what he was going to do about it. What could he say? That he'd just ordered a new home security system? Like hell he could. Maybe the best thing was to pull out of the neighborhoods until the shooting stopped, and then throw all the survivors in jail.

He filled a mug with steaming black coffee and topped it off from a bottle he kept in his desk for emergencies. The hell with it. He was through meeting the public today. All he wanted to do was go home, have a couple cold ones, and go to bed.

"Chief Slaughter," Angie shrieked over the squawk box.

He picked up the phone. "Yeah, what now?"

"There's an anonymous caller, Chief. Says he'll only talk to you."

Slaughter came to attention. A guy could always hope. "Is it about the Wrecking Crew?"

"He won't tell me. He says it's you or nobody, and you'll never forgive yourself if you don't talk to him. You want me to just put it down as a crank?"

Slaughter sighed deeply, wearily. "No, put him on."

The caller spoke in a gravelly whisper. "There's gonna be trouble, big trouble."

"When? Where? Who is this?" the Chief demanded, activating the tracer.

"This is a concerned citizen," the caller rasped. "Tomorrow. Two o'clock. County Building."

"All right, buddy. What's the story?" Slaughter slumped in his chair. Another crank. There was nothing going on at County tomorrow. Just a bunch of routine meetings, and another lousy demonstration by— "Wait a minute. Does this have anything to do with the Grasslands Alliance?"

Silence.

"Hello? Hello! Are you still there?"

"Yeah, but not for long. You got a fuckin' tracer on, aint ya."

"No, of course not. What's going down at the County Building?"

"Sort of a sixties revival, you could say."

"A what?"

"Jus' a little blast from the past, my man."

"You mean a bomb?"

"Gotta go."

"Wait, I'll shut it off."

"You shouldn't a lied."

"Wait, wait. Hello?" Slaughter pressed a button. "You get it?"

"Not quite, sir. If you could've kept him another thirty seconds—"

"No, he knew what he was doing." Slaughter ran his hands through his wiry gray hair, took another sip, then topped it off again. Then he pressed another button. "Angie, get Captain Richards up here, pronto."

Chapter Twelve

The bomb squad finished searching the County Building before the first employees dragged into work. When he received their report, Chief Slaughter sighed and said that would have been too easy. He turned to Captain Richards. "Well, Dan, I guess it's up to you. Remember, no force unless it's absolutely necessary. There's gonna be a shitload of media out there."

Richards went off to brief his Darth Vaders, who waited with riot sticks and tear gas launchers. He reviewed deployment and strategy, and stressed that crowd control was their primary duty. Then they trooped off to take up their positions around the building.

It was only ten and already the temperature was pushing ninety. Slaughter felt the humidity as he made his way to his car behind the County Building. Well, nobody expected that Honolulu weather to last forever. "God, I wish I was there right now," the Chief muttered to himself. "Spot on the beach, pina colada in my hand." He had a bad feeling about this demonstration. He told his driver to circle the block in order to see how things stood before heading back to headquarters.

The westbound lanes of Perryman Avenue were blocked off as a precaution. It had created a traffic jam and a hell of a lot of angry motorists, but it was better than having one of them catch a stray bullet. Slaughter winced. Surely it wouldn't come to that. He studied the vanguard of demonstrators. A lot of pretty, young suburban housewives with small children in tow, and clean cut college students. It looked more like a church picnic than a potential riot. Still, that voice. He couldn't forget that voice.

Chief Slaughter had logged a lot of hours listening to anonymous phone tips in his time. He'd developed an ear for fakes, and over the years had laughed off warnings of firebombed Thanksgiving Day Parades, assassinated Presidential candidates, poisoned water supplies and sabotaged nuclear power plants. He could tell a crank, and this one wasn't. This guy meant business.

Harry Bachman strolled the pavement in front of the County Building, greeting friends and the new supporters his frequent television appearances had attracted. Mya said he was telegenic. He didn't know about that, but it seemed like every time he talked to a camera, another hundred people volunteered. Grasslands Alliance membership was swelling, and it looked like they'd have a thousand bodies today. "That ought to make Patterson happy," he thought, scanning the crowd, wondering if the attorney would make an appearance.

Harry hoped he would, because this had all the earmarks of a great event. Already the gathering had a festive air. The banners and multi-colored clothing sparkled in the brightening sunlight. Soon the place would be overflowing with people celebrating their commitment to the environment. And with so many people, it shouldn't be hard to sneak a couple dozen into the building.

His contemplation of the speech with which he'd finally destroy Oak Grove was shattered by the sight of riot-clad shock troops cordoning off the County Building. "What the hell's going on?" he said aloud, thinking how much the Young Socialists would love this show of muscle.

Right on cue, Jack Rabinowski appeared at Harry's elbow. "No trouble, eh Harry? Got yourself a permit, eh Harry?"

Harry swung around and grabbed the kid by the lapel of his leather jacket. "You listen to me, Jack. I don't know what the hell they're doing here, but it doesn't change what I said. There won't be any trouble. You hear me?"

Jack smiled insolently. "Sure thing, Harry. No trouble. You got it. But who's gonna tell them?" He jutted his chin at the uniforms checking the identity and searching the belongings of everyone attempting to enter the building.

* * *

In the crowded basement meeting room of Perryman Park Baptist Church, Narrows was oblivious to the growing storm downtown. He was too caught up in the miracle of birth to give any thought to the potential death of his dream. Althea had done a tremendous recruiting job. There were twenty-five community residents in attendance. In addition to Narrows, non-residents included Krystal Williams, and one other guy in a suit and tie, who came in late, and took a seat next to her. The meeting started with a brief discussion, during which the new volunteers gave their views of the problems their community faced, their hopes engendered by this nascent endeavor, and a variety of suggestions to make the neighborhood a better place to live. Some of them merited action, including a Neighborhood Watch Program, a safe place for children to play, and something to keep the older kids off the streets.

As Cleve reviewed the by-laws, Narrows was surprised by his perceptive observations and additions, and he noticed the glow of fatherly pride on Peabody's face. After discussing a mission statement and tailoring the eligibility requirements to accord with the interests and capabilities of those present, Narrows took the floor and outlined the next steps the group should take.

"We need to take a survey of the neighborhood. We should document as thoroughly as possible the following areas: home ownership, the number and size of existing households, the percentage of residents employed and/or receiving public assistance, and the range of annual income. Not only will this give us a better idea of what we're working with, it will give us the sort of data bank which funding sources like to see."

Narrows was intrigued by the way the other suit nodded his head as he ticked off his points. When he was finished, Krystal announced that she'd learned the name of a contact person at Zenith Edison. "His name is Martin Perry—and here he is," she announced with a nervous laugh.

Perry said Krystal had told him all about what the Perryman Park Housing Corporation wanted to do. "Your goals dovetail nicely with my own views, and as the administrator of the Zenith Edison Community Support Fund, I'm in a position to be of assistance."

Among the areas in which the company was prepared to help were organizational strategies, the donation of office furniture and supplies, and the possibility of financial support. "Though I can't guarantee how the committee will react, I can promise a sympathetic review of an initial funding proposal."

"How much?" Peabody rumbled.

"As much as ten thousand dollars," Perry said, earning a vigorous round of applause from the group. "Now, I realize that's only a drop in the bucket for a program of this scope," he added. "But it should cover operating expenses for three months or so, which will help you get off the ground. I doubt you'll be doing any actual rehab work before then." He was interrupted by an upwelling of disappointed and impatient grumbling.

"I'm not trying to put a damper on your enthusiasm," he assured them. "But these things take time, maybe more than you realize. Just setting up the organization will occupy most of your time at first, that and writing more proposals."

Peabody interrupted at this point to say that he'd already identified a half-dozen target houses, and believed at least two of the owners would be willing to donate them."

Perry didn't try to conceal his surprise. "Then you'll want to get moving on filing for non-profit status."

"Already underway," said Narrows.

"Well, this is fantastic. You guys are in excellent shape for, what, two weeks?"

After the meeting, Narrows grilled Perry on what else Zenith Edison was prepared to do, and what other corporations would look favorably on a grant proposal. Perry, in his turn, grilled him about his interest in the organization. Once satisfied, he expressed his confidence that Krystal would prove an asset to the program.

"She already has," Narrow observed.

Krystal flashed her disconcertingly open smile, and said it was easy to talk about it because she believed in it so much. But she hesitated when Narrows suggested she should head the fund raising committee. Then Perry said he'd be glad to help her. That settled it, and it also marked the first corporate member of the Perryman Park Housing Corporation Board of Directors. Then Narrows looked at his watch and said he had to run.

Angela Duggins stopped him at the door. "My boy was askin' about you," she announced in a tone both suspicious and intrigued. Narrows said he'd run into Darrel after last week's meeting.

"He's a good boy," she assured him with an urgency which belied her assertion.

"He seemed okay," Narrows replied. "You think he'll want to get involved?"

"I don't know. Hangin' around a church aint real popular with his crowd." She shrugged. "He might. He say you one crazy man."

Narrows laughed. "Maybe I am. It's a crazy dream, but maybe we can pull it off." He tried to slip past her, but she grabbed his sleeve."

"Why you doin' this?" Her eyes were black, bottomless pools; a smile dropped into them didn't cause a ripple. "I want to know."

He wondered what difference it made to her, but simply said, "As soon as I figure it out, I'll let you know."

Emerging into the cloying noonday heat, Narrows was sweating by the time he reached his car. "Great," he thought. "Sweat buckets. That'll win 'em over." He hopped into his car, turned the air conditioner on high, and headed west on Perryman, trying to shift cognitive gears in anticipation of the commission's questions.

By all rights, planning commission approval should be nothing but a formality. It wasn't like he hadn't done his homework. He'd already checked out the environmental angle. He had an informal ruling from the DNR, a letter from Amanda Filcher, the department's Acquisitions Officer, stating that the DNR had no plans for that piece of property. The land had no environmental significance beyond the fact that it was pretty, and as far as Narrows knew, prettiness did not constitute legal grounds for an injunction.

Besides, he'd addressed that very issue in his planning. He was on the environmentalists' side. Oak Grove would be an example, not just to Zenith, but to the whole country, of how to develop a piece of property without destroying the environment.

The first thing developers did, at least in Zenith, was clear cut the trees. Well, Oak Grove wouldn't do that. Narrows couldn't wait to see the first houses go up, with 150-year-old oak trees in the front yard. They'd look like they'd been there for forty years. But they were brand new!

Narrows patted his briefcase. His report was compact, lucid and transparent. He wouldn't try to hide anything, because there wasn't anything to hide. The fact that it would make a profit wasn't a negative. It was the best thing about Oak Grove. No developer would willingly lose money, but if he could satisfy both the community and the bottom line, then everyone would benefit.

Narrows groaned and pounded the steering wheel. It wasn't fair the way that bastard Cooper had undercut him. He'd made Bachman a superstar, and Narrows one of the heavies. He hadn't yet been able to show off his plan. "I never will if this traffic doesn't start moving."

He checked his watch. It was already 1:08, and he was sucking exhaust fumes fifteen blocks from the County Building. He rolled down the window and craned his neck to see what was holding things up. Traffic jams weren't the norm in downtown Zenith, certainly not at one o'clock on a Thursday afternoon. There weren't enough workers left downtown to cause one.

But he was definitely in one now. He waited and fumed, switched the radio on and switched it off again, checked his watch every fifteen seconds, and covered an entire block in less than eight minutes. After 1:15. He had to decide. If he walked he could just make it, but he'd be drenched with sweat. He tapped the steering wheel, craned his neck, checked his watch again, and didn't move. It was now or never. He flicked on his turn signal, but there was nowhere to go. The cars in the right lane couldn't have made room for him if they'd wanted to.

The hell with it. He shut off the engine, grabbed his jacket and briefcase, and ignoring the insistent honking behind him, set off on foot through the murky heat. His car would be towed, but what was a hundred dollar fine when his life was on the line? He checked his watch after a block and picked up the pace. Sweat trickled down his face and began to dampen his shirt. No matter. He just hoped Diana had remembered to drop off the charts.

Over at the County Building, TAC Squad Chief Dan Richards peered at the crowd through his visor. He kept an eye on the two dozen black-jacketed youths drifting around the perimeters of the protesters. Led by a scrawny, greasy-haired kid, they were the most likely source of trouble. The only source, he reminded himself, watching Harry Bachman move from cluster to cluster, laughing and shaking hands. This wasn't a fucking riot, not in the least. There was no way around it. Chief Slaughter blew it. "We shouldn't be here," Richards muttered while observing the crowd control officers doing their usual fine job of keeping the peace. "We are the problem."

He glanced at his troops. They'd trained for years for a shot at civil disturbances. They'd kept in shape. They'd spent a half-dozen hours a month practicing—everything. With the exception of the Barons' winning the Super Bowl four years ago, they'd kept their powder dry and their high tech gear in the locker. They were like nuclear missiles. Nice to know we got 'em, but hope to God we never have to use 'em. Today was the closest they'd come to launching, and if they did, it was their own damn fault.

The young toughs clustered around their leader, who kept his arm around the waist of a skinny blonde girl. Occasionally they ventured close to the line and tossed a few experimental taunts before Harry rushed over to move them away from confrontation. For a moment, Richards viewed Harry as an ally. His fingers twitched on his riot stick. How he longed to return the favor. Bust that greasy head and they could all go home. Damn that Slaughter.

He shrugged and moved down the line. Had to keep his boys in check. There was a commotion in front of the main entrance. A stocky, red-faced man in a rumpled suit was arguing with Sergeant Porphus. Porphus was a type: ex-special Forces, walk around the house in fatigues, drill on weekends with the National Guard, take his machine guns out in the forest type. He was also a good sergeant. He knew the value and meaning of discipline, and was damned loyal to his superiors.

Porphus gazed impassively at the frantic civilian."What do you mean I'm not on the list?" the man demanded, mopping his face with a sodden handkerchief.

Porphis scanned the list of names again. "Sorry, pal. I don't see no Burton."

Richards approached. "What's the problem, Sergeant?"

"Guy says he's s'posed ta be in there, Cap'n. I don't see his name."

"Well, your list is mistaken," Narrows said icily. "I'm the reason they're meeting today."

"What did you say your name was?" Richards asked. He scowled over Narrows' shoulder at a pair of black jackets edging near.

"Burton. Narrows Burton. The developer."

"Hey, Harry. It's the developer," Jack cried. "Narrows Burton!"

The Young Socialists began chanting:

Hell no, it's our land,

Go build houses in Japan!

Narrows turned in time to see half the minicams in the state chase Harry as he ran, shouting, "Cool it, Jack!" He saw Narrows and stopped short, stunned to see a man younger than himself playing the role of voracious plutocrat. Narrows gestured helplessly. He still wanted to reach out, but events had moved too quickly. The reporters bustled forward, microphones thrust before them like lances. "Mr. Burton, why do you want to kill all those trees?" "What kind of name is Narrows, anyway?" "Hey, Burton, you pull wings off flies, too?"

He turned to Richards. "Satisfied?"

The policeman gave a curt order and Narrows was admitted. He passed through the revolving door and crossed the lobby to the elevators, mopping his face and trying to absorb the sensation of a thousand people shaking angry fists at him. At him. He recalled Cindy's accusation: "You've never, ever, done a single thing wrong."

"Tell it to them," he muttered. "Tell it to them."

Outside, Richards exchanged coolly appraising glances with the demonstration leader. He wanted more than anything to apologize, to explain. But a lifetime of training made him scowl instead. Cops don't apologize, and even if they do, TAC squad officers don't. The slightest hint of weakness and a mob like this would tear him apart. He didn't want to be there, but since he was, he knew how to behave. Besides, judging by this guy's face, there wasn't any room for compromise.

Resentful was a charitable term for Harry's feelings. Unabashed hatred was closer to the mark. He felt betrayed by the very values he'd labored to uphold. Richards' presence was a gauntlet hurled at the peaceable intentions of the Grasslands Alliance. It was an insult, and an eloquent statement of the establishment's attitude towards environmentalism. All his life he'd tried to walk the line between justice and radicalism, to keep things in perspective, to keep from going over the edge, as so many of his colleagues had done. He'd always been a believer: in justice, in peaceful agitation, in the system. If this was the way the system treated its friends, the ramifications were frightening, too frightening to contemplate at the moment.

One last slit-eyed glare and Harry spun on his heel and marched back into the crowd. Richards watched him go, relieved at least that the chanting had died down, but now convinced that there were two people out there who bore watching.

The conference room was only half full, but buzzing with the residue of tension each person had carried in from their interrogation at the door. Narrows scanned the crowd, relieved to see a preponderance of men and women attired in sober business suits. No radicals here, just the usual smattering of reporters. Print reporters only, he noted. The electronic media were outside, where the action promised a better story. He saw Curtis Gentry, but none of the other investors had shown. "Makes sense," thought Narrows. Gentry was the key. The others would follow his lead.

After making sure his charts were in place and in good order, and reviewing the procedure with Melissa Neusome, Onganaw County Planning Commission Chairperson, Narrows fended off another assault from the press. This time, without the backing of a mob, they were relatively polite, even respectful of his reluctance to speak. "My presentation will explain it all," he insisted. "The Grasslands Alliance is mistaken. I'm actually on their side."

Leaving them scratching their heads over that one, Narrows headed over to Gentry. Extending his hand in greeting, he said, "How are you, Curtis?"

Gentry ignored the proffered hand, and apparently of the opinion that Narrows was outside the need-to-know loop regarding his health, replied, "Nice little reception committee outside. That your handiwork?"

Narrows shook his head. "I don't know what's going on out there, but I don't like it."

"He doesn't know what's going on," Gentry remarked pleasantly to his companion, a little ferret-faced man in an Armani suit. "Guy's trying to pass himself off as a grand-a-day consultant, and he doesn't know what's going on."

His companion sniggered, then leveled a pair of empty gray eyes at Narrows. "You want to know what's going on out there? I'll tell you what's going on out there. We're getting fucked over royal, that's what's going on out there." He crooked a forefinger at Narrows and added ominously. "You know what happens when somebody fucks over Curtis Gentry? Somebody pays, with interest."

Narrows tried to muster a hearty assent, but had to settle for something closer to a strangled gasp. He wiped his face again and glanced at the crescent-shaped table where the balance of the commission was assembling.

Gentry broke off his merry chuckling and said, "By the way, Burton, this is Gary Kilton, one of my attorneys. I call him 'damage control.'"

Narrows nodded and moved to his assigned seat at the desk facing the commission. He wiped his face again and tried to concentrate.

Before she convened the hearing, Melissa Neusome dabbed her own face and suggested it might be better to put up with the noise and open some windows. The hearing commenced against a muffled backdrop of chattering, laughter, and honking horns.

Harry's lieutenants returned from reconnoitering the building with the expected news that all the other entrances were locked and guarded. The only possible entrance was in front of them. Harry groaned. He glanced up at the digital watch face on the sixth floor of the Flood Building across the street: 2:05. The hearing was already underway, and he was stuck outside. "Patterson should have thought of this," he thought. It was an uncharacteristic oversight by a man who was usually obsessive in his attention to details. The entire event would be useless if they managed to push Oak Grove through upstairs.

He ran his hands through his bristling black hair and announced to his crew, "I guess we'll have to bluff our way in." A few demurred, but he still had a dozen supporters as he approached the TAC Squad.

For the past twenty minutes Richards had been concentrating on the bearded activist's activities. He'd observed the crew he'd assembled, and the scouts he'd dispatched. He'd received reports from the north, east and south entrances, and knew something was afoot. As Harry's squad broke away from the crowd and approached him, Richards cursed. "The little shit wants to come inside." He told his men to stand firm, and reminded them not to use violence.

Richards wasn't the only observer who took an interest in Harry's advance. Jack Rabinowski nudged his companions and said, "The dumb fuck's actually going to try it. Keep your eyes open."

Derek Kimball whistled for his Eye on Two minicam and said the same thing in pretty much the same words.

Up on the eighth floor of the Holiday Inn a pair of pig eyes peered through binoculars at the scene a block away. He grinned, congratulated himself on selecting such a compliant dupe, and poured himself a scotch. "It's show time," he remarked to his elfin companion.

In the hearing chambers, Narrows moved easily through his introductory remarks, the same pitch he'd used to sell Oak Grove to his investors. He'd stopped sweating, his hands had stopped shaking, and he sensed that he was winning. He was bouyed by a sense of relief. After all the setbacks and obstacles, he was finally telling his side of the story.

"Now, as far as environmental impact is concerned," he continued, pleased to note Neusome's encouraging smile.

Richards met Harry at the top of the dozen marble steps leading to the entrance. Come down hard or jolly him along? He opted for routine. "May I help you?" he asked pleasantly, as if he didn't know who Harry was and what he wanted, as if he didn't know that this was the confrontation nobody wanted which could no longer be avoided.

Harry responded in kind. "I'd like to attend the public hearing of the Onganaw County Planning Commission."

Richards took the checklist from Sergeant Porphus. "Name?"

Harry frowned, but he gave his name. Richards made a show of checking the list, then announced, "Sorry, but I don't see your name here."

"But it's a public hearing."

"It may be a public hearing, but this building is closed to all unauthorized personnel."

Harry gazed at the officer a moment, then flashed a smile. "We have a right to be in there," he said pleasantly.

"Not today you don't. I have my orders."

"Just following orders, eh?" sneered Harry.

"Yeah, buddy. Just following orders." Richards' voice carried a menace it had hitherto lacked. His troops heard it and closed ranks behind him.

Harry shrugged. So it had come to this. He retraced his steps in his mind, but no matter how he looked at it, this was where he ended up. His dozen disciples were arrayed on the steps behind and below him. They gazed up expectantly. Some were starting to edge away. Others, their faces reflecting a dawning sense of outrage, moved forward to take their place. Behind them, a thousand demonstrators watched and grew silent. A half-dozen cameras stared at him, their red lights silently goading him on. Then Jack called, "Got a permit, right Harry? Work within the system, right Harry?"

Harry shrugged again and said flatly, "We have our rights."

Richards saw what Harry saw and he didn't like it. Somebody had painted him into a corner. If this bastard wanted to come in, he couldn't stop him. Not on TV he couldn't. But he didn't have to roll over and die, either.

"You cross this line and you're under arrest."

Harry laughed. "You haven't got the horses." He indicated the crowd with an idly waved hand. "They won't like it."

Richards stepped closer and said in a low tone, "When it happens it will be very quick and very quiet, but you will spend the night in jail."

Staring into the cop's eyes, Harry knew it was true. He also knew it didn't matter. Besides, a little martyrdom, especially mild martyrdom, the kind that didn't result in broken bones or funeral processions, could only help his cause. He stared at the cop and the cop scowled back. It was the only weapon he had left, and it wasn't enough to deter the activist. Finally, with a slight shrug and a downward flicker of his eyes, Richards gave in. Harry snorted and brushed past the vanquished sentinel.

Sergeant Porphus' strong suit was loyalty, not subtlety. Though he'd watched the exchange from a distance of just eighteen inches, all he saw was a goddam whale hugger resisting arrest. Sergeant Porphus knew his duty in situations like this. And he did it. All he really wanted to do was stop Harry. All he did was plant an open hand on the guy's chest and snarl, "Hold it right there!"

Maybe if Harry hadn't been enthralled by the narcotic effect of power, he would have been better prepared. Maybe Porphus did put a little too much force into his straight arm. Still, if Harry had only taken one step back instead of two, or if he had remembered he was at the top of a dozen marble steps, he wouldn't have tripped. Then again, if Richards hadn't chosen that moment to turn and reprimand his subordinate, he could have grabbed Harry's arm. As it was, Harry twisted his ankle on the top step and went over backwards. He took out a pair of his supporters, who had started moving forward while waving at the cameras behind them.

As they tumbled down the steps, Jack screamed, "They got Harry!"

He and his comrades produced rocks from their pockets and started hurling them at the riot cops. Richards, turning at the sound of Jack's voice, forgot to flip his visor down, and caught a lucky shot in the left eye.

The television crews converged on the bodies sprawled at the foot of the steps. Harry tried to sit up. He was dizzy and nauseous, and had trouble seeing through the blood flowing from a gash in his forehead. Chelsea, her face streaming with angry tears, led a hundred protestors in a rush towards their fallen leader. Sergeant Porphus misread their intentions and led his troops to meet them.

Jack's Young Socialists pelted the cops with stones until twenty uniforms broke ranks and came after them. Jack led his squad into the thickest part of the crowd. The uniforms pursued them until they were surrounded. They had to defend themselves. Even the inquiry set up by Mayor Brown agreed with that.

Upon reaching the bottom step, the rest of the troops began moving the onrushing protesters back. Some, attempting to protect Harry, pushed back. That's when the cops started swinging their clubs, and that's when things got out of hand. No one had thought to remove the pile of rubble from the parking lot construction site next to the County Building, and of course, most of the protesters had come prepared for a day in the heat. Soft drink, water and beer bottles joined chunks of concrete in an improvised arsenal as hundreds of debutante demonstrators became suddenly radicalized rioters beneath the jackboots of a TAC Squad running amok.

Narrows had undergone a grilling from the Planning Commission on Oak Grove's environmental impact. The questions had been sudden and incisive. He'd dispatched them with ease because he wasn't trying to protect a hidden agenda. That 400 acre park was set in concrete, so to speak, he'd stressed. When his quip earned generous laughter, from the commission and the audience, he knew he had won. "There is no way anybody can alter this layout," he continued. "Not for a hundred years at least, and after that they'll have to fight the Oak Grove residents."

He was elaborating on the development's esthetics when the outside noise escalated. The chants were replaced by screams and the sound of breaking glass and wailing sirens.

Someone went to the window and shouted, "My God, there's a riot out there!" The reporters led the charge to the windows, followed by most of the observers. Neusome pounded her gavel to no avail until, with the defection of the commissioners themselves, she gave Narrows an apologetic shrug and joined the rest of the spectators. Narrows sat down and buried his head in his hands. He was finished. Oak Grove was history, and he was forgotten.

Almost forgotten. He turned at the tap on his shoulder, and looked up at Gary Kilton's sneer. "Mr. Gentry says to tell you we'll be in touch."

Narrows went to a window. It was a full-fledged riot. Led by the Young Socialists, three hundred people fought a pitched battle with the TAC Squad in front of the building. Squads of police were taking up positions at the perimeters, clubbing and cuffing panicked demonstrators who ran towards them in an attempt to flee the melee. Cameramen, several of whom were bleeding themselves, scrambled about in search of safe vantage points. The Derek Kimballs of the world had called in reinforcements, and soon police helicopters hovered rotor to rotor with crafts from Channels 2, 6, 8 and 13, and radio stations WCXY, WZNT, and WZAZ.

Up on the eighth floor of the Holiday Inn, Rob Patterson put down his binoculars and poured two more hefty scotches. He handed one to Darren McCafferty and said, "Time to call the guv?"

At Police Headquarters, Chief Ernest P. Slaughter rummaged through his upper right hand desk drawer while keeping the phone wedged against his ear. His face was set, his brow more furrowed than usual. Finally he said, "All right. I've heard enough."

He hung up. No histrionics this time, he gently cradled the receiver and removed a single typed sheet of paper from the drawer. He inserted it in his antique Selectric—no need to involve Angie in this one. He typed the date and sealed it in a hand-addressed envelope.

On the way out of the office he asked Angie to get someone to run it over to the mayor's office, pronto. Then he rode the service elevator down to the garage and took the back way home.

Chapter Thirteen

The flames melted the snow up to fifteen feet away. Beyond that it remained packed two feet deep and the water had nowhere to go. The fire fighters rumbled up in their chartreuse machines and added to the lake. Finally, someone dug a trench to the street, where the water ran down the gutter to pool around the frozen drain. By morning it would be ice, and children would slip and slide and frolic on it all day long.

Narrows parked a half-block away, in the Perryman Park Baptist Church parking lot. That was as close as he could get to the fire. The street was blocked by fire trucks and police cars, and the hundreds of people who'd flocked to the sound of sirens the way children had to chiming ice cream trucks in a more innocent time.

As he picked his way around patches of ice and chunks of frozen snow, Narrows decided that inner city arson couldn't be fully addressed without understanding the social dynamics. As much as a blackened, burned out shell contributed to the blight, as much of a tragedy as it was for any occupants, a fire was undeniably a social event. It would be anywhere, he reasoned, but all the more so in an environment cut off from more traditional entertainment outlets.

It was one of the many insights he'd gained in the past six months of near-total immersion in the Perryman Park Housing Corporation.

* * *

By the time the smoke had cleared and the dust had settled, all agreed that the Oak Grove Riot, as it was immediately labeled, was the worst civil disturbance since the race riots in the sixties destroyed much of the city. Most experts agreed that this time the damage wouldn't be so severe and long lasting. This wasn't an outburst against systemic racism. Blacks were now a majority in the city, and the entire power structure was black. Besides, this wasn't a race riot. If anything, it was a white riot. The final toll counted 17 police and 157 civilians injured, 27 severely. There were 297 arrests that day, though most observers were confident that the bulk of them would be released without facing charges. The good news, all agreed, was that there were no fatalities.

Except Oak Grove, that is. The Governor acted precipitously to forestall any further discord over the controversial development by unearthing an obscure law, dating back to the Civil War, which enabled the state to seize any property which was contributing to public disorder. The County Board of Supervisors acquiesced in the Governor's decision. Whether the state would compensate the investors for the land would be determined by the courts.

Among other matters to be determined by the courts were Narrows' liability to his investors, which, with the damages that Kilton assured him that Gentry would be seeking, promised to run close to $10,000,000. A trio of personal injury lawsuits filed on behalf of Soccer Moms who got kicked in the stomach and face during the melee, merely added insult to Narrow's injury.

For awhile things got so out of hand that Gentry filed a suit against Ted Jr. claiming that the Arizonan had concealed the fact that the subject property had significant environmental qualities which mitigated against development. Ted turned around and filed a $1,000,000 lawsuit against Narrows, for the same reason.

Having achieved pariah status literally overnight, Narrows hadn't been too surprised when Thompson Properties fired him. They couched the dismissal in terms of necessary cutbacks due to the changing commercial real estate market, but he knew what was behind it. Oak Grove. It was the same thing behind the sudden silence which would descend upon the Men's Grill whenever Narrows made an appearance there. Those appearances had become less frequent of late as Denny had informed him that he could not or would not be making any more squash dates.

Suddenly the ZAC, formerly one of his favorite retreats in the city, had become a burden. The social burden was reason enough to resign, but when he lost his job, there was the financial burden to consider, too. Narrows had been surprised at how easy it had been to let it go.

He let so many things go in the riot's aftermath. He had intended to include the Perryman Park Housing Corporation in the list. During a long, lonely weekend, following the riot, Narrows decided that continuing his association would be an act of selfishness. He had to find some other means of salving his wounds. Allowing his name to remain attached to the project would be disastrous. If he really wanted it to succeed, he had to let it go. When he submitted his resignation to Peabody though, the preacher surprised him by refusing to accept it.

"But my name is mud out there, John. Won't I hinder you more than help?"

Peabody laughed. "Son, in case you didn't notice, none of us are climbing high on the social ladder. What's that term you used? A pariah? Yeah, that about sums us up. Don't run away from us. Embrace us. Who knows, maybe your problems will help you understand what these people are going through. Whether it does or not, though, the important thing is that you continue to give us the technical expertise which only you can give."

Peabody's advice was a saving grace, and Narrows devoted himself to the project. He had enough money to last for a while, thanks to his savings, and Denny's continued run of good luck with his stock picks. The work was real and true and far beyond merely restorative. Narrows continued his labors, albeit exclusively behind the scenes. He advised on development mechanics and grant writing. He also threw himself into fund raising, including handling all the details of a reception in the atrium of the Thompson Building, which netted the corporation $50,000.

Narrows took particular pleasure in holding the event there, not only because it was the eponymous building of his former employer, but also the lair of the Grasslands Alliance. That last factor wasn't quite as satisfying as it might have been since Harry Bachman was no longer served as Director. He had resigned in order to focus on his political career.

In the days following the Oak Grove Riot, Bachman held interviews with all the local media from his hospital bed, to which he was confined while he recovered from his injuries. After a visit from the Governor, Harry announced his candidacy for State Senator for District One, which included Zenith's University and Cultural Districts. The announcement had a sensational impact on the public. Supporters flocked to his campaign, and political experts called his election as close to a sure thing as any race in the past forty years.

Even though his nemesis wasn't there to see that Narrows was still on his feet, the event was tremendous. More than just the money raised, though that was certainly a gratifying and necessary achievement, was the number of people who attended, to whom they had a chance to tell their story. The event gave Perryman Park crucial momentum, and enabled them to move rapidly ahead, beginning rehab work on three houses, and acquiring a dozen more, all in the first six months.

Narrows hit the trifecta with the fund raiser. It provided enough money to cover expenses for the next six months, he found a friend where he had never expected to, and maybe, just maybe, a way out of his legal problems. And then there was Cindy. Perhaps the most pleasing aspect of the fund raiser was the fact that she made an appearance. She'd told him she wouldn't. She swore she wouldn't. She said she just couldn't get involved, not on that level, not now, so just stop asking. He stopped asking. He stopped hoping. He started doubting again if things would ever work out between them. They were just too different. And then she showed up.

Among the many losses he had chalked up while watching the riot, Cindy had been near the top of the list. She won't have anything to do with me, now that I've failed, he had told himself. She is done with me, and I don't blame her. So it was with some surprise that during the darkest hours in the week following the collapse of his dream, Narrows took a phone call from his ex-wife, and amazingly, loyal friend.

She came and gave him sympathy and—face it, love—and kept him from running off the rails. And she came to him, that was crucial. If she wouldn't make the effort to come downtown, then they couldn't see each other. That much was clear. There was no way he would undergo the abuse and humiliation of returning to Wellington Lakes, to the Country Club and all her favorite watering holes. He wasn't a Seneca Doane. He couldn't put himself out there to let the harping public throw pies in his face.

But Cindy did come to Zenith. More than just come, she made an effort to understand his mission. While not yet, or likely ever, ready to visit Perryman Park, she listened to him speak, and even wrote a check for the fund raiser. She supported him and tried to see his side of things, even though it went against the grain of her class, her culture and her upbringing.

Her culture was so foreign to the culture of urban poverty that it was hard to believe they shared the same planet, let alone the same country. The urban poverty culture had to be experienced on a daily basis; it had to be lived, not studied in books and articles. There was a plethora of learned reports, but few not written to support one agenda or another. Narrows enjoyed a unique perspective. He was among members of a separate, distinct, though surprisingly open and welcoming society, yet he remained sufficiently detached, by mutual consent, to observe it dispassionately.

* * *

His dispassionate posture began to melt however, as he neared the fire. The flames from the abandoned house were spreading to the second Perryman Park house next door. They'd already begun referring to it as Angela's house, though it remained as yet uninhabitable.

He joined the group of Perryman Park Directors huddled to one side of the mass of spectators. "Thanks for calling me, John," he said to the preacher. "I came as quickly as I could."

The others greeted him negligently and continued to stare at the roof of Angela's house. "Maybe they can save it," Narrows offered when the fire fighters trained a hose on the structure.

Peabody turned a weary face to him and said, "I hope to God they can."

"They got to," Angela cried. "We're being put out."

"When did this happen?" asked Narrows.

"I just found out today. You know how Mr. Philips been tryin' to sell?"

"Yeah, we've been negotiating a price."

"Well, you can stop now. Somebody beat you to it and they say I got to be out by the end of the month."

Narrows glanced at the roof, where the flames seemed to be losing their battle with the hose. Why would anyone want to evict Angela? She paid her rent on time, or rather the state did, under the vendored shelter payment program. She took pride in her home. She kept it clean and attractive. She planted flowers and made sure Darrel mowed the lawn, taking advantage of the community lawn mower which the housing corporation had purchased. Did they want to jack up the rent? If so, they were crazy. The DHS set the rates in the neighborhood, and anyone who could afford more chose to live in a better part of the city. Did the new owner want to move in? The same principle applied. Anyone who could meet Philips' price wouldn't want to live there.

He shrugged. Plenty of time to explore that mystery later on. "Maybe you can still move in if they get the fire out." Narrows' words were lost in the explosion. Later one of the fire fighters said it must have been a bunch of oil rags or a can of paint thinner left in the attic, but something blew the roof off the abandoned house. Screams collided with shouted orders and the runaway-train rumble of the flames. In no time at all, the roof of Angela's house was burning out of control.

"Son of a bitch," Narrows muttered as Angela began to cry.

Darrel put his arms around her. "Aw, Ma. It's okay. We'll get the next one."

"Goddam son of a bitch," Narrows repeated.

Peabody moved next to him. "It's a setback," he soothed. "Just a temporary setback. It's insured."

"For the purchase price," Narrows spat. "For five hundred lousy bucks. We've got a couple thousand in it already."

"So what? It's only money." The preacher spoke with a harshness belying his own sunny words. "If we can't salvage it, we'll get another one."

"It's just not fair."

"Whoever said life was fair? Do you remember what God said to Job? 'Where were you when I laid the foundations of the earth? Where were you when I hung the stars in heaven?' Answer that, and then you can tell me what's fair."

Narrows stared at him. Why did simple faith make a man seem wise? "I just wish something would go right for a change."

"Something has gone right. You're blind if you can't see it." He pointed, and Narrows saw Darrel consoling his mother. The boy had become a man by his sixteenth birthday. He was a mainstay of the program. He pitched in on weekends and after school, painting, sanding, hammering nails; anything to help, anything to learn a new skill. Angela said he was going to school every day now. His grades were improving, and he'd stopped running with those punks. He'd even brought some of the local boys into the program. "It's going to work out for Angela," Peabody said softly. "Thanks to the boy, it will work out."

There was nothing to say as the house burned down. "I'm sorry, John, but I haven't got your faith."

"Then you got nothing, son."

"Yeah, maybe that's it." He searched for a way out, but the old man's face offered nothing. "You're right, I've got nothing. Nothing but a shitload of lawsuits, so what am I doing wasting time with you?"

Peabody put his arm around Narrows' shoulders and guided him towards the church. "This isn't about you," he said gently. "It's about people reclaiming their dignity, and you can't do that. Nobody can except them. You can help. Your expertise, your organizational abilities, your contacts—"

Narrows snorted.

"Don't sell yourself short, Burt. You aren't used up, not by half you aren't." He stopped after they'd covered fifty yards. "Look," he said bluntly. "I'm an old man. All my life I had a dream. Yeah, just like King did, I had a dream. Only I didn't put my life on the line for it. I just dreamed it. I dreamed it until maybe it was too late. Then Elvie died and everything I'd worked for died with her. All I had left was the dream, and now I'm living it. I'm fighting the odds. You don't know how hard it is. No, wait. You listen," he said harshly when Narrows started to protest.

"You've been down here a lot and you've worked hard. I'm not denying it, and let anybody say you aren't here for the right reasons and I'll be the first to shut him down. But, and this is where I draw the line, you don't live here. You go home to your tower and you look down on where we—where I—live, and I don't know what you think. Maybe you feel proud of yourself. Maybe you despair. Maybe you wrestle with the same doubts and fears that I do. Maybe you just sit there feeling sorry for yourself. I don't know, and I don't care. You got that? I don't care!" He snarled the last and glared.

Narrows stared back. His mouth twitched. He licked his lips and tried to think of something to say. He wanted to defend himself from this assault, but he couldn't understand it. He wanted to ask what he'd done wrong, but he was tired of whining.

"All I know," Peabody resumed in a tired voice. "All I know is you will never truly understand. You'll never be a part of us. Not even if you came down here and lived in one of these rat holes."

Narrows found his voice. "No offense, John, but I wouldn't want to."

"Exactly, and I don't blame you."

"Then what the hell are you trying to say?" he demanded. "First you say you don't need me, then you say you do. You say I can't help you because I don't know what's going on, because I've never been on welfare, or because I live downtown. You want me to suffer? Well, I am suffering, John. I'm facing half-a-dozen lawsuits. I'm talking about millions of dollars here."

"That doesn't mean anything to us, Burt. We don't have that kind of money."

"Neither do I, John. Neither do I."

"We all bleed red, don't we."

"Well, you can go to hell." Narrows started to walk away.

"Burt, wait!"

Against his will he stopped, and turned. Peabody lumbered over the icy sidewalk. "Listen, I don't want to make light of your problems."

"Then why do you? You act like it's a personal affront for me to have any. Like I'm white so everything is hunky-dory. Like because I've never gone to bed hungry I've got no room to complain."

Peabody shook his head. He reached for Narrows' hands with both of his, and squeezed them gently. "See those people back there? They need me. They come to me with things you'll never know. Husbands, lovers, fathers, sons in prison. Someone's boyfriend rapes her eight-year-old and she won't report it. Crack. Heroin. You name it. They come to me and I do what I can. It takes everything I have, and just a little more." He sighed, and went on like a mountain climber covering that last thirty yards. "I haven't got time for your problems, Burt."

"You haven't got time for my problems," Narrows repeated woodenly. He shrugged and extended his arms, with his hands held out plaintively. "I thought you were my friend, John."

Peabody's eyes glistened, and his voice shook when he said, "I love you, Burt, but I can't be your friend because a friend takes time out for problems. It's not that I don't want to help you, I can't. See, I need your strength. I need the support you've given me the past six months. If you come to me with your problems, it's not just a drain on my compassion, you're taking away my resources. Do you understand?"

Narrows nodded and turned away again.

"Will you be back?"

He shrugged and kept walking.

* * *

Seneca Doane was dressed in a cable knit cardigan, a brown and yellow checked flannel shirt, brown cords and a pair of battered loafers. He stood at his window and watched the early afternoon sunlight sparkle on the snow-covered city. He smoked a cigaret and sipped coffee from the ceramic mug Krystal had given him last night. Life hadn't been this good since—he grinned suddenly. Life had never been this good.

He hadn't realized how much he'd missed the full-contact-chess atmosphere of the courtroom until he got back inside one, until he found a client with a cause worth fighting for. He hadn't realized how much he'd missed love until he found it. Or it found me, he thought. He rubbed his face—his clear, smooth face. Well, not smooth. The pockmarks would never go away, but there hadn't been any outbreaks for three months now. Not since he met Krystal.

It had been in the lobby of the Thompson Building. That was so typically Burt. Thompson Properties fires him and he throws a party in the lobby of their White Elephant. And Burt couldn't keep him out this time. Not when he bought a fifty dollar ticket with a ten-thousand dollar check.

They had wall-sized charts and sketches of what Perryman Park could look like in just three years. Doane had been impressed. Burt did good work. And the fund raiser was good PR. Someone had done some heavy selling—not Burt this time. He was still too closely connected with the Oak Grove Riot to find much of a welcome within corporate hallways. Probably Martin Perry had pulled in all those bankers and executives.

Doane had worked the edges, nipping over to the bar for another glass of wine, watching Perry steer Rev. Peabody from one mover to another shaker. He'd looked for Burt and found him standing between the two best looking women in the place. Cindy, overdressed in her usual fund raiser gown, looking exceedingly uncomfortable with the people who kept coming up to Burt. What do you say to an African-American who is neither a maid nor a bartender?

The other woman was Krystal. She had honey brown skin and a butter yellow dress. Her hair was done up in intricate lacy curls above her head, ringlets fallen here and there—by design? Who knows? It worked. They graced her fine cheekbones and spilled down her long, elegant neck. She'd laughed easily and extended her hand with a natural grace. Her eyes were bright and brown and widened slightly when she said, "Seneca Doane? As is Seneca Doane the radical lawyer?"

"My grandfather."

A tremendous smile. Doane had felt like giggling. "My grandfather knew him. In fact, Seneca Doane kept him out of prison."

"Really? What was his name?"

"Marcus Williams."

"Oh my God, Marcus Williams? Gramps used to tell me about that case, how the Zenith Traction Company sent thugs around to beat him up when he tried to organize the conductors. About the explosion on the streetcar, how they'd arrested him in the hospital, said he'd placed the bomb himself."

Her eyes flashed a hint of fire. "Even though he was on the car himself. We didn't have to blow ourselves up to be martyrs in those days. Just speaking out of turn was good enough."

"That was the only case he argued before the Supreme Court," Doane said wistfully. "He said that one victory helped him endure all the defeats. It kept him working for justice."

"And what about you, Seneca Doane III? Are you still working for justice?" The smile had gone and so had the brightness in her eyes. She knew what he was.

Looking back on it, Doane knew that was when things finally began to change. He stopped running that night. He stopped apologizing for not being his grandfather, and that whole dead weight was lifted. That had been a different era. It was a different kind of fight now, but it was still a fight for justice, and he had reenlisted that night. He saw her again at the next Perryman Park Housing Corporation board meeting. Burt hadn't fought his appointment this time. He'd said, "I've been wrong about a lot of people lately. Maybe I was wrong about you, too."

"Maybe you weren't Burt. Maybe I've changed." And to prove it, he signed Burt on as his newest client.

He didn't ask Krystal out until the annual Christmas performance of "The Nutcracker" at Zenith Auditorium. After that, a couple of dinners, a play. Then last night she showed up unannounced at his apartment. She gave him the coffee mug and a kiss, and said, "I thought you'd be alone?"

"How'd you know?"

She just smiled mysteriously and said nobody should be alone on their forty-seventh birthday.

She left at noon and Doane spent the next hour standing at the window, smiling. Then the intercom buzzed. He answered it and said, "Send him up."

* * *

Jaroslav Klima, the sensational rookie center for the Zenith Flash, broke up a pass at the blue line and skated in alone on the Red Wings' goalie. He deked left and cut to his right. The goalie guessed correctly, slid across the crease and poke checked the puck clear. Klima tried to avoid the net but caught it with his left skate and somersaulted into the end boards, breaking his leg, fracturing his collar bone, and ending any chance the Flash had of escaping from the Central Division Cellar.

Rob Patterson pounded the bar at Wilder's Sports Bar and cursed.

"Didn't know you were such a hockey fan," Ernie Jacobs remarked. He hadn't taken the attorney for any kind of sports fan at all. Sure, he knew his history, but in all the years he'd known the big man, he'd never heard him make a single reference to any of Zenith's professional teams. Aside from the odd, and usually penetrating sporting analogy, you'd be forgiven for thinking he had never set foot on a playing field. Which had made it all the more surprising to see Patterson at the bar when he walked in for his usual Saturday afternoon of sitting at a table with his pals and yelling at one of Wilder's sixteen giant plasma TV screens.

Ernie had reflexively veered away from the bar, hoping to make it to a table without catching the big man's eye. Wednesdays at the Round Table was one thing, but this was down time, and he certainly didn't want to spend it in the company of that bitter, sarcastic slob. On the other hand, what if Rob saw him and thought he was avoiding him? It wouldn't do to have the guy pissed at him. Especially not these days, when you didn't know who he'd lash out at. Patterson may have been a lousy friend, but he could be far worse as a foe.

Grabbing a seat at the bar, he greeted the attorney and offered to buy him a beer. "Make it a scotch, and you got a deal."

"Scotch? At two o'clock?" Ernie asked before he could stop himself.

"You got a problem with that?" challenged Patterson.

Ernie assured him he didn't, and placed the order, asking for a Bud Light for himself.

"Why not just drink water?" Patterson muttered.

"Hey, I like the taste, plus it keeps me fresh for tonight. There's that

175

big party at the Country Club tonight. You going?" he added before he could stop himself.

Patterson scowled. "I'd sooner sit down to dinner with Narrows Burton than attend the Winter Ball." He sipped his drink, muttering to himself. His lips worked feverishly, and Ernie thought, not for the first time, that the big man wasn't well. "You know what the definition of a human body is?" Patterson asked. "It's a machine to turn good beer into Bud Light."

Ernie grinned in response to Patterson's hearty laughter. "I may borrow that, use it for Miller."

He was just about finished with his beer and ready to make his getaway when Klima had his accident. Ernie was a big hockey fan. He lived and died, and mostly died, with the Flash, the way most Zenithites did with the Barons. He was excited about this kid Klima, who had looked like a shoo in for Rookie of the Year, and promised to be the foundation around which the team could build a real contender.

"I don't care if the Flash never win another game," Patterson said bitterly. "But, God, I hate to see a kid get torn up like that." His tone was wistful, and Ernie could tell he was thinking of his own career.

"Maybe it won't be so bad. He's a kid. You know how they bounce back."

Patterson leveled such a baleful glare at him that Ernie offered to buy him another drink, and then mentioned something about meeting some friends for lunch. Patterson didn't seem to care one way or another, so Ernie skunked off, relieved not to have to share any more of his afternoon.

Sipping his fourth scotch of the afternoon, Patterson mulled the irony of running into that asshole here. He'd suggested Wilder's figuring probably nobody he knew even knew where it was, let alone was likely to show up on a Saturday afternoon. Stuck in the middle of a strip mall in the heart of Crystal Heights, Wilder's was the kind of place catering to factory workers and carpenters, not bond traders. Probably it would have been better meeting at his house, he thought. Only he didn't have a house. The bitch got that. Leave it to her to hire Ben Wethers. The bastard was going to break the prenup, he just knew it. Shit, that should have been ironclad.

Oh well, he'd get his. Yes, he would. Just as soon as he was finished with Narrows Fucking Burton, old Ben would find himself looking at a gaping hole in his briefs.

Right on schedule, Darren McCafferty clambered onto the stool Jacobs had so recently vacated. "My God, Rob. You sure know the most unlikely of places."

"Yes, for the unlikeliest of associates," Patterson replied, drumming home the oft-repeated fact that they had never talked about these matters. "So, what have you got for me?"

McCafferty frowned. "Things are proceeding as directed. Acquisitions are moving efficiently. Buyer's market doesn't begin to describe the situation. You're paying twice what these people are asking, begging if you want to know, so they don't look twice at the terms."

"Cash. No names. Dummy corporation."

"As per your instructions, yes." The little man paused. He told himself to keep his mouth shut. He was making good money for this job, and really nobody was getting hurt. Still, it bothered him. Patterson was a good client. Okay, he paid well and he offered plenty of work. But this project just didn't pass the smell test. He sighed and made up his mind. "But tell me, Rob. Why go through with this? I mean, you already won."

Patterson turned, a slow, ponderous rotation on his stool. "You don't win until the game is over," he breathed, his face just inches from his companion. McCafferty struggled not to recoil from the ghastly presence. "He's still on his feet, the game's still on," the attorney pronounced. McCafferty shrugged his compliance.

"And the rest of it?" Patterson persisted.

"You, of course, do not wish to know the details," the diminutive fixer assured him. "But things are proceeding according to plan."

* * *

After he left Peabody, Narrows went home and poured himself a drink. High noon on Saturday, a good time for a tumbler full of whiskey. He lay down and thought about the people he'd built his life around the past six months, the money they'd run through to achieve two finished houses, one smouldering ruin, and a four person staff. He thought about liability insurance and workers comp, and how much less time Cleve had to spare since he got that job reading meters for Zenith Ed.

Then he picked up the paper and turned to the stock tables. Denny was right again. Dynographics was up eight on takeover rumors. That made another sixteen grand. He wondered why, if this was really the result of Denny's own research, he never let him pick up more than two thousand shares. Hell, why tell him at all?

He didn't see much of Denny anymore. Quitting the ZAC had driven the final wedge in their friendship, and one too many arguments about him throwing his time and money away on "a bunch of lazy niggers" had reduced their association to a series of phone calls. Always the same thing. Buy this stock, now. Two thousand shares. Never more than that. Why? Why just two thousand? Somehow, the voice of caution didn't ring true, but what the hell. He really didn't want to know.

Then he remembered Cindy's big party at the club tonight. He groaned and rolled over on the bed, and stared at the alarm clock and the phone until he made up his mind.

"Narrows!" Cindy cried. "I can't wait for tonight. It's going to be so much fun. Denny's coming—with Peg! It's like their coming out party."

"I don't think I'll be able to make it."

"Oh, no." Her voice dragged in a pathetic little whine. "You aren't sick, are you? You sound awful." It was an approximation of maternal concern by a consummately bad actor.

"I just don't feel up to it, that's all."

If he wasn't sick then he was just being selfish again. "Oh Narrows, you've got to come. It'll be so much fun. The whole gang will be there."

"All the more reason why I shouldn't—"

"Narrows Burton, I'm getting a little tired of you feeling sorry for yourself. You can't hide forever. You agreed with me that six months has been long enough. Everybody's forgotten about that stupid riot!"

"It's not that, Cindy. I just don't feel like partying tonight. Things are—I—well, I just got some bad news."

"Not about the lawsuit?" This time the concern was genuine.

"No, one of our houses burned down."

"Oh God, not that again," she groaned. "Listen, Narrows, I'm sure it's just awful for you right now, but I've got a million things to do for tonight and I have to pack for France—I'm leaving tomorrow you know—and I got a late start because Jenny and Rina are in town and they kept me up late last night drinking champagne—they made me, they absolutely forced me to, and you know—"

"Plus, I just lost a friend," he said softly.

"—and I'm late for the hairdressers and you know how busy Tracy is and I don't know when I'll get by the cleaners—"

"Make that two." He hung up and felt the sting of regret in his eyes. He got up and stated out the window at the frosty glitter of Zenith in winter and decided to consult with his attorney.

* * *

Doane let Narrows in the door and said, "God, you look like you could use a drink."

"Another drink."

He frowned and said, "Yeah, sure, another one."

Narrows wandered through the living room admiring Doane's collection of pastels. There were three by Marnie Johnson, studies of windows in varying gray-blue shades. There was a fourth one, he couldn't make out the name. An empty office, a rolled up carpet and dirty drapery, all done in dusty whites and grays. It was hauntingly stark and caught his mood. "One side of the room dominated by a window," he mused. "The other by windows." A joke?

Doane returned with two drinks. "You like it? It's called 'Waiting,' by a guy named Warren Dreher. A California artist."

"I suppose 'stunning' is an appropriate term."

Doane laughed. "I'm sorry, Burt, but I've never heard 'stunning' used with such lack of feeling."

Narrows gulped his drink. "I think it's tremendous, Seneca. Tremendous power. Such poignance. But the fact is, whenever I look at a painting these days I think of frames and that's how I feel, like I've been framed."

Doane's face wobbled slightly before giving way to a grin. "I suppose it's okay to be framed as long as you're well hung." He laughed so hard at his little joke that Narrows had to smile.

"Thought you'd given up morning drinking."

"I have," Doane replied, gasping for breath. He cleared a mess of papers to one side of the coffee table and motioned for Narrows to sit in one of the overstuffed Queen Anne chairs. "Fact is, I think you're right. I tried to cut a deal with Harry Bachman yesterday and—"

"And what did 'Senator' Bachman have to say?"

"Take it easy on the guy, Burt. He's a good man. He really cares about the city."

"He fucked me over royal, to borrow a phrase. He used Oak Grove as a springboard to the State Senate. He's a heartless, opportunistic bastard."

Doane stared at his client. "Finish your drink and I'll fix you another. We'll just get quietly pissed together." He cleared the table with a flourish, notebooks and papers falling ajumble to the floor. "This can wait until Monday."

Narrows buried his face in his hands. "I'm in a pit and I can't get out. No matter how hard I scrabble, I can't make the slope."

"I'll get you that drink."

He came back with another full glass, and the bottle. "Saves time," muttered the voice of experience. "Now, what's the matter?"

Narrows told him about the fire. He told him about Cindy, about Peabody. It wasn't just "the crusade" of Oak Grove, it was the simple fact that he'd tried and failed. "Jesus Christ, Seneca. I feel so goddam useless. You don't know what it's like to go out to dinner and have half the restaurant start whispering the minute you walk in. They cast these sly glances, thinking they're so goddam clever, like you don't even know they're doing it."

"Tell me about it." There was a suggestion of the old acerbity in Doane's tone. "That's the way my whole life worked." He paused to retrieve a notebook from the floor. "I'll grant you, there is a difference. I brought it on myself. You didn't do anything wrong."

Narrows laughed bitterly. "That's what Cindy always said, 'You've never, ever, done a single thing wrong.'" He stopped, and gazed off

180

somewhere out the window. "I'm surprised she put up with it as long a she did."

"Okay, so where do you go from here? How do you put your life back together?"

With a shake of his head, he said, "Hell, I don't know. I don't even know if I want to."

"That's bullshit, and you know it."

"Do I?"

"What are you saying? You want to die?" Doane got up. "Don't waste my time talking about it if you do. Listen, I've got a revolver in the closet. You can have it. Go blow your fucking brains out."

He stood there, waiting for Burt's nod. He'd get it. He would. He'd send him home with it. This was the new Seneca Doane, the guy who'd jump into a freezing river to save his worst enemy. But the guy had to want saving. He wasn't a saint.

"Sit down," Narrows decided. "I'm too much of a coward."

"There's always pills," he offered as he reclaimed his seat. "Gentle overnight action. Go to sleep and wake up dead."

"A friend in need, eh Seneca?" Narrows grinned. "So what do we do now?"

"Why don't we get down to business?" He opened the notebook. "I've got some good news."

"Okay, shoot."

Doane laughed. "That's more like it. Anyway, like I was saying, I talked to Harry. Oak Grove's a no go. He's got the governor behind him on that."

"So, what's the bad news?"

"Just wait a minute, wouldya? The thing is, he agreed, off the record, to back market rates for the land."

"Why?"

"Because he's an honorable man."

Narrows snorted.

"He is, Burt. You should have seen his expression when I showed him your plans."

"You what?"

"I laid it out for him. The park, the esthetics, the whole shooting match."

Narrows perked up. "And?"

"And he was plenty pissed. 'Then I've been had,' he said. He said the plan was beautiful. He said it was perfect, and he said, 'If only I'd known,' in a kind of wistful, dawn of understanding voice."

"I knew it! I always knew if I could just get through to him."

"But you never could, could you."

"Yeah, and I couldn't understand why. He always seemed so reasonable on TV. Even after the riot, I was half-tempted to vote for him."

Doane hunched forward, riffling pages in his notebook. It was more for show than to find a specific page. He knew what he had to say, but he had to do something with his hands. "You know who put the bug up his ass? Patterson."

Narrows' jaw dropped. "You mean it? I always thought he had something to do with it, but you got proof? We can nail the bastard?"

Doane shook his head. "Yes, we got proof. No, we can't use it."

"Why not?" demanded Narrows.

"It's part of the deal."

"What deal?"

"Sit down and I'll tell you." He flashed a smile. It was great to see Burt come back to life. "The deal is, Harry got elected on the basis of his opposition to Oak Grove. According to him he never even thought of going into politics until the governor suggested it."

"The famous bedside chat."

"Yeah, right. Big press conference in Harry's hospital room. Anyway, with the governor's backing he was a shoo-in. So he went along with it."

"But what's the deal?"

"The deal is, he likes it. He wants to go big time. He's talking US Senate, the White House, God. You name it."

"So he doesn't want to admit he was duped."

"Exactly. And in exchange, he'll make sure the state pays market rates for the land, which means matching your price."

"And Gentry gets his money back?"

"Bingo."

"But is that enough? He's a vengeful bastard."

Doane riffled the pages again. He couldn't sit still. "That's where I come in. I laid it out to Kilton yesterday afternoon."

"You met with Kilton?"

"Yeah." The attorney chortled. "What a punk. I used to eat guys like that for breakfast."

"What'd you lay out to him?"

"There's still the little matter of your consultancy."

Narrows waved his hand dismissively. "Oh, that? That's ancient history."

"Not necessarily." Doane rummaged around on the floor for the document. "According to your contract—and a contract's a contract—you're supposed to be paid two hundred bucks an hour, twenty hours a week for 'advice and assistance in any and all matters pertaining to development activity in Onganaw County.'"

Narrows mulled it over, then grinned. "That was Gentry's wording. I wanted him to specify Oak Grove, but he wouldn't do it. I thought I was getting hustled."

"You probably were, if things had worked out. But now, thanks to his greed, he's trapped."

"Because it doesn't mention Oak Grove?"

"You got it. Without Oak Grove, he has no legal basis for breaking the contract. It's still valid. So, you want to go work for Curtis Gentry?"

"If the alternative were a slow, painful death, I might consider it."

"That's what I thought, and from what I gather from Kilton, that's the first thing you and Gentry have agreed on in a long time. So I laid it out like this. Gentry gets his money back and drops his suit for damages. Otherwise we hit him with breach of contract, and double his damages."

"Okay, but what about Ted?"

"Ted's just pissed 'cause Gentry's suing him. It's purely defensive. When Gentry drops his suit, Ted'll drop his."

"You know this for a fact?"

Doane grinned. "Let's just say I'm privy to the thought processes of a skunk."

"I don't know, Ted sounded pretty angry when I talked to him."

"Well, you know how Arizonans are. They haven't got enough brains to hold a grudge."

"Okay, assuming you're right, that just leaves those three ladies from Merrydale who got injured in the riot."

"Forget it. They're just fishing. I know their attorneys. Maybe ten grand apiece if it comes to that, but I don't think it will. They don't want to go up against Seneca Doane, believe me." He put all the sheets into a neat pile and laid them to one side. "There's just one more thing."

"Yeah?"

"What about your commission?"

"What about it?"

"Seems to me you're out a half-million bucks here."

"Forget it," laughed Narrows. "I'm just glad to be out of this."

"Why? You were still on the Thompson payroll when the deal went down. They got their share, and yours. You earned it, and if they don't come across, they're breaking the law."

"You want to sue them?" Narrows said warily.

"No, simply ask for it. Politely at first, then just the suggestion of a lawsuit. Don't forget, I still have a reputation."

"Well," Narrows hesitated. He just wanted it over.

"It won't go to court. I promise you. Thompson's lawyers know the law." He waited for Narrows' response. In its absence he added, "We both know it'll go to a good cause."

In the end Narrows agreed. He laughed the manic's laugh and the morning was almost forgotten. But not quite. When Doane went into the kitchen for more ice, Narrows strung a series of coincidences together.

"How far would Patterson go?" he asked when Doane returned.

"How far in which direction?"

"Somebody's been buying houses in Perryman Park."

Doane stirred his drink, the ice cubes clinking metallically against the glass. "You think Patterson might have—"

"If his goal was to break me."

"You mean because you jumped into this after Oak Grove?"

"It could just be speculators, but the price is too high. Three, four times market value. We aren't that high profile."

"I hear he's pretty unstable right now," Doane conceded. "Especially since Peg threw him out."

"Well, why doesn't he go after Denny?"

"Give him time. It took him better than two months to get back at you, plus Denny's making him money." He swallowed and rubbed the bridge of his nose. "Maybe it's time to do a little title search."

Chapter Fourteen

Denny came up from behind and put his arms around her. She gave a squeak of surprise, then nestled in his arms.

"What's the matter, kid?"

She shook back her auburn hair. "Oh, I don't know, Denny. I just don't feel a part of it."

He stood beside her, leaning against the bar, and watched the frivolity unfold. Kerry Pullman and Ben Wethers stood on their chairs and sang the State fight song until Bob and Janey and Phil and Carrie unleashed a barrage of dinner rolls. Doug Jackman drifted through holding a bottle of Moet high. He poured when bidden, and shouted, "C'mon, drink up. Gotta whole 'nother case."

Peg held her glass greedily beneath the bottle while Ron Philbert held her greedily around the waist.

Cindy nudged Denny. "Better watch Ron."

"Let her have her fun," he said. "She's a free woman now."

"Nice of Rob to let her keep the house."

"For the time being."

"She told me Ben thinks he can break the prenuptial."

Denny stared at the cluster of ex-wives emptying their glasses over the slender divorce attorney's head. "If anyone can, Ben Wethers can. But he better watch his back."

"You think Rob will try to get back at him?"

"It wouldn't be Rob if he didn't."

Cindy shivered. "What a repulsive man," she said sadly, but then, she brightened, poking Denny in the waist. "At least Peg is free of him." She snickered. "And what a catch for you!"

Denny frowned. "You know what she said at dinner? When Rob moved out it was like a great weight had been lifted from her shoulders."

"That's what that explosion of laughter was about."

"She turned to me, very confused, and said, 'What's so funny?'"

Cindy poked him again. "Having second thoughts, Denny?"

Jenny and Rina came back into the room with rumpled skirts and wired eyes, towing their latest acquisitions. A brace of polo players up from Palm Beach, they were trying to parlay tales of chukkers with Charlie Wales into a budget champagne weekend.

Rina came over and squeezed her sister's hand. "I saved you some."

"Oh, you're too kind," Cindy replied sarcastically.

Rina gave Denny a kiss on the lips, and said, "Don't be afraid to share." Then she was off with a shriek and a lunge at an unclaimed bread basket, and came up firing. Someone answered with a dish of ice cream.

"You want to?" Denny asked as Peg and Ron disappeared through the far door. Cindy shrugged.

They went upstairs to the Map Room, a moderately sized drawing room done up in leather and oak, given over to a dozen framed antiquarian maps of England, donated by Colonel Wethers. Denny took the smallest one off the wall, and chopped up their windfall.

"Enough for two?" He indicated eight healthy lines. Cindy took half of one on her finger and rubbed it on her gums. She licked her lips and said, "You first."

He did two, quickly and efficiently, and nudged the frame her way. "So, why so glum party girl?"

She took her share, tapped her nose, and flounced around the room. "Did you ever feel corrupt, Denny? I mean, really corrupt? In the middle of dinner, listening to Kerry Pullman brag about foreclosing on a church, I looked around the room at what must have been a quarter of a million dollars worth of clothes—of clothes, Denny!—and by tomorrow morning most of them will be torn or hopelessly stained, utterly wasted, never to be worn again."

Denny bent over the glass again. "Burt getting to you?"

"He hung up on me today."

He glanced up, mid-snort. "Burt? Hung up on you?" He finished it. "That's a switch. You must have been furious?"

"I was ashamed. There I was, prattling on like a princess. He was in pain and I—"

"Burt's always in pain. It's part of his lifestyle."

She glared. "Denny Redmond, you take that back."

"Why should I? He's an old woman." He shrugged. "He's a sanctimonious fool and I'm getting sick of his sermons."

"I think you're drunk, Denny. Narrows is the only person I know who truly cares about people. Look what he's doing with that housing program."

"Burt's playing a game. It's called white guilt. He's just twenty years behind, that's all."

"What's he got to be guilty for?" she demanded. She fumbled for her cigaret case, broke the first one extracting it, and lit the second without even waiting for Denny to react. "He is the most decent man I've ever known."

"I wouldn't put any money on that, if I were you."

"And what's that supposed to mean?"

"Why don't you ask Saint Burton?"

"Because I'm asking you," she snapped, a little shrillness leaking in.

Denny glanced around the room nervously. "This is just between you and me," he said with an intensity which got her full attention. "I've been feeding him insider tips for the past eight months."

"I don't believe it! You, Denny?"

"He's been snapping them up as eagerly as Patterson has."

"Does he know?"

"How can he help but know? He's not stupid."

"Don't play that game with me, Denny Redmond."

There she was, deadly serious, defending the man she loved—he knew it, even if she denied it—stamping her feet like a caricature. Denny couldn't help but laugh.

"You stop that this instant!"

"Shake your curly little head again, I love that."

She burst into tears and collapsed on a leather sofa. True to form, right up to the end. Denny moved to her. He held her close and kissed her eyelids. "If it makes you feel any better, he asked me point blank, and I lied."

She opened her eyes. "See? He doesn't know."

"He doesn't want to know."

"He doesn't want to believe his best friend would lie to him."

Denny shrugged. "Whatever." He left her on the couch. "You going to finish this or what?"

"Go ahead," she said miserably.

He did, then walked to the door. He stopped with his hand on the knob, as if weighing the odds, then made up his mind. "Life isn't a game, you know," he exhaled wearily. "It's not something you do part time. Life is hard. It's full of risks. Sometimes you have to bet it all on a single roll of the dice. That's what I'm doing right now. It's a good system, well thought out. I'm part of a network. We feed each other information. It's more like a think tank than a scam. We aren't manipulating the market. We aren't big enough for that, and anyway, we don't want to. All we're doing is trying to get our share."

"But you already have your share," she protested. "Besides, isn't it against the law?"

He slumped against the door, fighting exhaustion. Too much to drink too fast, and the coke wasn't doing what coke was supposed to. He waved an ineffectual hand. "Yeah, well, that's the fun part, isn't it? That's what makes it so damned exciting. It's not the money, it's the risk. It's putting it all on that one roll. And if you crap out, you crap out. You start over again. That's how life works. You don't walk away. You don't quit when things go wrong. That's what Burt did. He was on the verge of something great, something that was going to put him in the big leagues. If he pulled off Oak Grove he would have been—" He groped for the words—"One of us. But look what happened. The first setback, the first sign of adversity, and he walked away. Like it was a game. He let himself down. He let me down, and you may not realize it, but he let you down, too."

Cindy shifted into a sitting position on the couch. She leaned forward, her arms extended downwards, hand clasped, elbows clenched between her knees. She turned her red-eyed, puffy face to him and said, "How did he let me down, Denny?"

"He opted out of the game. He found out how tough real life is, so he jumped into fantasy land. He thinks he's Mother Teresa, helping the poor little darlings who can't help themselves."

"I think it takes a lot of courage to do what he's doing."

"What a load of bullshit," Denny snorted. "If he had any courage at all he'd be trying to put Oak Grove back together. If he were a real man, he wouldn't give in. The system knocks you down, you get up and go at it again. Instead, he says the system's wrong. He's identifying with every loser out there. He wants the rewards without paying the price."

"I don't think you've been listening to what he says."

"Damn right, I haven't," he snapped. "I haven't got time to listen to his whining. And you shouldn't either."

He jabbed a forefinger at her, then clutched the back of a chair. He rocked back and forth, watching the room slowly revolve, waiting for everything to fall back into place. "I don't want to lose you, kid, but you can't run away from life. I don't want you to throw everything away on Burt's silly game."

"It's not a game," she insisted. The tears were starting again. She saw how ridiculous it was to defend Burt's beliefs now when she'd ridiculed them on the phone to him just hours before. She shook her head. "It doesn't matter anyway. He hung up on me. He won't give me a third chance."

Denny moved to her as she stood. He took her in his arms. "No, Cindy. You've got it all wrong. You won't give him a third chance. You're too good for him. He's a loser. He's not in our league."

He kissed her, hard. She opened her mouth to his, and sucked his tongue into her mouth. With a moan, and a groan, of disgust and contempt, for Denny, for herself, for the whole shabby affair of her life, she locked her hands behind his neck and pressed against the length his straining body, kissing him soulfully, passionately. Their breaths came hot and fast. He enveloped her in his arms, and ran his hands down her back. He cupped her buttocks in his hands and ground her pelvis against his groin. She gyrated her hips against him until he reached up and unzipped the back of her gown. She gasped, and tensed, and murmured, "Oh, Denny, no," but otherwise didn't resist as he slipped the thin straps down her shoulders, then slid the dress to the floor. She stood there, tears running down her face, idly holding his head as he kissed her breasts. Then she pushed him away from her.

"I'd think you'd better go, Denny," she said coolly. "You're starting to lose control."

He reached for her. She stepped away. His face turned rigid, set and blank. He went to the door. "You just made a choice, kid. I think you blew it."

After he left, Cindy stepped back into her gown. She reached behind her and zipped it, and crept down the back way to the Ladies' Cloakroom. She snuggled into her full length sable coat and went to find the doorman. She went home to pack, went home to get some sleep. She was off to Paris tomorrow.

Denny returned to the dining room where the festivities continued unabated. The band had started again, and couples were dancing, or trying to. They tried to hold each other up, but more often pulled each other down. Some gave up the struggle and lay in the dust and spilled wine, getting all those expensive clothes horribly stained and torn. Others stumbled over the prostrate forms until it looked more like a battlefield than a dance floor. White-jacketed black men moved from table to table collecting plates and glasses, leaving white tablecloths stained red and yellow, brown and green. An undercurrent of giggling ran through the room. It sounded like weeping to Denny.

There was still no sign of Peg, so he gave up and headed for the front door. He passed Kerry Pullman who said, "Check out the pool."

"Why the hell not?" he thought, and descended the stairs to the basement pool. Steam from the heated water hovered above a dozen writhing, splashing bodies. The surrounding ledges and benches were heaped with jumbled clothing. Again, no sign of Peg. He walked alongside the pool, noticing a healthy preponderance of female bodies in the water. When he reached the saunas, what he felt more than anything was regret. There were three doors. He opened the last.

They were there, on a bench in the dressing room. Peg's hands stroked Ron's back. They gripped his buttocks. They fluttered feverishly over his body. His muscles bunched and flattened as he thrusted and grunted. He pulled her short yellow hair and she bit his shoulders. Denny watched them, unnoticed. "It the same room," he mused.

Peg's eyes were open and empty and staring without seeing. At him. He shut the door and went back the way he came. He wanted to go home and forget it all, but stopped instead by the pool and took off his clothes. "Fuck corruption," he thought as he slipped into the turgid water.

* * *

Peabody found it increasingly difficult to keep his two roles separate. The Housing Corporation was moving upstairs. He set aside his sermon draft and stared at the people who'd burst into his office. With a bit more bulk on his bones, Cleve looked younger, and healthier than before, though his expression didn't bode well for a long, happy life. It was one of rage, cold, murderous rage, and the object of his rage sat slumped in a chair, holding a hand to his bleeding face. Cleve gripped one of the youth's arms. The other was held by Darrel. He too was angry, and being younger and more recently buffeted by adversity, was much more likely to vent that anger in violence. Completing the tableau were two of Darrel's contemporaries, DJ and Iron Man.

They were graduates of Zenith's street culture. They'd rolled crack. They'd driven hot Mercedes' and Cadillac Escalades. They'd carried beepers and uzis, and maybe even used the latter. Peabody wasn't inclined to pry.

Together they represented the hope of Perryman Park. Though they remained aloof, quick to anger, not far removed from the killing fields, they were making an effort. Beneath their mask of ferocity, the macho posturing prevalent amongst the disenfranchised men and boys of the ghetto, was a tacit surrender. It was evidenced in the alacrity with which they threw themselves into rehab work. Their willingness to scrape, sand and paint, to run errands, to do the grunt work of lifting and carrying, served as a renunciation of the fleeting wealth and inevitable ruin of the streets. When they discovered their gold chains carried no weight in the housing corporation, they put them away. They had turned their backs on violence. Until today, Peabody thought, gazing at the broken youth in the chair. Yet even this outburst was a healthy sign. They had acted in self-defense, to protect the community. If he could derive satisfaction from that fact, it didn't ease the task before him. It didn't lessen the pain of interviewing Robbie Rollins.

Peabody accepted the chalice. The words, though difficult to speak, came easily enough. "Why, Robbie? Why you of all people?"

Robbie replied with a sullen stare.

"Don't you realize what we're trying to do here? Why'd you want to burn that house?"

"I didn't burn no fuckin' house."

"You lyin'—"

Cleve moved fast to keep Iron Man from inflicting further damage. He had changed so thoroughly that, even at this unhappy juncture, Peabody enjoyed watching him in action. Cleve had achieved such a quiet authority that one word was enough to quell Iron Man's rage.

Peabody studied the battered youth. Even now, having been caught entering an abandoned house with a gas can in his hand, he sought to brazen it out. Frowning, the preacher decided to wield his most effective weapon, the one he'd hoped he wouldn't have to use. First, he needed to get rid of the others.

"DJ, would you go and get a wet cloth for Robbie? We have some talking to do and I don't want him to get blood on my furniture."

When he left, sniggering, Peabody turned to the others. "Cleve, this has gone on too long. Twelve fires in two weeks. It has to stop."

"Yeah, but how?" he complained. "We can't buy 'em, and the city won't give them to us."

"The city doesn't own them anymore," countered the minister. "Anyway, it's gone beyond ownership." He took out the corporate checkbook, signed one, and handed it to Cleve. "Take the van down to Schettler's Lumber and get enough plywood to board up all the vacant houses in the neighborhood."

Cleve grinned. "'Bout time, Rev."

"Take these guys with you." Addressing Darrel, Iron Man, and DJ, who'd just returned with a towel, he added, "It'll count as rehab hours."

"What about him?" asked Darrel, nodding menacingly at Robbie.

"I can take care of him," he assured them. When the door closed on the departing crew, Peabody leveled his most severe glare. "Robbie, I'm shocked to find you here like this. More than shocked, I'm severely disappointed."

"Big fucking deal."

It was time to unsheath the sword. "But most of all, I'm just glad your father didn't live to see this."

Robbie came to life. "You leave him out of this," he cried, leaping to his feet. "You just shut your mouth about him!"

There were tears in his eyes. A good sign. "Your mother says you quit school," he remarked softly. "She says all you do is sit around playing your tapes. You go out at night and sometimes you don't come home 'til dawn." He watched Robbie struggle for composure. His heart went out to him. But he knew he had to remain firm. "It must be hard to lose your father, Robbie. It must be worse than almost anything. But it's not the worst thing in the world."

"What you mean by that, muthafucka?"

"Don't use that gutter crap with me!" Peabody roared. "Your father made damn sure you got an education. The least you can do is use it."

Robbie backed down. He returned to his seat. Peabody may have been aging, but he remained a powerful presence; his rage was still frightening to observe.

"You know what's worse than losing your father? Never having one. Those guys who just left, none of them ever knew their fathers, yet they've overcome their environments. I guess you have too, in a way." He paused to let that sink in, then demanded, "Why, Robbie? Why torch that house?"

"'Cause I need the money."

Patterson sat up straight. "You mean somebody's paying you to burn these houses? Who? What's his name?"

Robbie shook his head. Peabody stood up. "Don't make me do this, son. It'll kill your mother, but I'll call the police right now." He reached for the phone.

"Wait!" cried Robbie. "Don't do that. Don't hurt Ma!"

"Then tell me about it."

Robbie recounted his life since his father's death. At first, it was a game. Running with a rough crowd. Being cold. Going as far as the others, then a little further. Suddenly it wasn't fun anymore. He was getting scared, but he didn't know the way out. Peabody listened to Robbie's story and ached for his anguish. He knew he was, at least in part, at fault. He hadn't given the boy the time he deserved. He'd been so caught up in his mission that he'd neglected his flock.

"How did you get messed up in arson for hire?" he asked.

"This dude at the Projects, he told me how to get some easy money. Just go down to the Games Center, on Perryman, and ask for work. So I did and this little white guy he say he give me five hundred if I go torch this house. I go look at it. I mean, I don' wanna hurt nobody—"

"Robbie," Peabody chided. "Don't talk nigger."

"Okay, sorry." He shrugged. "The house was deserted. No doors. No windows. Brick thieves had already cleaned off one wall. So I figure, why not? Place is gonna fall down sooner or later anyway. I came back that night and torched it."

"Was it in Perryman Park?"

"Uh huh, on Skidmore. 321 Skidmore."

"The day before we were going to buy it," muttered Peabody. "What happened next?"

"I went back to the Games Center a few days later, and Mr. Henry, you know the dude what—the man who runs the place—he gave me an envelope."

"Sealed?"

"Yeah. Mr. Henry might let things happen there, but he keeps out of it. That way he stays alive."

Peabody nodded. "It should be shut down. Too many good boys get messed up down there."

"They got to go somewhere, you know."

"Yeah, I know. This old place isn't good enough for them anymore." He waved his hand dejectedly, then said, "go on."

"I didn't open it right away. I was kind of scared. But next day I went down to Jefferson Park, down by the river. I sat on bench and there it was. Five one hundred dollar bills, and another address, on Merritt."

"What'd you do?"

Robbie hung his head. "First I cried. Then I went and torched it."

"How many have you burned?"

"Six. Woulda been seven if they hadn't caught me."

"Okay, what now?"

Robbie held out his hands. They were empty, as empty as his life at that moment. "I don't know, man, but I'm scared. Nobody said nothing, but I think they'll kill me if I stop."

"Who's they?"

"I don't know. Just a lousy envelope. I don't know nobody."

"What about the first guy, the white guy?"

"He was this little guy, with red hair. Real slick dresser and he had this funny accent. But I don't know him. I never saw him before and I never saw him since."

"You think Mr. Henry knows?"

Robbie shrugged. "If he does or doesn't, he'll never tell."

"What about you? Who knows you're involved?"

"Nobody." Robbie looked shocked. "You think I went around advertising?"

"If you wanted to be 'the baddest dude they is' you would."

"Well, I didn't," he said with some heat.

"Okay. What do you do now?"

"I don't know. I don't know. Quit askin' me 'cause I don't know."

"Maybe you should disappear for awhile."

"I can't leave Ma and Tina alone," he protested.

"Isn't that what you've been doing lately?" Robbie hung his head. "Anyway, you won't be going far. Just off the streets for awhile." Peabody didn't give much credence to Robbie's fear, but all the same, taking him out of that environment for a week or two would do him a world of good. "Some place they won't think to look."

"I'll still be in Zenith?"

Peabody nodded. "If the guy'll do it." He picked up the phone.

* * *

Walt Simpson sat in his office smoking another cigaret and drinking another cup of coffee. He glanced up when Steve Jacobs entered. "Got something for me, Steve?"

"Yeah, I just got the readout on Dynographics."

Simpson stubbed out the half-smoked cigaret. "And?"

"We got the same activity we had before."

"Zenith?" Simpson asked with growing excitement.

"Yeah. Looks like your hunch paid off. This Redmond guy's been trading along with the rest of 'em, ever since Carlisle."

"Okay, okay. How do we play this?"

"Wait. It gets better. What was the one before Carlisle?"

"Herringbone. The big one. The one that tipped us to the network."

"Right. So it turns out, he's got a Herringbone for a client."

Simpson grabbed a pen and started scribbling. "Okay, now we're getting somewhere." He frowned. "But it's still circumstantial. It could be a coincidence. Carlisle MedTech, Ryan Systems, Midwest Healthcare, Wheeler Oil and Dynographics, they all made sense as legitimate investments. Plus there wasn't any secret that they were targets. It wasn't necessarily the result of inside information."

"You don't believe that," scoffed Jacobs.

"I'm just trying to look at it from the other side. We gotta have an airtight case. You know Sanguinetti's been kinda gun shy since that beauty queen fiasco."

"Ass licking piece of shit."

Simpson chuckled. "Yeah, but he's our ass licking piece of shit."

Jacobs helped himself to one of Simpson's Camels. "So, where do we go from here?"

Simpson scanned the printout. "Beats me. This guy's shrewd as the rest of 'em. No new clients. No big trades. The only thing we got's a pattern. Unless—" He tapped the printout. "This guy Burton. Why's that name ring a bell?"

Jacobs shrugged. "Beats me."

"Well, find out," snapped Simpson.

* * *

"I just dropped by for a minute," Doane said, declining a drink. "I'm s'posed to meet Krystal at the Art Institute. Can you believe she's never been there?"

"Well, go easy on the Hudson River School, or she'll never go back," Narrows replied with a laugh.

"Try to give a lowbrow some culture," Doane said with exaggerated scorn.

"So, what's up?"

"Title search."

Narrows went to the bar. "Sure you don't want one?"

"All right," Doane decided. "Lots of water."

"Keep talking," Narrows called from the kitchen.

"I tracked down every house in the neighborhood. In the past three months the city's sold thirty houses to three different property management companies. All thirty are sitting empty."

"Empty," said Narrows as he returned with the drinks. "They're obviously not being renovated. What gives?"

"What gives is all three companies are based in Chicago."

"Zenith is unloading property to out-of-town investors? So much for land banking."

Doane sipped his drink and sighed. "God, I love the taste of scotch."

"Too bad you wanted water. I was going to open a bottle of Laphroiag I picked up in Scotland last summer."

"Single malt," Doane said longingly.

"You wouldn't expect me to pollute it with water." He sat down across from the attorney. "So, who's behind these companies?"

"Wanna guess?"

"I bet I know, but what have we got?"

"Oh, you're gonna love this," Doane said with a grin. "When I was in Chicago last weekend—took Krystal to the big Sargent retrospective—I looked them up. All three addresses are bogus. Two vacant lots and a gas station." He paused. "They're dummies."

Narrows nodded. "Now all we have to do is catch the big dummy."

"That's not our job."

"You think the police are going to lift a finger to help me? Or you, for that matter?"

"Why don't we tap his phone then?"

"Forget it. Patterson's too smart for that. I doubt he—" Doane's laughter brought him up short. He grimaced, and said, "Point to Mr. Doane." Narrows sipped his drink and strode about the room. "But we have to do something. Perryman Park has all this momentum now, and nowhere to go." He slapped the back of Doane's chair. "The bastard's got the whole neighborhood locked up."

"Why don't we go someplace else? There's no law that says we have to stay between Perryman and Cumbria, is there? Why don't we go north of Cumbria?"

Narrows gazed at his friend. That's what the man is, he realized. A friend. It was going to take some getting used to. "We can't just pick up and move, Seneca. It takes a hell of a lot of ground work. We got lucky with people like Cleve, and Angela, and Darrel, and Althea. They're a nucleus, something to build on. That's a prerequisite. Otherwise we're just fixing up houses. Otherwise we're just a charity."

"Who's to say there isn't a nucleus the other side of Cumbria?"

"Cleve, and Angela, and Althea." He gave a sad sort of smile. "One of the most devastating things I've learned about Perryman Park is that it's not really that bad of a place, relatively speaking. For people like Althea, north of Cumbria is the other side of the tracks."

"You mean, it gets worse?" Doane couldn't conceal his surprise. If he were to drive up any of the streets, except maybe Wright, he would be hard pressed to say why it was worse. The same dilapidated housing, the burned-out shells, the preponderance of vacant lots...

"Then if we ever get Perryman Park off the ground, that's it? I always thought we'd move on up those streets."

"That's the plan."

"Then why not now?"

Narrows sat down again. There was no way around it, the project was a part of him now. How did Althea put it? "It's like cancer. Pretty soon it eats you up." Maybe not the most apt analogy. Certainly not the kind of quote you want to read in "The Zenith News," but that was how the program took over your life. And it had taken over his, he realized. He hadn't been back to Perryman Park in the two weeks since Angela's house burned, but it hadn't been far from his mind. He decided to call John. As soon as Seneca left, he'd call him and—

"Are you still there, Burt?"

"I'm sorry, Seneca. I was back in Perryman Park."

"I was wondering why we can't cross Cumbria now."

"Oh, right. The way we planned it was we'd use the nucleus to build a community. Ideally people over there will notice the improvements—fixed up houses, new housing, lower crime. If so, maybe some of them will come over to see what we're doing. That way our achievements will serve as our own PR. By the time we're ready to move, there should be a nucleus in place."

"If we're ever ready to move."

"There's that," Narrows agreed. "We can't do a thing without houses." The discussion died as they silently confronted the barricade Patterson had erected. Each wrestled with his rage at the prospect of a genuine solution to Zenith's greatest problem failing because of on mans greed and his selfish passion for vengeance. There had to be a solution. There had to be a way through to justice.

"Wait a minute, wait a minute," Doane shouted as the phone began to ring. "I've got it!"

"What's that?" Narrows asked, moving to the phone.

"We'll take it public."

"Take what public? Our suspicions? Patterson'll sue us for libel. You got to know he's covered his tracks."

"We don't have to use his name. We'll just borrow a page from his book." He stood up. "Better get the phone. I'll explain it later."

Narrows picked it up on the sixth ring. "John!" he cried. "I was going to call you. Yes, everything's fine." Then, more seriously, "I took my medicine. I'm okay now." He motioned for Doane to stay, but pointing at his watch, the lawyer moved to the door. "Just a second, John. Seneca's here. He's just leaving."

Covering the mouthpiece with his hand, Narrows said, "You can't leave me hanging like this."

Doane shook his head. "Just don't say anything about it until you hear from me."

"How can I say anything? I don't know anything."

Doane left the apartment, leaving a frowning Narrows listening intently to the preacher's pitch.

It was a frightening proposal. It also directly addressed John's accusation the day of the fire. If Narrows accepted the kid, he'd be bringing the street inside. His last refuge gone. He threw up some obstacles, but Peabody was ready for them. In the end, all Narrows had left was fear. Fear of the consequences. Fear of exposing himself finally and irrevocably to what he was trying to fight. In the end he had to agree.

Chapter Fifteen

The fat man rolled over several times in a subconscious attempt to evade the glare of the morning sun. In the end, sleep surrendered and he sat up with a start. He glanced wildly about the tiny room littered with discarded clothing, his eyes dull beneath the panic. It took some time for them to focus. When they did, and he recognized his surroundings, he groaned. He rolled over to a sitting position and began his morning routine. He rested his flabby forearms on his naked, pasty thighs, and stared at the railroad tracks crisscrossing his right knee. He groaned again.

That was history. He could hide the trophies and burn the clippings, and enough years had elapsed for the American fan to forget. Rarely did anybody come up and say, "Hey, didn't you used to be…" anymore. And his recent campaign to keep himself out of the papers had worked all too well. He wasn't there to remind anybody of who he had been. No, all he had left were those goddam scars.

Finally, he stood up. He clutched the headboard, leaned on the end table, and knelt torturously to retrieve the cane from the floor. Mornings were the worst. Next to the nights, when the bars finally closed and he had to admit that he couldn't get drunk, and the afternoons, when there was nothing for him to do, mornings were the worst. He could barely move. He screamed, "Foul!" He looked for the flag. The goddam flag. There should have been a flag. Look at me, I can hardly fucking walk!

Mornings were the worst. Sometimes, when the lousy sun wasn't streaming through the lousy window—it wouldn't be so bad if it wasn't fucking freezing outside you'd think it was eighty degrees outside the way it shone, the naked sun mocking you with false promises—sometimes when he first woke up he'd lay his hand on her hot little thigh—she slept hotter than anybody he'd ever known, goddam little furnace inside her, didn't even need covers—and she wasn't there. Of course she wasn't. Bitch threw me out. Lousy goddam bitch throws me out. She can't throw me out. I left her. I threw myself out. Let her have the fucking house. Hell with that. She signed that paper, let her go find a flat. Sleep on the street for all I care. Go sell real estate and sleep with every aging cock in town like every other ex-wife in Wellington Lakes. I'll break her. She sues me, I'll break her. Like I broke all the others.

Mornings were the worst. Hobble to the bathroom and grip the curtain rod while the water streams over you. Like to sit down. Take a lousy bath but the lousy tub's too small. Pieca shit. Eighty bucks a night for a rathole like this? Then you get dressed and take the elevator one measly floor. Can't take the stairs. Are you kidding? With this lousy knee?

12:30. Just in time for breakfast. "Jerome! Bloody Mary. Pronto!"

"Yessir Mr. Patterson."

Damn right, yessir. You always say yessir to me, boy, or your ass is out the door.

Round Table empty. Look out the window. Snow piled up at the edges of the lot. Sooty, ice-encrusted. Looks solid enough, but the water trickles out underneath and flows down to the drain in the center of the lot. Not many cars yet. Give 'em time. They'll be here yet.

"Here's your Bloody Mary, Mr. Patterson. Extra spicy the way you like it. And I brought your paper." Jerome placed the drink on the table, slid the salt and pepper shakers within reach, and produced a bottle of Jamaica Hell Fire because Mr. Patterson always found something wrong with his Bloody Mary. "Will you be having lunch today? The special? Tagliatelle, with ham and cream sauce. Nice bottle of Chianti Classico to go with that, sir?"

Patterson glared at the white jacket and graying head as it disappeared into the kitchen. He glanced at the headlines. Another famine, another war, and more Greenpeace bullshit. Same old world. Then something caught his eye:

ZENITH FOR SALE:
City unloads Properties to Chicago Interests
A Zenith News Exclusive, by Stewart Cooper

What the fuck? I own that bastard. What's he think he's doing? Patterson scanned the article. "According to Perryman Park Housing Corporation President Cleve Clifford, out-of-town speculators are gobbling up inner city Zenith properties. 'We're trying to help people move into the economic mainstream… Our goal is to make the inner city a decent place to live… Make the welfare class into the middle class…'"

Patterson read on. "Seneca Doane, attorney for the non-profit group, stated—" He snorted. The little worm went through with it. He shook his head and read on. "Rev. John H. Peabody, senior advisor to the corporation, points to a conspiracy against the program. 'I have proof that somebody is paying kids to burn down houses in Perryman Park. These aren't speculators. Someone is actively destroying our efforts. Someone is trying to keep decent people from climbing onto the economic ladder.'"

Patterson drained his drink and barked for another. He folded the paper to page 13 for the rest of the story. Cooper wrote:

> Peabody's allegation about the red-headed man was supported by several youths at the Games Center, on Perryman Avenue. They confirmed that he offered them five hundred dollars to burn specific houses on the city's east side. "Yeah, I seen him here lots of times," stated Antwan McDonald, 15. "I told him I don't want nothing to do with him."
>
> Gerald Henry, the Games Center's proprietor, denied any knowledge of the mystery man. "We got a lot of people passing through here. I don't know nothing about nothing."

"The little shit," Patterson muttered. "Why not just take out an ad, McCafferty?" He read on.

> Will Lippman, press secretary for Zenith Mayor Jeremiah Brown, expressed the City's outrage at the charges. "It's not our policy to sell valuable development sites to out-of-town

speculators," Lippman stated. "The Mayor has ordered an investigation of the Land Bank program. If there is any truth to these allegations, the City will take appropriate legal action."

Lippman declined to elaborate on what form such action would take.

Patterson roared as he crumpled the paper.

"Trouble with the crossword?" quipped Ben Richards as he walked in the door.

Patterson hurled the ball at the manufacturer's rep, but it was too bulky to do much damage. Ben deflected it easily and pulled out a chair. "Looks like I'm early."

Patterson laughed like he was at peace with the world, and said, "Siddown, siddown. What are you drinking?"

The Round Table gradually filled with the regular Wednesday crowd. They counted themselves fortunate to find Patterson in such good spirits. He hadn't been this jovial since the day he drove Seneca Doane away. He insisted on buying not one, but every round of drinks. His tongue was as sharp as ever, but his insults were so benign that none of them minded being the target. In his magnanimity, he even let them snipe back, though Ben nearly pushed it too far with a quip about Peg. They held their breath as the fat man's face darkened. Then he unleashed a barrage of laughter and hollered for another round.

Narrows grimaced at the sound. He hated to hear him laugh. He wanted him to be miserable. He wanted him frightened. When he saw "The News" this morning he'd been tempted to call Denny and cancel. He didn't want to risk a confrontation with Patterson just yet. Seneca had said to avoid him at all costs. But he couldn't cancel. He hadn't played squash with Denny since he resigned from the Club.

Although he had described it in his resignation letter as a cost-cutting move, the act was long overdue. The novelty of acceptance, long since exhausted, had been replaced at first by the comfort of ritual but with the passage of time and the alteration of his perspective, it had become increasingly more difficult to make the transition from Perryman Park to the ZAC. It required a much longer journey than the twenty minute drive allowed. He no longer enjoyed his proximity to Zenith's best and brightest; he no longer wanted to be one of them, and with Oak's Grove's denouement, he no longer could.

His letter had been proper and apologetic, citing a change in business and increased obligations. He had expected the board members to snicker when they read it, so he hadn't been surprised when Denny said they'd posted it on the bulletin board next to Seneca's. When he added that within a week it had been obscured by written comments such as "Good riddance" and "Goddam socialist," Narrows hadn't been as hurt as Denny had expected, certainly not as hurt as he was by the fact that Denny had expected, had wanted him to be hurt.

The pain had helped prepare him for Denny's rejection. At first he mourned the loss of twelve years of friendship. Later he concluded it had been twelve years wasted. He had never been Denny's friend. He'd only been window dressing. How else to explain the abrupt rejection? Once Narrows left the ZAC, they simply didn't see each other. If Narrows made it out to Wellington Lakes at all, it was to spend a quiet weekend alone with Cindy. More often than not, she came downtown. With her increased interest in his work, and in him, Narrows had found himself slithering back down that slope towards love. Until that phone call shut the door.

When the other phone call came, at the beginning of March, Narrows agreed without hesitation to meet Denny at the club for squash and lunch. He climbed the marble steps to the carved oak door on a sparkling morning. The temperature was in the seventies, a far cry from last year. The cloudless sky was a rich shade of blue. A gentle southerly breeze barely stirred the banner adorning the facade. Narrows was surprised when Henry, the porter, greeted him with a nod, as if he'd been there just last week, instead of last year. He didn't know what he'd expected Henry to do. Certainly not slaughter the fatted calf, more likely a show of hostility, or even a refusal of admission.

The casual acknowledgment restored his confidence. He could blend into the background. It would be as if he'd never left, or had never been there before. Just another anonymous body, one of a thousand men and women who frequented the place.

He found his old locker, as yet unclaimed, in the dingy, neglected locker room. As he changed into his gear he realized how much he'd missed the place. Not the club itself, not even playing squash with Denny, more the homey comfort of changing clothes in the musty, cramped locker room.

There was an intimacy about it reminiscent of the best of his college days, before he left the dorm. Before the money stopped coming from home and he got a job working graveyard at an all-night gas station. Before going to school became just another job.

He was lacing up his shoes when Denny rushed in. His face was thinner than before, with a grayish tinge to it. "Sorry I'm late," he said, slinging his bag into the corner and ripping off his jacket. His eyes didn't quite make contact as he rattled off the appointments, phone calls and mishaps which had delayed him.

Narrows wondered if Denny's blustering itemization was supposed to be an indictment of his own apparent inactivity. It was as if he was trying to erect a wall to preserve their separation. If so, what was the point of being here? The intimacy was shattered. The locker room was now just a moldy closet, and Narrows simply wanted to get it over with.

His mood picked up on the squash court, however. Though his game was rusty at first, he was moving well. He'd shed the requisite twenty pounds, and so far, it hadn't come back. His speed made up for his reflexes and shot selection, and as play continued, his game returned. It helped that Denny was distracted. He frequently forgot the score, served from the wrong side, and did little more than go through the motions. Narrows refused to let it bother him. He made Denny work for his points. He made him sweat. He even took a game off him. He said the six month layoff had done wonders for his game. "I've forgotten all my bad habits," he chuckled. "I should have done this years ago."

Denny scowled and said, "Just serve the ball."

When they sat down to lunch, Denny plumped for the special while Narrows stuck with the diet plate, "For old time's sake." They talked about the market, interest rates, the trade deficit, the Chinese, and the earthquake in Los Angeles over the weekend.

"Wasn't the big one, though," Denny said flatly, almost as if he were disappointed.

"Still, six hundred people dead, thousands injured, and it'll be months before their freeway system's straightened out."

"Bet your heart's just bleeding away. I'm surprised you're not out there directing the reconstruction."

Narrows wanted to laugh. He would have if there had been the slightest hint of mirth in Denny's voice, the slightest suggestion of friendship in his expression. There was only a sneer. Narrows pushed his cottage cheese into a mountain. He squashed if flat on the lettuce, spread the tuna over the plain, and topped it with a beet. He cut a slice and put it in his mouth. Chewing slowly, methodically, he tried to decipher Denny's veneer of hostility. What exactly had he done to earn this hatred? He hadn't said anything. He hadn't done anything, except quit the Club. It could only be his involvement with Perryman Park. Was his refusal to accept the legitimacy of a permanent underclass that much of a threat?

He understood the mentality. Most ZAC members shared it: people are on welfare, are tearing up their own lives in the squalor of the American inner city because they choose to do so. They are lazy. They don't want to work, or they suffer from some genetic deficiency. Accept that premise, and it is easy to continue as you have been, raking in the money, buying a new BMW or a cottage up north. Then it's easy to give money to the poor: soup kitchens and Christmas baskets, summer camps so little ghetto children can see what life could have been if they hadn't been born of inferior breeding stock.

That was why he found it so difficult to raise money from traditional charitable sources. If you acknowledged that the only thing Perryman Park residents needed to participate in the American Dream was the simple opportunity, and the belief that they were in fact eligible, then that became an indictment of the system whereby people who contributed to traditional charities profited.

Narrows tried to catch Denny's eye across the table. He wanted to stare him down. He wanted to make him so damned uncomfortable that he had to say something, had to tell him why he was so angry. Denny kept his eyes averted, either concentrating on his tagliatelle, or studying the birch paneling. Finally, Narrows said, "So what is the purpose of this charade?"

"What charade?"

"You obviously didn't call me because you missed my pretty face, and you certainly aren't enjoying yourself, so unless you've become a masochist recently, you must have had a specific reason for dragging me down here."

Denny didn't answer. He took another bite of pasta and sipped his wine. "Maybe you wanted to get a piece of my commission?"

Denny glanced up in surprise. "That came through? I thought Thompson cut you off."

"I got a good attorney." Narrows frowned. "You really didn't know? I thought Cindy would have—" He stopped short. Cindy didn't know. She was still off in France. That's how much of a habit she'd become, again. Until he threw her away, again. He nearly succumbed to the urge to confess that latest blunder. But no. Cindy wasn't something they had in common anymore. She was only one more thing they no longer had in common.

"A year ago you would have been the first to know, Denny."

"A year ago you would have been the first to crow."

"A lot changes in a year, doesn't it?" Narrows said bitterly. A year ago he was one of them, a real contender, waiting in the wings for a shot at a starring role. Now he was an outsider, sitting where he no longer belonged, a sheep in wolf's clothing. He shook his head slowly. Nothing was the same. His apartment? Same address, but it had changed too. It was no longer a refuge. Not with Robbie Rollins sacked out on the couch. He grinned suddenly. Too bad about Cindy. It would have been fun to see how she would have reacted.

Then Patterson bellowed his laughter. That was something that hadn't changed. Patterson was still the same, still mocking his dreams, blocking his efforts.

The big man's jollity seemed to shake something loose inside Denny. "Did you know I was sleeping with Peg?"

Narrows nodded, then said, "Was?"

Denny shrugged. "I got bored. Anyway, she's starting to make the rounds."

"Does Rob know about you?"

"Who gives a shit?"

"Pretty blase, aren't you?"

"A woman's one thing, a wife's another, but money's a different ball game altogether." He finished the last of the wine. "I've been making him a ton of money."

"Yeah, me too."

Denny's eyes were cold and hard as he stared at Narrows. "One thing about Patterson, he figured it out from the start. There was no bullshit."

A little electric spark went scurrying around at the base of Narrows' neck. He rotated his head to make it go away, but it wouldn't. Now comes the confirmation, he realized.

"Maybe he didn't respect your abilities."

Denny snorted. "You flatter me, Burt. All this time you thought I was a financial genius?"

Narrows shook his head. "I guess I just didn't want to believe my best friend was lying to me."

"That's what Cindy said."

Narrows pushed himself away from the table. "You told her?"

"I was trying to disabuse her of the notion that you are an honorable man."

"What did I ever do to you, Denny?" His question was almost a whine. "You act like I betrayed you."

"You did," he snapped. "Not only me, you betrayed yourself, everything you—we—stood for. You let your conscience take over, and the hell of it is, it isn't even your conscience. It's Cindy's conscience. You appropriated her heiress' guilt, like you appropriated everything else of hers, and then you went off trying to make amends. But you don't have to make amends, Burt. You don't owe those lazy shits anything."

"I don't owe anyone anything," Narrows replied in a level tone. "It isn't a matter of debt, it's a matter of compassion."

"You don't get to the top worrying about compassion, buddy."

Narrows tossed his napkin on his plate. "I guess I'm not cut out for the top, then."

"Well, you certainly proved that."

Narrows stared at him. Denny stared at the wall. He wouldn't meet his eyes, and that was infuriating. Narrows found it hard to believe that this had been his closest friend. He'd shared so much with him: goals, dreams, secrets. "I can't believe you told Cindy about it," he said flatly.

Denny shrugged. "I didn't plan to. It just leaked out. She was going on about what a saint you are, and I got pissed."

"When was this?"

"That big party at the club."

"After I hung up on her," murmured Narrows. An inkling of hope stirred unexpectedly.

"Hanging up her was the best thing you could have done. It really shook her up."

"Shook her up? You should have seen what it did to me."

"The girl is truly smitten. Don't ask me why." Denny smiled ruefully. "She's there for the taking, and this time I think it'll stick."

"Why tell me this, Denny? I'd think you'd want to protect her from the clutches of a reprobate like me."

"Oh, I tried. Believe me, I tried." He grinned, just a hint of the old Denny. "Anyway, call it a going away present." He laid his hands on the table and turned them palms up. "I'm clearing out."

"Clearing out?"

"Skipping town, going on the lam, ducking out one step ahead of the law." He laughed bitterly. "I'm a cliche. Just another headline in a small suburban daily. They caught me."

"What are you—Where are you going? Who caught you?"

"The SEC. Ron's got a man inside, and he says they're gonna nail me. So I'm splitting."

"How'd it happen?"

"They have a computer that can trace even a single share transaction. I guess they found a pattern and decided I was the weak link." He waved his hands aimlessly. "A friend of mine in Florida has a boat. He'll take me sailing and I'll just drop out of sight on one of those little islands."

"You're giving up everything?"

"I don't want to go to jail, buddy."

"How will you live?"

"Don't worry about me. I've got enough squirreled away to buy a little bar somewhere. Something I always wanted to do…" His voice trailed away. "I'll be okay. Just worry about your own ass."

Narrows slumped in his chair. He hadn't even considered that. "That's just what I need," he muttered. His name was already tarnished by Oak Grove, now this. Insider trading. He'd have to dissociate himself from Perryman Park, the only worthwhile thing in his life. No way would the city ever help if there was a crook running things. He groaned.

"I wouldn't get too upset," Denny counseled. "Give me a day, then go to the feds. Tell 'em the truth—you didn't know. I was your best friend. You thought I was some kind of fucking genius. Give 'em everything you have on me and—"

"I couldn't do that, Denny."

He laughed. "You don't know anything, Burt. You don't know where im going, where my money is, anything that matters. All you'll have is the letter I put in the mail this morning. That'll be enough to exonerate you." He waved his hand when Narrows started to speak. "It's the least I could do. You're fucking up your life enough on your own. You don't need any help from me."

Denny's voice trailed off again. He pushed his plate aside and tried to take a sip from his empty glass. Taking one of Narrows' cigarets, he looked him straight in the eye for the first time that day. "Look, I—I'm sorry, Burt. I never meant for this to happen. I didn't think we were big enough. What can I say? I blew it."

With that he got up and left. He left his life behind, left his friends, his enemies, his unrequited love. Narrows watched him go, and realized he didn't care.

Then a heavy hand clapped onto his shoulder. Startled, he whirled around and out of his chair so quickly that Patterson lost his balance and crashed onto the table. Plates were smashed and glasses tipped over. They rolled off the table, and shattered on the floor. The buzz of conversation ceased abruptly. Narrows could feel every eye in the place staring at him.

Anonymity was gone; he'd made a sensational return. He laughed. "I didn't think you could get drunk, Patterson."

The big man clambered back to his feet, expelling lungs full of fetid breath. His face reddened from the exertion, his eyes rolled. He lurched forward and gripped Narrows' arm. "I'm going to break you," he snarled. "I'll snap you like a toothpick."

Narrows laughed again. "Not this time, fat man. This time you went too far." He shook Patterson's hand off his arm. It was surprisingly easy to do. The big man had no strength left in his grip. He clutched the chair back for support and glared at Narrows, who realized his adversary wasn't at all well.

"Be seeing you," he said cheerfully. Then he turned and headed for the exit. Someone started to applaud. Slowly at first, a single pair of hands clapping. Then some else joined in. As he passed through the dining room the sound of it grew steadily louder until it was a cacophony, with intermingled cheers. It sounded like they were calling his name, Narrows thought, though he looked neither left nor right, and continued on his way. He left the club, for the last time.

Outside, in the sunshine, he walked along the boulevard, past crumbling hotels and vacant office buildings, trying to decide what to do. Call Seneca? Call Peabody? Call Stewart Cooper with a juicy scoop? Or just enjoy the weather? In the end he decided to get out of the city. He went home, fetched young Rollins, and drove to the site of the future Oak Grove State Park.

As they hiked over the rolling hills, Narrows told Robbie how his dream had died on the battlefield of the Oak Grove Riot. From the top of a hill he pointed out the site for the new school, the shopping center, and the park. "Down there, among those trees, is a pond teeming with wildlife; fish and birds, even a beaver dam."

"Really? Can we go see?"

Robbie could barely contain his excitement. He hadn't been out of the city that often, but he loved the outdoors and couldn't wait to see the pond. Two weeks had made a world of difference. His dark, sullen expression had been replaced by an easy smile. He was smart, quick-witted, articulate. Once the mutual uneasiness wore off, Narrows had found himself enjoying Robbie's company. They'd spent a great deal of time talking about life in Zenith. Narrows had wanted to know what it was like, growing up black in the big city. Robbie had said he really didn't know, not in the way Narrows was asking.

"I didn't grow up in the slums. I went to a good school. I went to church. I stayed home and studied. My father wouldn't let me go out at night. It was like he was afraid of the street." Robbie hung his head. "He had good reason. The street will eat you alive."

They only rarely spoke about Rollins, until that afternoon, sitting on a rock beside the pond. Then the questions poured out. Robbie wanted to know about his father's job. What exactly had he done? How had he acted? How did you guys treat him?

Narrows answered him honestly and at length. He talked about Rollins' integrity, his decency, the grace with which he'd handled the transition from Parisienne maitre d' to Men's Grille Steward, and the pride he'd struggled to contain. "If he hadn't contained it, he would have walked out. I don't think he wanted to do that. I think he would have considered that a defeat." Narrows winced and admitted his own culpability. "He had to put up with a lot of bullshit. Some of the guys treated him like dirt, and even the decent guys didn't defend him."

"Yeah, I got that feeling. Mostly he wouldn't talk about it. When I pressed him he'd always say he was doing it for me. That I deserved better than that. That's why he worked so hard to get me into college."

"What happened with that?"

For a second the bitter street punk came back. Robbie scowled. Narrows pursued it until the kid barked, "I blew it. I blew the scholarship. At first, when he died, I told Ma I was gonna be the kind of man he wanted me to be. But it kept getting harder. I started listening to all that bullshit out there. I mean, you don't what it's like to feel ashamed for trying to make it. Everybody says a college degree aint worth shit. You know, the stuff on the street, like, those assholes wearing suits and driving BMW's, they aren't really black. They're like, Oreos, black on the outside, white on the inside?"

Narrows pounded his fist on his thigh. "So what are they saying? You have to be on welfare to be black?" He grabbed a stick and switched the reeds growing at the edge of the pond. "That's bullshit. That's what the guys at the Club would say." He turned to Robbie. "Do you believe that?

He shook his head. "Not now. For awhile I did, or tried to convince myself I did. But it's all a dodge. I'm not sure they even know it's a dodge, but it's just a way of running away from trying, of justifying going nowhere. I mean, it takes a lot of work to make it."

"Tell me about it."

"You don't know," Robbie bristled. "You can't begin to understand. You don't know what it's like to have a security guard dog your steps every time you walk into a nice store. And I mean every time. You don't know what it's like to go to a good school and have all the white kids buddy up to you only to figure out that the only reason they're being friendly is because they think you can score some drugs for them. You don't know what it's like when you got everything, and I mean everything, going against you. Look at me. I blew it, and I had things those guys never had. Like a family, some money, and my father worked hard to give me goals. And I still blew it. These guys on the street, they got nothing. So they just say, man, I wouldn't want to be a house nigger like that, and then they don't even need to try. Why try when chances are you're gonna fail?"

Narrows stared at the shoots of grass pushing up through the spongy soil at his feet. Spring had arrived. Everything bounced back from the death of winter. Soon this grass would be two feet high and the air filled with flying insects and a hundred species of birds to feast on them.

He glanced at the young man sitting next to him on the rock. His knees were drawn up to his chest. He hugged them and gazed at the mirror-smooth water. His face was smooth and contented, a little smile on his lips as he watched a pair of mallards swoop in for a landing. He didn't know the power of his words. He didn't realize how hopeless he'd made things sound. Even if they got Perryman Park off the ground, it was just a tiny square in the huge, metastasizing slum of Zenith. It seemed like there weren't enough decent people to make a difference.

"It's so peaceful and quiet here," Robbie said softly. "It's almost terrifying."

"You want to go?"

He grinned. "Hell no!"

Narrows gestured at his watch. "We have to. Got a board meeting tonight." He paused. "Wanna come?"

"I'm not sure they'll want me."

"Bet they will. Come on."

Narrows stood up and offered a hand to the younger man. He grinned, slapped it, and jumped up on his own. As they trudged back to the car, Narrows asked what he planned to do.

"Go home," he said emphatically. "Tonight. Then back to school. But first I need a job. The scholarship's gone, and Ma needs my college money to live on. So I have to pay my own way."

Chapter Sixteen

Robbie's appearance at the Perryman Park Housing Corporation board meeting certainly was sensational. People began shouting at him as soon as he walked through the door. People shook their fists. Angela shrieked at him, and Darrel and Iron Man had to be physically restrained.

"I think I better go," the young man whispered as tears welled up in his eyes.

"No, you stay right there," Peabody intoned. Addressing the angry crowd, he continued, "Young Mr. Rollins has come to us tonight to offer his apology. He did us wrong, I won't deny it, but he is here to try to help make things right. And remember this, if Robbie didn't burn those houses down, somebody else would have. We have to stop those people, and thanks to him we have evidence that may lead to the arrest of the people behind these fires." The minister paused, gazing at the crowd whose members, though still grumbling, were no longer shouting, no longer threatening violence. "Beyond that, Robbie needs to stay because his staying is essential to this program. We're not just about fixing up houses, but about renewal. By coming here, Robbie brings us a sign of that renewal. By accepting him, and forgiving him, we will take another step on the long, hard road to becoming a community."

Despite Peabody's words, or possibly because of them, they decided to vote on whether to accept Robbie's presence. After a half hour of discussion, a painful session for the young man to endure, votes were cast, not just by the directors, but by all present. It wasn't unanimous, but nearly so, and Robbie took a seat.

Narrows was pleased to see that Angela and Darrel voted in favor of his staying, even though they were currently living in the church basement. They had little choice. Their new landlord had followed through on his threat, and there wasn't anywhere else to go in the neighborhood. They didn't want to leave it because it was their life. Darrel wore a perpetual scowl these days. There's thirty houses just sitting there, he complained. And the lousy landlords won't rent them.

However, Peabody announced that night, that situation might change, and soon. "A couple of lawyers from the city were here today to look into this Land Bank scandal. Mayor Brown is furious and he's demanding fast action."

"Where does that leave us?" demanded Darrel. "When are we going to get some houses?"

"I think I can answer that," announced Doane. "I sat in on the meeting today, and I gave them everything I've come up with. You know the addresses for the property management companies are fake, right? So it looks like the city's going to cancel the sales. Now, it'll be tied up in court for some time, but I convinced them that we should be allowed to manage the properties for the city. That means we can fix them up, rent them out, and someday, the tenants will probably be able to buy them from the city. It's not quite the way we planned it, but it's moving in the right direction. We're in good shape financially, so when we move, we'll be able to move quickly."

"What makes you so sure the City's gonna help?" Althea interrupted. "They never helped us before."

"Things are changing. Housing's a hot issue right now, and we're already in place. Everybody wants to see us succeed so they can take credit." He hesitated before deciding not to bring Patterson into it. That their enemy was also the Mayor's nemesis gave him an added incentive to come down on their side. But that was just a complication. So he went on to his last piece of news. "Plus we've got a friend in the state capital, Senator Bachman. He'll be at the City Council meeting next week, and we should be there, too. There might be some good news."

At the end of the meeting, Narrows submitted his resignation. He promised to continue his support, "But for the good of the organization, I feel I must resign."

* * *

Five days later the sun was still shining brightly, keeping the high temperature in the seventies. Already there was talk of a drought, and the supermarkets were preparing their customers for higher food prices mid-summer. The sun shone on Narrows and his attorney as they passed through the granite portals of the Federal Building in downtown Zenith. Narrows shifted his briefcase from hand to hand as they waited at the bank of recalcitrant elevators, and his hands weren't sweating because of the warm weather.

Doane grinned at him. "Nervous?"

"I still think maybe I'd be better off with a criminal lawyer."

"Don't worry. We've been over this before. It's strictly routine. They don't want you. You're small potatoes."

The bell chimed and they entered the empty elevator. "I feel like I'm entering a trap," Narrows whispered.

"Relax. I'll be there with you. Anything goes wrong—" Doane grinned—"and I'll sue the bastards." He laughed, and Narrows joined him. Then the elevator stopped at the seventeenth floor.

Walt Simpson had flown in from New York to interview his quarry. He had the clipping which Steve Jacobs had scraped up for him. The headline read: "Riot Rocks Midwestern City." Three paragraphs in "The New York Times," not a bad piece of notoriety for a small time crook; not a bad tool to use if this guy's even thinking about holding back.

They gave him an office in a neglected corner of the seventeenth floor. Not a bad view, he'd thought, peering out the dusty window. Too bad there's nothing to see. The office was little more than a spacious closet, with a battered gunmetal gray desk and three plastic chairs. It wasn't much, but with a few little touches Simpson had managed to make it just like home. By the time Narrows arrived the office was filled with smoke, ashtrays heaped with butts. Smoking bans be damned. Empty styrofoam coffee cups were scattered about, and sheets of paper and computer printouts littered every available space.

Simpson jumped up, shook hands with Narrows, scowled at his attorney, and lit another cigaret. "Have a seat. Glad you could make it. You know, you didn't have to bring your lawyer. This is just a routine interview."

"Yeah, that's what he said." Narrows nodded at Doane. He coughed nervously, and reaching for his own pack, added, "Hope you don't mind if I smoke."

Simpson thought that was hysterically funny, and went off in a riot of laughter until a fit of coughing broke it up. He gulped some tepid coffee and said, "Okay, whatcha got for me?"

Narrows told his story, and Simpson scribbled notes, nodded, and muttered, "Uh huh," throughout. Then he flipped the pen on the desk and said, "So this 'buddy' of yours skips out and leaves you a letter?"

Narrows nodded. "Sounds like a load of crap to me," Simpson decided. "You don't know where he went? Somewhere in the Caribbean? Well, that narrows it down, Narrows." He chuckled at his little pun. "So how do you get in touch with the guy?"

"I don't."

"Your buddy splits and that's it?"

"Yeah, well, he wasn't really my friend by then, see. We'd had a falling out over, well, a lot of things, I guess." Narrows told Simpson how Denny got so upset about his involvement in Perryman Park. Doane fought back laughter as Narrows went through the details. He couldn't believe Burt was turning the interrogation into a fund raising pitch.

Simpson let him run with it. This wasn't what he expected, a do-gooder. He was supposed to be a conniving, cheating rat. "Sounds like a worthy project," he said when Narrows wound down. "I wish you luck."

"Then you understand my position," Narrows replied. "I'm willing to pay back my profits, plus any penalties or fines—I don't know how this is supposed to work—and to help your investigation any way I can, but I don't want any hint of scandal to affect this program.

Simpson stubbed out his smoke and lit another one. He tapped his notebook with his pen and said, "Okay, I see your point. Hell, we don't want you anyway. Guys like you don't go to jail for insider trading. Not if you cooperate." He rested his chin on his hand and took a deep drag. He blew a couple smoke rings, then said, "So, we got the goods on Redmond. We don't know where he is, but you're pretty sure wherever he is won't have an extradition treaty." He flipped his pen in the air and caught it after a triple somersault. "Well, hell, we wouldn't extradite him anyway—not worth the expense. And we got this friend of his named Ron who you think's the ring leader." He glanced at Narrows. "You're prepared to testify in court?"

"If it'll help."

"If it'll help." Simpson guffawed. "Aren't you a fucking little saint."

Doane spoke up for the first time, dangling Patterson's name. "If you're looking for a name, this is it. This guy'll get you headlines. Plus he's particularly vulnerable at this time."

"Oh yeah?" Simpson smelled blood. "What's his story?"

"He's a lawyer, filthy rich, sort of a celebrity. Going through a nasty divorce right now, plus the city's about to nail him on a land fraud scheme. He's a natural. Last thing the guy needs is the SEC breathing down his neck. You even look at him and he'll tell you everything he knows. That's a guarantee." He flashed his trademark vulture's grin.

Simpson scrunched around hi his chair. "Yeah, maybe so. Maybe this is a guy we can use." He grinned. He could see the headlines already. Nail this guy and he could see himself moving into Sanguinetti's office real soon.

* * *

The little redhead scurried down the dark, musty corridor, peering at the brass plates on the doors until he found number 21. He rapped softly and stood glancing left and right until the door opened. He stepped inside and stared in disgust at the squalor which greeted him. Clothes and empty bottles, broken glass and fast food wrappers littered the room. He declined when the berobed blimp offered him a drink and a chair.

"This better be good," McCafferty said, giving the room another derisive glance. "I've spent enough time in the slums for you already." He shrieked when Patterson backhanded him, then cowered in a corner. "My God, have you lost your mind?"

Patterson loomed over him, swaying and gulping his scotch. "You fucked up, McCafferty. I'm in deep shit, thanks to you." He flourished a ragged copy of "The Zenith News." "'A little red-haired man,'" he read savagely. "You call that discreet?"

McCafferty waved helplessly. "That doesn't mean anything. Nobody knows my name. What are they going to do, pull in every redhead in the state? I can't believe you called me down here for that."

"I didn't," snarled Patterson. "Not just for that. They're all over my ass. They know about the dummy corporations. They know about the arson. They know everything except my name."

McCafferty got slowly to his feet. Who would have thought there'd be so much interest in a bunch of crumbling houses? Hell, he pulled off scams like this all the time. He rubbed his already aching jaw and remembered why he didn't like vendettas. People didn't think things through when it was personal. He glanced up at the fuming giant. There was something Patterson wasn't telling him, and that something was crucial. That something had led to his failure, and there was a good chance that it might get him killed.

"What do you want me to do?"

Patterson turned with surprising speed. The little man cringed against the wall. "I want it to stop," he roared. "I want you to make it go away. All of it."

"How do I do that?"

"I don't know. You're the fixer, so start fixing." Patterson towered over the Irishman, panting and snarling. Then, muttering to himself, he retreated to the bed. He flopped down on it, the springs shrieking in protest. McCafferty took advantage of the opening and sidled closer to the door. If he could get that far, he'd have the courage to speak. He could beat Patterson in a foot race.

Leaning against the door frame, he said, "This isn't my responsibility, my friend. You hired me for a job, and I did it. 'Strictly routine,' you said. Well, I took care of it. If something's gone wrong, it's not my problem. It's your mess. You'll have to solve it yourself." He opened the door.

"Wait," Patterson rumbled. "I need you."

McCafferty rubbed his jaw. "You should have thought of that a couple of minutes ago."

Patterson raised his open palms and smiled his winning smile. "I'm sorry, Darren." He managed a jolly chuckle. "Been under pressure." His voice turned wistful, distracted; he couldn't sustain the act. "I—I don't want to go to jail," he pleaded.

It was a pathetic appeal, and the fixer didn't have the stomach for it. He walked out, but froze when the lawyer bellowed, "I won't go alone."

McCafferty returned to the doorway. "Meaning?"

"Meaning there are certain aspects of your illustrious career that won't stand the light of scrutiny."

McCafferty shuddered. "You wouldn't—you couldn't. You don't have anything on me."

Patterson gestured at the cassette recorder on the bed stand. "Handy little gadgets. Great for backing up an informer's testimony."

"What do you want me to do?"

"Fix it. Destroy the evidence. Keep my name out of it."

"Destroy the evidence?" McCafferty scoffed. "There is no evidence. You think I put things in writing? There's nothing with your name on it. Just a couple kids with some walking around mon—" He stopped short. "Surely you don't mean—"

Patterson sneered. "Destroy the evidence, Darren." He peeled some hundred dollar bills off his money clip, and threw them at the fixer. "Here, this ought to do it. Haven't you heard? Life's cheap in the hood."

McCafferty's hands were shaking. His voice was shaking. He was trapped and there was no way out. He'd always had his doubts about this guy, but he'd paid good money for relatively easy assignments. Until now. "It's impossible," he confessed. "I've seen the press. It's too late. I can't turn back time. I can't save your property. I can't—"

"Fuck the property," Patterson bellowed. "Save my ass!"

A few phone calls, a few more miles on the odometer, a visit to a dark, ramshackle arsenal on the southwest side of Zenith, and the process was set in motion. Darren McCafferty went home and washed his hands and hoped the fat man was sick as he looked.

* * *

Dinner at the Hotel Thornleigh seemed a suitable extravagance for such a propitious meeting, and Narrows was hosting Doane and Krystal, and at last, Harry Bachman. The Senator and his wife had separated recently, so Harry came solo, providing an illuminating contrast to the billing and cooing couple.

Doane had the enthusiasm and even innocence of a teenager bathing in first love. First love, or at least first requited love, was something he'd missed out on in those years. He'd spent the requisite hours bashing away at himself, cursing his pimply visage in the mirror. When the irruptions failed to cease in concert with those of his peers, when the blemishes became pockmarks and would not stop, Doane had relinquished love as something beyond his reach. Krystal had changed that, and being loved, he became lovable.

He served capably as mediator between Narrows and Harry. They had as much in common as Narrows had suspected, and the dinner was a success. The four of them discussed their game plan for tomorrow night. They respected Narrows' concerns, understood his reasons for backing away from Perryman Park, but in the end, collectively overrode his arguments. Maybe it was best that he resign from the board, they conceded. "But only for six months," Krystal insisted. "Burt, we need you."

Doane said he'd seen his latest drawings, more detailed than those for the fund raiser, and assessed them as brilliant. "You're giving the kind of expertise we can't afford to buy."

"Take them," Narrows urged. "Take what I have and I'll give you more. I don't need the credit. I'm perfectly content to sit on the sidelines. That's one thing I've learned."

Harry gazed reflectively. "So many things happened so quickly," he mused. "Things could have turned out so differently."

"Forget it," Doane interjected, knowing the Senator was thinking of Mya. "It would have required another universe, and we've only got this one."

Harry smiled appreciatively, and spelled out the situation as he saw it.

"We can get you those houses. Not the deeds, not yet, but you already know that," he told the attorney. Then, to Narrows, he added, "You ought to come to the meeting. Your name's not mud, at least, not as muddy as you think it is."

After he gave in, Narrows leaned back in his chair, ordered another round of port, and felt content and warm and loved. It had been such a long, roundabout road to satisfaction. So many disruptions, setbacks and failures for it all to turn out so right. He shook his head in wonder, and raised the glass the waiter had just poured. "To understanding. Of ourselves, of our friends, of our place in the world." He glanced at each of them in turn. The glance was eloquent, and the sentiment reciprocated. "To Perryman Park," he added. "To our grand experiment. You know, for the first time I really and truly believe it will work. We can be an example. We can change lives, and maybe, just maybe, we can help turn Zenith around."

After they drank to his toast, Harry promised to do what he could on the state level to help replicate the project throughout the city. "I may be just a freshman senator, but I have the governor's ear, and I know he's searching for a program like this.

It was the kind of night that shouldn't have to end, but must, due to the inexorability of time and the conspiracy of circumstance to destroy happiness and trample aspirations. They returned, separately or in tandem, to their respective homes, to dream of tomorrow's victory. Narrows stood at his window and watched the insomniac city toss and turn again. "You, Zenith," he said. "You'll come back. You'll make it. We'll survive."

* * *

The following afternoon the doubts crept back. So many things to go wrong. So many intangibles. How much influence did Harry really have? Was Peabody's eloquence up to the challenge? And what of that loose cannon, the unknown factor? What did Patterson have up his sleeve?

He pondered the imponderable and slowly dressed. The phone rang as he knotted his tie; as the sun dipped beneath the horizon and the sky caught fire; as a young man with a jagged scar on his cheek checked his weapons and realized with a start that it was his fifteenth birthday. For a moment Narrows considered letting it ring. It was bad news and he didn't want to hear it. But maybe it was Robbie. He'd gone to a job interview at Winston Brewing today. Maybe it was good news after all.

"Narrows! I'm so glad I caught you," she cried. "Narrows? Narrows are you there?"

Narrows gazed at the man in the window holding a phone to his ear, his tie half-tied and a silly grin on his face. The room revolved a turn or two, but the grin wouldn't fade.

"You're back," he croaked.

"I'm in New York. I just got through customs. Two hours, Narrows! Can you believe it? It gets worse every time." He laughed. It was so good to hear her voice. "My flight leaves in fifteen minutes, and, um, can you pick me up? I'm sorry, I'm so tired and worn out and depressed and I'd just like to see a friendly face at the airport." A pause, then, very softly, "I've been doing a lot of thinking, Narrows, and—Oh, I hope you'll be there."

It wouldn't be hard to muster a friendly face for her. Not hard at all. But what about the meeting? Didn't matter. They didn't need him. He wasn't a central player this time. He was a controlled risk. "I'll be there," he promised, and hung up when she heard her flight announced.

He called Seneca with the news and drove out early for a drink at the bar. Something about airports, all those people rushing about wanting or needing to be somewhere else in a hurry, always gave him a sense of anticipation, the sense that something good would happen soon.

* * *

When the phone call came the first thing Robbie did was call Narrows, but there was no answer and he had to decide. He couldn't tell his mother. She didn't know—anything. And yet, he couldn't stay home. He had to get out of the house. He had to run and there was only one place he could think of to run.

Out on the darkened street, waiting in the sudden drizzle for the bus, he wrestled with injustice. It wasn't fair. On this day of all days, the day he'd gotten a job. Not just any job, not a job slinging burgers, but a real job, a job in an office. It wasn't fair. It wasn't fucking fair. He wanted to cry out in the darkness. It just wasn't fair. Couldn't a guy make one lousy mistake?

The bus pulled up with a rumble and a hiss and the doors eased open on a littered, well-lighted place. Robbie paid his fare and slumped into a seat halfway back and opposite the exit. He stared at his reflection in the wind-and-dust-scarred plexiglass window. The bus rolled along, shattering the silence of deserted avenues, carrying the young man on his flight from fear.

He could hear that voice. The voice on the phone which had obliterated the reconstructed calm of home. His mother had welcomed him back, no questions asked. His sister had cried and asked with her tears for him to be the anchor she needed. He was home, easing into the role his father had left for him: provider, counselor, solid rock of stability. And then that voice.

"They gon' get you ass," it said, softly, full of fear and menace. Who was it? Just one of the nameless bloods from the hood. One of his former running mates, one of the losers going nowhere, destined to end in jail or death, and which was worse? He didn't have a name, but he had a job. Just for the night, but a job was a job, and maybe after he flushed the quarry they'd give him another one.

Robbie ran. He got off the bus, pulled his jacket collar up around his ears, and waited for the transfer. It came, he rode, and jumped off at Portman and Cumbria. He hurried down the sleeping block. Doors were shut and locked and barricaded. Porch lights on, street lamps out; burned out or shot out. Robbie hurried down the block. The only sound was the echo of his footsteps on the broken pavement. He breathed a sigh of relief when he reached Peabody's house. He rang the bell and waited. He rang again, and again, forgetting in his panic that the City Council meeting was tonight. He rang again, but it was no use. Peabody was out. Everybody was out. Everybody he'd come to trust and rely on was out.

What could he do? He sat on the top step, under the overhang out of the rain. Here was as good as any other place.

He noticed the figure detach itself from the shadows of the church across the street. Too small for the preacher, maybe it was Cleve. When he stood, the figure gave a friendly wave and started trotting across the street. Robbie moved down the sidewalk to meet him. "D'you know where Pastor John wen—"

It wasn't anyone he knew. But that face. He remembered that scar from somewhere in the background, somewhere at the projects or the Games Center. Robbie started running again.

* * *

After the meeting, members of the Perryman Park Housing Corporation remained in the chambers locked in excited, and exciting conversation with Senator Bachman and five of the nine members of Zenith's City Council. The meeting had gone better than anyone had hoped or prayed. Simply put, Perryman Park had dominated the session. Peabody's message of hope and regeneration had been simple and compelling. Darrel and Cleve had served as witnesses to the transforming power of the preacher's mission. Doane had provided the legal backing, and Bachman the blessing of the governor. Councilmen and women had climbed all over each other in their eagerness to align themselves with the program.

By the time it was over, Perryman Park was back in business. There were new prospects of city funding, real prospects, not pipe dreams. Doane was going to work out the details with the city attorneys, but those were mere formalities. Tomorrow the neighborhood would once again resound with whining power saws and pounding hammers. There were thirty houses waiting to be cleaned, painted, and put back in working order. The dream was beginning again.

They left City Hall and went their separate ways. Doane, Krystal and Martin Perry drifted off to their apartment towers after a final round of congratulations and celebration. The rest piled into the Perryman Park van. Peabody dropped Cleve, Althea, Iron Man and

DJ off on the way home. He parked and locked the van, then double-locked the garage, and saw Darrel and Angela to their lodgings in the church.

"Won't be long now, Ma, and we'll be in our own house." Angela hugged and kissed her son and Peabody laughed in agreement.

Then, singing a triumphant hymn to himself, he crossed the street and trotted up the steps, an old man grown suddenly young. He stopped short when he noticed the blood, then sank to his knees sobbing when he saw the face of the body lying on his porch.

AND GOD SAW THAT IT WAS GOOD

by Sherry Pryor

Be reminded of God, the Creator. He has a vision and a plan for the world He created, which includes His children. He has given us life and the right to make choices. As you journey through this book you will watch as God says the words, "Let there be..." and His creation comes to life in six days. You'll learn about your place in God's plan, and the choice He gives you.

Paperback, 59 pages
6" x 9"
ISBN 1-60703-143-4

About the author:

Sherry Pryor and her husband Michael live in Sarepta, Louisiana. They have three grown children and one daughter-in-law. Sherry discovered her gift of writing in 2002. It is truly a gift from God and a gift that she dearly loves.

THE TATTOOED CONSCIENCE

by Mark Granberry

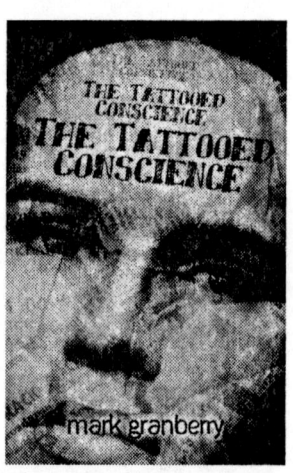

It's not a matter of whether our conscience has been branded or designed by external influences, but by how much. *The Tattooed Conscience* is a collection of poems that attempts to awaken our conscience.

Paperback, 120 pages
5.5" x 8.5"
ISBN 1-60610-751-8

About the author:

Mark Granberry was born and raised in St. Louis, Missouri, and graduated from Northeast Missouri State University. He now resides in Naperville, Illinois, with his wife and two children. His friends, after reading some of his poetry, encouraged him to write a book. This is his first compilation.

Also available from PublishAmerica

PARALLEL JOURNEY
by Joyce Isaacson

Is Todd Anderson crazy?

Todd Anderson wakes up in a mental institution. He is told he is really Todd Bergstrom, a famous author. Todd refuses to take his medicine. After doctors show him news clippings and news footage of his suicide, he believes he is crazy and must stay at the hospital and accept their help.

Part of him still wants to know why he is hospitalized, and another patient gives Todd clues that everything isn't what it seems in the hospital. Todd climbs through air ducts to find the truth.

After being caught, he is subjected to harsh treatments. An unseen person tells him if he would give up a certain code, he would be discharged from the hospital. Todd decides to comply, but he still has his doubts, and discovers something much bigger going on.

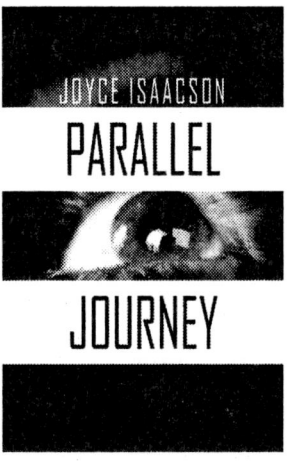

Paperback, 270 pages
6" x 9"
ISBN 1-60441-186-4

About the author:

The Chicago Tribune inspired Joyce Isaacson to be a writer. When she is not writing, she spends her time with her husband and her son, watching TV or going to the park. Her hobbies are drawing, surfing the net and talking to friends on the phone.

Available to all bookstores nationwide.
www.publishamerica.com

SHANNON: SHAMAN WOMAN
by Michael J. Paton

Tommy and Shannon, two young frontier teenagers fleeing from a violent family member who intends to kill them, seek out a tribe of Cherokee Indians who will protect them. On the way, they discover a long-building love between them as well as the gift of "sight" that the girl is just becoming aware of. This gift that saved their family now saves the lives of several members of the tribe and assures their survival as well as the friendship of the entire tribe. The Cherokee host a shaman priestess, who trains Shannon in the use of her fledgling abilities and discovery of what she truly is: more than just the seer she believes she is, while warriors train Tommy in warfare so he may better deal with his violent family. With the help of white trappers, they band together to crush the terror reigning over the area. The final confrontation will pit family against family as well as friends against old enemies. Together they strive to fulfill the old prophecies and return balance and peace to their world. Right must survive or all may die.

Paperback, 372 pages
6" x 9"
ISBN 1-4241-6889-9

About the author:

Michael J. Paton has spent fifty years in the Detroit area of Michigan. He works there, but his mind lives in other times and spaces. His profession is a technical position in a major health care facility. There are gaps in time between jobs being processed that allow his mind to wander (just don't tell his boss that). He believes that he has lived in the past and is still thrilled with the experience of living in the forest. He loves camping and being outdoors when possible, this love reflecting in some of the stories he has written. He has been writing since he was about fifteen years old.